"Damn, damn, dar

Quinn shut the drawin
against it. He closed h
was Serena looking more beautiful than he had
ever seen her, with her eyes sparkling and the
flawless skin of her shoulders rising from the deep
dusk-pink silk gown.

By heaven how much he wanted her, but he had
given her his word that he would not make love to
her until she was ready. When that lecher Dineley
had leered at Serena, he had seen the panic in her
eyes. The woman she had once been would have
laughed it off, sent the fellow on his way, but she
had lost her confidence and he had stepped in,
carrying her off to dance with him.

And his efforts had been rewarded. By the end of
the evening, she had regained much of her sparkle
and self-assurance. That pleased him but it had
also roused his desire. He shook his head. Much
as he wanted to make love to Serena, he dare not
rush her.

Upstairs was his wife, the most desirable woman in
London. And he could not have her.

SARAH MALLORY

---

*Beauty and the
Brooding Lord*

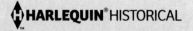

Recycling programs
for this product may
not exist in your area.

ISBN-13: 978-1-335-52297-9

Beauty and the Brooding Lord

Copyright © 2018 by Sarah Mallory

Printed in U.S.A.

Sarah Mallory was born in the West Country, UK, but now lives on the beautiful Yorkshire moors. She has been writing for more than three decades, mainly historicals set in the Georgian and Regency period. She has won several awards for her writing, most recently the Romantic Novelists' Association RoNA Rose Award in 2012 (*The Dangerous Lord Darrington*) and 2013 (*Beneath the Major's Scars*).

Books by Sarah Mallory

Harlequin Historical

The Scarlet Gown
Never Trust a Rebel
The Duke's Secret Heir
Pursued for the Viscount's Vengeance

Saved from Disgrace

The Ton's Most Notorious Rake
Beauty and the Brooding Lord

The Infamous Arrandales

The Chaperon's Seduction
Temptation of a Governess
Return of the Runaway
The Outcast's Redemption

Brides of Waterloo

A Lady for Lord Randall

Visit the Author Profile page
at Harlequin.com for more titles.

To L.F., my lovely editor. Your patience, help
and guidance have been invaluable

Chapter One

London—1816

Serena stepped out on to the terrace. It was a warm night and the earlier rain had passed, leaving only a few small clouds scudding across the sky. She hesitated, her heart beating rapidly. She knew she was risking her reputation, but how could she know if Sir Timothy was the man for her unless they kissed? She ran lightly down the steps at the end of the terrace, where a path led away from the house to a leafy arch set between high hedges. A slight breeze ruffled her skirts and she gave a little shiver as she stepped through the arch. Surely there could be no danger in one little embrace?

The rose garden looked very different from when she had been here a few days ago with her brother and sister-in-law, Lord and Lady Hambridge. Henry had been keen to see the paintings Lord Grindlesham was selling and, while the gentlemen went off to the gallery, his wife had shown Serena and Dorothea the gardens. Now, in the moonlight the paths gleamed pale silver and the roses themselves ranged from near black to pale blue-grey. But if the flowers had lost their colour, their scent was enhanced and Serena breathed in the heady fragrance as she made her way along the path, but when she reached the turn in the path she was aware of something else besides rose scent in the night air. A faint hint of tobacco.

Ahead she saw an arbour surrounded by climbing roses and her heart gave a little skip. There, in the shadows, was the unmistakable figure of a man. His upper body was hidden, but his crossed legs in their light-coloured knee breeches and white silk stockings were plainly visible in the gloom. Serena had expected to find her swain pacing up and down, impatient for her to arrive, but here he was, sitting at his ease. She quashed the faint ripple of disappointment and hurried up to him, smiling.

'Forgive me, I was delayed. I—' She broke off with a gasp as she peered into the shadows. '*You* are not Sir Timothy.'

'No, I am not.'

The reply was an irritable growl. The figure rose from the seat and Serena took a hasty step backwards. She realised now that he was nothing like Sir Timothy Forsbrook. This man was much larger, for a start, although his upper body was so broad that he did not look overly tall. Where Sir Timothy's glossy black locks were carefully styled about his head, the stranger's hair was lighter and too long to be fashionable. And as he stepped out of the arbour she thought he was not at all handsome. In the moonlight his craggy face appeared harsh, as if he was scowling at her.

He towered over her and she took another step away.

'Excuse me—' She would have walked on but his next words stopped her.

'There was a fellow here, but he has gone.'

'Gone?'

'Aye. He had the impudence to suggest I should vacate the seat, so I kicked him out.'

She swallowed. 'Literally?'

His great shoulders lifted in a shrug. 'No. Mere jostling. He retreated rather than have my fist spoil his face.'

She sucked in a long, indignant breath. 'That is disgraceful behaviour. Quite boorish.'

'I suppose you would have preferred me to give way. But why should I? I came out here to enjoy a cigarillo in peace. You two will have to find some other place for your lovemaking.'

His voice dripped scorn. Serena's face burned with mortification.

'How dare you! It is nothing like that.'

'No?'

Knowing she was in the wrong did nothing for Serena's temper. She drew herself up and said angrily, 'You are odiously rude!'

'If it's soft words you want I suggest you go and find your lover.'

'Oh, I shall go,' she told him in a shaking voice,' and he is *not* my lover.'

He grinned, his teeth gleaming white in the moonlight. 'No need to be coy on my account, madam.'

Serena gasped. 'Oooh, you...you...'

He folded his arms and looked down at her. 'Yes?'

For a moment she glared at him, her hands closing into fists as she tried to control her rage. It would be

most undignified to rip up at him. Resisting the urge
to stamp her foot, she turned and swept off, muttering
angrily under her breath all the insults she would like
to hurl at the odious creature.

Serena hurried back to the ballroom. It was half-
empty, most of the guests having gone in to supper.
Those who remained were talking in little groups and
she prayed no one had noticed her entry, for her agi-
tation must be evident. She slipped away to the small
room set aside for the ladies, where she had earlier left
her cloak and outdoor shoes. The looking glass showed
that her cheeks were still flushed and her brown eyes
sparkled with anger. She made a pretence of tidying
her hair, although in truth her honey-gold curls were
remarkably in place.

Really, she thought indignantly, it was most frus-
trating. All she wanted to do was to find an interesting husband, one who would not bore her silly within
a week, like the exceedingly correct suitors her half-
brothers insisted upon presenting to her. These respectable gentlemen were to be her dancing partners for the
whole evening, which was the reason Henry and Dorothea had thought it safe to go off to the card room and
allow Serena out of their sight. But a short break in the
dancing had given Serena the opportunity to slip out
and meet one whom she knew to be a rake and who was
therefore *much* more interesting.

Serena remained in the retiring room until her indignation had died away, then she shook out her skirts, put
up her head and sailed downstairs to the supper room
where she found her brother and sister-in-law enjoying
a cold collation in the far corner. Nearer at hand, Eliz-

abeth Downing and her brother were part of a lively group gathered about one of the larger tables. Elizabeth waved and Serena walked over. Immediately Jack Downing sprang up and pulled out a chair for her, then he proceeded to hover solicitously until Serena had been provided with a plate of delicacies and a glass of wine.

After the incident in the rose garden such attention was balm to Serena's spirits. Mr Downing was a serious young man whom she had previously apostrophised as stuffy, but at least he was not *rude*. She now thanked him prettily and allowed him to engage her in conversation until the musicians could be heard tuning up again and everyone began to drift back to the ballroom.

The dancing recommenced and Serena looked around for Sir Timothy. Imagining his ignominious departure from the rose garden, she was not surprised to learn that he had gone home, but she felt no sympathy for him. She wished he had come to blows with the rude stranger and knocked him down rather than walking off and leaving her to endure a most unpleasant encounter. However, when she recalled the size of the stranger, she doubted Sir Timothy would have got the better of him.

The evening was proving to be exceedingly tedious and after a couple of dances Serena excused herself and went in search of her sister-in-law.

'What, you wish to leave, before the dancing is ended?' Lady Hambridge gave the loud, irritating laugh that announced she had enjoyed too much wine this evening. She shook her head at Serena and said playfully, 'This is most unlike you, Serena! No, no, we cannot go yet, for you are engaged to stand up with Lord Afton. I should be failing in my duty if I were to take you away before he has danced with you.'

Viscount Afton was the highest-ranking bachelor at this evening's ball. Serena thought him dull, pompous and old enough to be her grandfather, but it would do no good to say as much to her sister-in-law, so when the time came she pinned on a smile and went off to dance the quadrille. As the dance ended she spotted a familiar figure at the side of the room. She touched Lord Afton's arm.

'Tell me, my lord, do you know that gentleman, the large man talking to Lord Grindlesham?'

'What's that, m'dear?' The Viscount looked about him and gave a disdainful grunt. 'Do you mean that great bear of a man? That's Lord Quinn. Damned unpleasant fellow. No one likes him.'

She was pleased that Lord Afton shared her opinion of the stranger from the rose garden, but curious, too.

'If that is the case, why is he invited?'

'Rich as Croesus,' he replied shortly. 'He don't often show his face in town, but Grindlesham is selling off his art collection and that will be the reason he is come. Rufus Quinn is considered to be something of a connoisseur, I believe.' He huffed. 'Well, he can afford to indulge himself.'

There was a bitter note in the viscount's tone, but since it was well known that Lord Afton had little fortune, it did not surprise Serena. As he led her back to join Dorothea and Henry, she took the opportunity to study Lord Quinn from a safe distance. In the blaze of candlelight, it was clear to see that he was no arbiter of fashion. His coat of dark blue superfine fitted well enough across his impressive shoulders, but no servant was needed to ease him into it and the simple arrangement of his neckcloth would not rouse envy in the breast of any aspiring dandy. His brown hair was not brushed into artful disorder; it was positively untidy. His face was rugged, his nose not quite straight and his brow fierce. He looked impatient and she already knew his manners were abominable. All in all, Serena decided, he was a man not worthy of her attention.

At last the evening was over and Serena accompanied her brother and sister-in-law to the hall. It was crowded and noisy, and the servants announcing whose carriage was at the door were obliged to bellow over the chatter of the guests. There was much pushing and shoving and Henry guided his ladies to one side, away from the throng.

'It's like a dashed cattle market,' he muttered. 'Whatever persuaded Grindlesham to invite so many? And that reminds me.' He turned a frowning gaze upon Serena. 'I saw you talking to Forsbrook earlier. Who introduced you to him?'

Serena spread her hands. 'I really cannot recall, but it is impossible to avoid such introductions in town.'

'I suppose you are right,' he agreed grudgingly, 'but he's a dashed Lothario and you'd be advised to stay away from him.'

'Indeed, you would,' added Dorothea. 'He has the most unsavoury reputation.'

'What of it?' Serena countered. 'Most gentlemen in London have an unsavoury reputation. Even Russ, before his marriage.'

Henry scowled. 'That was different. Forsbrook is an out-and-out libertine. Russ was never that.'

'The pity of it is that such men are so attractive to a large number of our sex,' declared Dorothea repressively.

'Well, they would have to be,' reasoned Serena. 'One can only conclude that they are experts at making love to a woman.'

Henry spluttered and Dorothea said in a scandalised voice, 'Serena, *hush*. You cannot say such a thing—it is most unladylike.'

Serena begged pardon and closed her lips upon any more unwise utterances. Clearly it would not do to admit that she thought she might like to marry just such a man. She had been out for two years and was still unmarried. Oh, she had had offers, but all the men Henry and Russ considered eligible were so very *dull*. In fact, Serena was finding life in town rather dull, too.

It had not been so bad when she had been staying with Russ, for although he was ten years her senior both he and his wife were lively and quick-witted. But Russ had taken Molly to the north to await the birth of their second child and Serena was now living in Bruton Street with Henry, who was her guardian and eldest half-brother. Having married off their own daughter very successfully two years ago, he and Dorothea were keen to find a respectable husband for Serena.

She understood perfectly the reason for this. The Russington family history was tainted by scandal and they were anxious to avoid adding to it. Good birth was considered essential, a title an advantage, but respectability was prized higher than a fortune and Serena was kept well away from any gentleman whose reputation was less than spotless, with the result that she had not yet met any man whose company she enjoyed for more than a very short time. Naturally, she wanted her husband to be handsome, but she also wanted a man of wit and intelligence. An educated man with a sense of humour, with whom she might enjoy lively conversation.

Finally, she wanted him to be skilled at pleasuring a woman. Not that she knew a great deal about what went on in the marriage bed, because young ladies were not supposed to be interested in such things. What she *had* learned was all very confusing. If Dorothea was to be believed, it was a wife's duty to accept her husband's attentions with fortitude, whereas Molly had told her that the union, when a husband and wife truly loved one another, could be beyond wonderful. It seemed that love was the answer, but none of the suitors presented to Serena had roused the faintest flicker of interest. She had therefore decided she must take a hand in her own destiny. Russ had been considered a rake before he had married his beloved Molly and Serena thought such a man would suit her very well.

Therefore, whenever she could escape Henry and Dorothea's watchful eyes at any ball, breakfast or assembly, she sought out the rakes and gentlemen of more dubious reputation. The problem was that it was so difficult to be alone with any gentleman in town. Her flirtation with the dashing Lord Fyfield, for example, had been going well until they were spotted by one of Dorothea's bosom friends in Green Park and Serena had to account very quickly for being alone with a gentleman. Word of the assignation had soon reached Bruton Street and Henry had lost no time in putting an end to Lord Fyfield's attentions before he had even kissed her.

It was all most unsatisfactory and Serena's spirit rebelled against being so confined. She wanted to marry, but not one of the milk-and-water sops that her family put forward. No, she wanted a man who could hold her interest. One who knew how to make love to a woman. Was that too much to ask? Her musing ended when a servant announced Lord Hambridge's carriage.

'At last,' said Henry. 'Come along, my dears, let us get home.'

Serena followed as he pushed his way towards the door with a word here and there to clear the path. A large, commanding figure stood in their way. Serena could only see his back but she immediately recognised Lord Quinn's tousled head. A word from Henry and he stood aside, but there was no smile, no word of apology. His rugged face was stony and although his gaze moved over Serena, she had the impression that he was looking through her. However, she did note that those eyes, which had laughed at her so insolently in the rose garden, were a warm brown, the colour of fresh hazelnuts.

Serena decided she would strike Sir Timothy from her list of prospective husbands, but at the Downings' party the following day, he sought her out and told her he had come with the sole intention of apologising for his absence from the Grindleshams' rose garden. He begged for the opportunity to make it up to her and Serena decided she would at least listen to what he had in mind for her entertainment. After all, he was extremely fashionable and very handsome, with his black curls and Grecian profile, and there was no denying that he had about him a dangerously rakish air. She decided to give him another chance.

His proposal that he should escort her to Vauxhall when it opened for the Season was too tempting to resist. He painted an alluring picture of the two of them, cloaked and masked, wandering through the gardens and marvelling at the mechanical exhibits such as the famous waterfall.

The clandestine escapade appealed to Serena's adventurous soul and she dismissed the tiny voice inside that urged caution. She must allow Sir Timothy to kiss her, just once, for how else was she to know if she would like him as a husband? And from all she had heard there was no better setting for a romantic interlude than Vauxhall, with its shadowy arbours and dark avenues hung with coloured lights.

Serena knew it was one thing to allow a hopeful young man to steal a kiss in a shadowy alcove of a private ball—which she had done once or twice—quite another to go off alone with a gentleman to Vauxhall, but Elizabeth had already told her that she and her family were going to the gardens that night and if it went horribly wrong, if she found she did not like being kissed, or Sir Timothy should become importunate, she would seek them out and beg their protection. That would be humiliating and once Henry knew about it he would probably banish her to the country for the rest of the Season, but one must be prepared to risk all in the search for a husband. All she needed now was to work out a way to slip out of her brother's house without raising any suspicions.

Her plans came to fruition two days later, at breakfast, when the butler brought in the post and delivered a letter to Serena. Dorothea looked up.

'What have you there—is it a love letter from one of your beaux, perhaps?'

Dorothea's arch tone grated, for Serena knew quite well that correspondence between herself and any gentleman who was not related to her would be highly improper. However, she replied calmly and with perfect honesty, 'It is from Mrs Downing. She invites me to join her party at Vauxhall tomorrow evening.'

'Vauxhall?' Henry looked up from the perusal of his own post. 'It is not at all the place for young ladies, especially tomorrow, for it is May Day, when all sorts of common folk will be out celebrating. I have no doubt that the disreputable among them will be masked, too.'

'Mrs Downing sees no harm in it,' replied Serena. 'Mr Jack Downing will be with them, too.' She glanced at her sister-in-law, upon whom the young man's name acted like a talisman.

'Henry, my dear, I do not see there can be any harm in it, if she is with the Downings. And I believe Madame Saqui is performing. I confess I should very much like to see her myself. I am told that last Season she ended her display by running along the tightrope with fireworks exploding all around her.' Dorothea picked up her coffee cup. 'Perhaps we should go as well, I doubt we would be able to obtain a supper box at this late notice, but we might enjoy the spectacle.'

Serena held her breath. Her own plans for tomorrow evening would have to be drastically changed if Dorothea and Henry decided to go to Vauxhall.

'To go all that way and not be able to sit comfortably for supper?' Henry's mouth turned down. 'Bad enough that we should be mixing with heaven knows what class of person, but if we cannot sup in our own box it would be insupportable. Besides, I am already promised to dine tomorrow at White's.'

'I could report back to you upon Madame Saqui's performance,' Serena suggested. 'Then you may decide if it is worth the effort for another time.'

Henry turned an approving gaze upon his half-sister. 'An excellent idea, Serena. I am sure, if this rope dancer is any good, you will wish to see her again.'

She gave him a dazzling smile. 'Indeed I shall, Henry. And perhaps you will order the carriage to take me to the Downings' house tomorrow evening. Since they live *en route*, I do not wish to inconvenience them by making them come out of their way to collect me.'

With the matter thus settled, Serena breathed a sigh of relief. So far, everything was going to plan. Her hints last night to Elizabeth had resulted in the Downings' timely invitation, which had aroused no suspicions. Now she must carefully pen a note to be delivered tomorrow evening, regretfully crying off because of a malaise. She sipped her coffee. A malaise called Sir Timothy Forsbrook. She did not like deceiving her friends, but it must be done, if she was to find lasting happiness.

Serena dressed with care the following evening, choosing a high-waisted evening gown of lemon satin with an overdress of white gauze. As befitted a demure young lady she tucked a fine white fichu into the low neck of her gown. Lemon satin slippers, white kid gloves and a white crape fan completed her ensemble and over everything she wore a cashmere shawl, its wide border embroidered with acanthus leaves. Sir Timothy had promised to provide a domino and mask for her, because for Serena to carry such items would only invite comment from her brother or his wife.

Darkness was already falling when the Hambridge carriage pulled up at the Downings' house in Wardour Street. Serena stepped down and airily told the coachman there was no need to wait. She stood on the pavement, making a show of fussing with her reticule until the coach was out of sight, then she turned and ran quickly back to the chaise waiting further along the street. Sir Timothy jumped down as she approached.

'You have come!'

'Of course, did you doubt it?' She laughed as he handed her into the chaise. 'I sent my letter of apology to the Downings this morning. They will have set off for Vauxhall a good half-hour since.'

'So, no one knows where you are. My clever, adorable angel.' Sir Timothy tried to take her in his arms, but she held him off.

'Not yet, someone might recognise us!'

He released her and threw himself back against the padded seat. 'Little chance of that in this poor light. But there is no hurry.' He lifted her fingers to his lips. 'We have all night. Tell me instead what you have been doing since we last met. I want to know every little detail.'

It was already growing dark by the time Rufus Quinn left London. The meeting at the Royal Society had gone on longer than he had anticipated, but he could not pass up the opportunity to talk with the celebrated astronomer Miss Caroline Herschel, who rarely came to London. After that he had taken advantage of the moonlight to drive home, rather than spend another night in town. He had no time for society, everyone was too set up in their own importance. If people weren't vying for superiority they were all wishing to line their pockets at someone else's expense. Quinn hated it, and had only allowed himself to be dragged to the Grindleshams' ball because he wanted the Titian. In the event, Quinn had merely told Grindlesham to name his price and the painting had been his. He had wasted an evening watching the overdressed popinjays cavorting around a ballroom when he could have been at home enjoying a glass of his excellent claret and reading a good book.

Even when he had slipped away to enjoy a cigarillo he had been interrupted by an insufferable cockscomb who had wanted him to make himself scarce. Quinn had soon sent him about his business, but damme if the fellow had not gone off with never a thought for his mistress! A smile tugged at his lips as he remembered her reaction when she arrived. Spirited little thing, though, the way she had stood up to him. No tears or vapours. Reminded him of his Barbara, God rest her soul. His good humour faded, but he shook off the threatening black mood, blaming it on fatigue.

By nursing his team, Quinn usually managed the journey into Hertfordshire without a break, but tonight he felt unaccountably tired. Another yawn broke from him. Confound it, he would have to stop if he was not to fall asleep over the reins. He gave a grunt of satisfaction when he reached Hitchin and spotted the Swan ahead of him, light spilling from its windows. He guided his team into the cobbled yard, where torches flared and ostlers came running out to attend him. The landlord appeared, wiping his hands on his apron.

'Evening, my lord, trouble with your team?'

'Nothing like that, Jennings, but I need a short rest.'

He saw the landlord look past him and anticipated his next question. 'I left my tiger in town. Clem follows on tomorrow in the carriage with Shere, my valet. They have a rather valuable cargo.'

'Been buying pictures again, my lord?' The landlord gave him a fatherly grin. 'I think what you're wanting now is a bite to eat and a tankard of home-brewed, sir, to see you on your way.'

'Aye, you are right. Lead on, Jennings. Find me a table and somewhere quiet to sit, if you will.'

'No difficulty there, sir. It's fair quiet here tonight, it being May Day. The night mail's due in later, but there's never time for the passengers to get out. No, the only other customers I'm expecting tonight is a honeymoon couple, travelling from London.' Jennings winked and tapped his nose. 'A servant rode ahead to say they wouldn't be here 'til late and that they'd take a cold supper in their room.'

It was gone midnight when Quinn walked out of the inn, refreshed and ready for the final stage of his journey. It was very quiet and the yard was empty save for the ostler looking after his curricle and pair. As he crossed the yard Quinn heard a faint cry.

The ostler looked up towards the gallery and grinned. 'Sounds like someone's having a good time, m'lord.'

Quinn grunted. It was no business of his. He merely wanted his own bed. He stopped to pull his gloves on and give the greys a critical glance. They were rested well enough and should carry him home in well under the hour. He was just about to step into the curricle when a shrill scream rent the air. It was cut off almost immediately, but there was no mistaking the terror in the voice.

Quinn did not hesitate. He raced up the stairs. A disturbance could be heard from the first door he reached, but it was locked. Quinn launched himself at the door, which gave way with a splintering crash. The inrush of air caused the candles on the table to flicker, but he took in the scene in one glance. The meal laid out on the table was almost untouched, but the two chairs were overturned and a drift of white gauze lay on the floor, like a wraith.

A man scrambled off the bed and hurled himself at Quinn, fists flying, but one blow to the jaw sent him crashing to the floor. Quinn stood over him, hands clenched, but his opponent was unconscious.

A whisper of silk made him look towards the bed as a figure scrabbled away and huddled in the corner of the room. In the gloom he could make out nothing but a mass of fair hair and a pale gown, and the fact that the woman was shaking uncontrollably.

He untangled a wrap from one of the chairs, a large cashmere shawl, heavy and expensive. This was no drab from the stews picked up for a night's gratification. He shook it out and approached the woman, who was fumbling to pull together the torn pieces of her bodice.

'Here, let me put this around you.' She did not respond, but neither did she shrink away as he threw the shawl about her shoulders. Gently, he led her out of the shadows. 'Are you hurt?'

'N-no, not really. I…he…' Her voice failed and he caught her as she swayed.

'You need not worry about him any longer,' he said. 'Come, I will take you out of here.'

He escorted her from the room, keeping one arm around her, lest she stumble. The landlord met them at the bottom of the stairs.

'The lads said there was some trouble, my lord.'

'The lady is, er, distressed.'

'Ah.' Jennings nodded wisely. 'Had a falling out with her husband, has she?'

'Is that what he told you?' Quinn was surprised to hear the woman speak. The voice, coming from behind the tangled curtain of hair, was quiet but firm. She put a hand to her head. 'He is not my husband.'

The landlord regarded her with disapproval and Quinn's arm tightened protectively around the dainty figure.

'I came upon the lady defending her honour.' His tone dared Jennings to dispute the fact that she was a respectable female. The landlord met his eyes, considering, then shook his head.

'She needs a woman to look after her, my lord, and since the wife died...' He spread his hands in a helpless gesture. 'I'll find a chaise to take her home...'

Quinn glanced down at the hunched figure beside him. She was calm enough now, but he doubted she would endure the long drive back to town.

'Is there a maid you could send with her?'

'Nay, my lord. As I told you, they'm all out, it being May Day.'

'Then I will take her to Melham Court and put her in the care of my housekeeper.' Quinn guided her to the curricle and lifted her, unresisting, on to the seat. As he took his place beside her he glanced up at the gallery. 'Her companion is unconscious at present, but when he wakes—'

'Don't you worry about that, my lord. We will deal with him. I don't hold with such goings on in my establishment.'

'And. Jennings…' Quinn gathered up the reins '…the lady was never here.'

The landlord nodded. 'My lads'll do as I tell 'em.'

With that Quinn whipped up his team and the curricle bowled out into the night.

Chapter Two

Quinn drove steadily, but as the curricle rounded the first bend he felt the figure beside him sway and he quickly put an arm about her shoulders.

'Easy now. I don't want you falling out on to the road.'

'No, of course not.' She sounded very calm and made no move to shake him off. 'I do not feel quite myself.'

'That is understandable.' He frowned. There was something familiar about her voice, but he couldn't quite place it.

'No, what I mean is, my head is swimming. He made me drink the wine. He was trying to get me drunk.'

'Did he succeed?'

'Not quite.' There was a long pause. 'You must think me very foolish.'

'I do. But you are not the first.'

'I should have known better. Molly—my sister-in-law—is patroness of Prospect House, a refuge for women who have, who have been…' A shudder ran through her. 'I have met some of them and learned their history, but I thought it could never happen to me. I thought I knew better.'

She was talking quite naturally, as if they were old friends, but Quinn guessed that was the shock. It would not last. Reaction would set in at some point and he must be ready for that. For now, talking was a way to distract her from her ordeal.

'It is common among the young,' he remarked, 'to think they are awake upon every suit.'

'Where are you taking me?'

'To Melham Court. My housekeeper will look after you. I am Quinn, by the way.'

'I know. You were pointed out to me at the Grindle-shams' ball.'

So that was it! He felt a stab of shock. The hair, the voice—he could place her now, the outraged beauty from the rose garden. Well, however wilful she might be, it was clear she had got herself into a situation far beyond her control.

She said now, 'I was told you are the rudest man in London.'

'Which was your own opinion, when we met in the garden.'

'Ah, yes. Do you wish me to apologise?'

'No. I admit it, I *was* rude to you.' He glanced down at her. 'You have the advantage of me. I do not know your name.'

'S-Serena Russington. I am Lord Hambridge's ward. But I pray you will not blame him for my present pre-dicament.'

'I don't. I have no doubt you told him some tarra-diddle so you could slip away this evening.'

She tensed, and said coldly, 'I think you should re-lease me. It is most improper for you to have your arm about me like this.'

'Improper, perhaps, but necessary. In the dark you will not be prepared for the twists and turns of the road. My team, however, are very familiar with this route and need little guidance from me.'

'You can drive one-handed?' Her indignation died away as quickly as it had come. 'I am impressed. Not that you wish to impress me, do you, Lord Quinn? You think me a sad romp.'

'No, I merely think you foolish.' The stiff little body beside him drooped a little and he softened his tone. 'Perhaps you should tell me how you came to be at the Swan this evening. And who was your companion?'

He thought at first she would not reply. Then she began to speak, her voice low and tightly controlled.

'The man was Sir Timothy Forsbrook. He said he would take me to Vauxhall Gardens, but instead he was going to carry me off to Scotland. I did not realise the deceit until we were out of London.' She added bitterly, 'He tricked me finely! He *said* that he thought I wanted to elope with him, so he had arranged it all. Elope!' She shuddered. 'I am sure I gave him no such indication!'

'Yet you agreed to go to Vauxhall with him.'

Silence, then, 'Yes.'

'And would I be correct in assuming your dowry is…substantial?'

'Of course. I know *now* that is why he ran off with me, but he d-did not admit it at first. When I told him I did not wish to elope he begged pardon and said he had quite misunderstood and we would go back just as soon as we had changed horses. When we reached the Swan, I wanted to remain in the carriage, but the night mail followed us into the yard and he said I would be sure to attract attention. He…he had bespoken a room where I might rest in private.'

'And you believed him?' He could not keep the incredulity out of his voice.

'He had given me no cause then to think he would not respect my wishes. He was so polite, so remorseful that I truly believed he was in earnest, that he really was protecting my honour. Instead he…he t-tried to…'

She began to shake, quite violently, and his arm tightened.

'Enough. I can guess the rest.'

With relief he saw they were approaching the gatehouse of Melham Court and he slowed the greys. The bridge and archway leading into the courtyard were narrow, but at least there were no tight corners to negotiate one-handed. He brought the team to a stand before the door and a servant ran out to take their heads. Serena was still trembling. Quinn picked her up and carried her into the house. It was the work of a moment, but he was aware of two things. She weighed almost nothing in his arms and she smelled of summer meadows.

If Dunnock thought it unusual for his master to arrive with a strange woman in his arms, he was too wise a butler to show it. Quinn made directly for the drawing room, requesting that the housekeeper should attend him.

It was his custom whenever he was returning to Melham to send word ahead in order that the principal rooms could be prepared, so he was not surprised to find a good blaze in the hearth. He lowered Serena gently into a chair beside the fire and she huddled into her shawl, leaning towards the flames. She barely seemed to notice him.

His housekeeper came bustling in and he explained without preamble.

'I found Miss Russington at the Swan. She is very distressed and I need you to take care of her, Mrs Talbot. She will need a hot brick for her bed.' He glanced down at the dishevelled figure hunched over the fire. 'And a bath.'

'Aye, of course, my lord. I always make sure there is hot water when you are due back, but 'tis only enough for one. And…' She stopped, consternation in every line of her kindly face.

'Yes?'

'Everything is set up in your dressing room, my lord. I can easily have the hip bath removed to the guest room, but there is no fire burning there and it will take a time to get it warm.'

'Bathe her in my rooms, then, while you have the guest room prepared. And be sure to have a bed made up in there for one of the maids. She must not be left alone—do you understand me? I will remain here until you have finished.'

'Very good, my lord.' The housekeeper turned to Serena. 'Come along then, my dear, let us get you into a warm bath and you will soon feel better. And perhaps we'll find you a little soup afterwards, what do you say to that?'

Serena made no response, but she allowed Mrs Talbot to help her out of the room. Quinn threw himself into the vacated chair. All this was a damned nuisance, but what else could he do? A hired coach would have taken several hours to get her back to town and, aside from the perils of making such a journey alone and at night, there was no telling what distress she would be in by the time she reached her home. He was not prepared to have that on his conscience.

It would not do for him to remain here, though. As soon as the women had finished with his dressing room he would pack himself a bag and remove to Prior's Holt. Tony Beckford and his wife were still in London, but the staff there knew him well and would not deny him, even at this late hour. He closed his eyes, too tired to consider anything more right now.

An hour later Mrs Talbot's tactful cough roused Quinn from his sleep.

He sat up in the chair, saying irritably, 'What is it now?'

'I beg your pardon, my lord, but 'tis the young lady. She is still in the bath. I've built up the fires in the guest room—and in your bedroom, too, my lord—but the bathwater is turning cold now. I've looked out one of my dressing gowns for her, too, but she won't budge. I'm afraid she will catch a chill if we don't get her dry soon.'

'For heaven's sake, woman, can't you get her out of the water?'

'Every time anyone goes near her she screams fit to bust.' The housekeeper wrung her hands. 'She keeps scrubbing away at herself, sir, and muttering. I'm sure I don't know what to do for the best.'

Smothering an oath Quinn pushed himself to his feet. 'Very well, let me see her.'

The steamy warmth of the dressing room hit Quinn as soon as he entered. Serena was sitting in the hip bath but facing away from him, the smooth skin of her neck and shoulders golden in the candlelight. Someone had pinned up her fair curls to keep them dry and she was rubbing at her arms with the sponge. A young maid was in attendance, watching Serena with an almost frightened intensity. A screen was set up to protect the bather from the draughty window and thrown over it was a large towel and a bundle of white cotton that he assumed was Mrs Talbot's dressing gown.

The housekeeper picked up the towel, saying cheerily, 'Now then, miss, time we wrapped you in this nice warm sheet.'

'I am not yet clean.' Serena rubbed even harder at her arms.

'You'll take the skin off if you scrub yourself any more, miss. Come along.'

Serena lashed out, shrieking, and Mrs Talbot backed away, turning an anguished face to Quinn. He took the towel from her.

'Leave us, both of you.'

The maid scuttled out, followed more slowly by the housekeeper, and Quinn moved around until he was facing Serena. There was a livid bruise on one cheek and she had rubbed her arms until they were red, but he saw marks on her neck and arms that had not been caused by the constant scouring. He wished now that he had spent longer punishing Forsbrook rather than knocking him out with a single blow. Serena ignored him and continued to rub the sponge over her body. He knelt beside her.

'Miss Russington, Serena, you must get out and dry yourself.'

'No, no, not until I have washed it away. I c-can still feel his h-hands on me.'

Quinn gently touched her cheek. 'Did he do this?'

She pulled her head away but did not answer him. Instead she gripped the sponge even tighter as she scrubbed at her skin.

'What did he do to you, Serena? Tell me,' he commanded.

She stilled, although she did not look at him. A shudder rippled through her.

'He k-kissed me. When I told him to stop he—he laughed and t-tore my gown. Then he grabbed me.' She put her hands over her breasts.

'Did he do anything else? Serena?'

He spoke sharply, demanding a response and she gave a tiny shake of her head.

'He—he tried, but I scratched and bit him. That was when he hit me. Then he t-tried to ch-choke me.'

Her hands crept to her throat and Quinn felt his anger growing. He fought it down.

He said calmly, 'You showed great courage, Serena, but you must be brave again now. We must get you dry or you will be very ill and all your fighting will be in vain. You do not want that to happen, do you?' He had her attention now. Her dark eyes were fixed on him. He rose and held out one hand. 'Come.'

He held her gaze, willing her to obey. Slowly she took his proffered hand and rose from the water. He had the impression of a womanly form, all soft curves and creamy skin, but he kept his eyes on her face. She was on the verge of hysteria and the slightest error on his part could overset her. As she stepped out of the hip bath he wrapped her in the towel. She did not move but looked up at him with eyes so full of trust that the constriction around his chest was like an iron band.

Panic shot through him. She was relying upon him to act honourably and just for a moment he doubted his ability to do so.

She stood motionless while Quinn dried her body, steeling himself not to linger over those luscious curves. When he had finished he dragged the wrap from the screen.

'Put this on. It belongs to Mrs Talbot, so it will be far too large, but it will keep you warm.' Briskly he helped her into the dressing gown and knotted the belt. He tried not to think about her tiny waist or how easily his hands could span it.

'There, now you are—' He had been about to say *respectable* but that was wholly inappropriate. And untrue. Even in the voluminous robe, her cheeks flushed and wisps of errant curls framing her face, she was undeniably tempting and desirable. He cleared his throat and stepped back, ready to turn away.

'Th-thank you.' Her face crumpled. 'Everyone has been most kind.'

She gave a wrenching sob and Quinn could not help himself. He gathered her into his arms, where she remained rigid and tense against him.

'It is all right, Serena. You are safe now.'

He cursed the inadequacy of the words, but she leaned into him while hard, noisy sobs tore through her. He continued to hold her, but the room was cooling rapidly, so he swept her up and carried her through the adjoining door into his bedchamber. She clung to him as he used one foot to push the large armchair closer to the fire, then sat down with Serena across his lap. The sobs had turned to tears and she was weeping unrestrainedly, but at least with the warmth of his body on one side and a good fire on the other, she should not become chilled. She huddled against him, clutching at his coat. The curls piled upon her head were tickling his chin and he reached up to pull out the pins. Her hair fell down her back in a thick curtain of rippling gold that shimmered in the firelight.

At last the weeping stopped. She gave a sigh, muffled because her face was still hidden in his shoulder.

'I beg your pardon,' she muttered. 'I *never* cry.'

'You have had a trying day.' His lips twitched at the understatement. He shifted slightly so that he could reach into his pocket. 'Here. I would rather you blew your nose on this than my coat.'

She gave a watery chuckle as she took the handkerchief.

'That's better,' he told her. 'Now, can you walk, or shall I carry you to your room?'

Immediately she clung to him.

'Not yet.' Her voice was breathless with fear. 'Please, may we stay here for a little longer? I do not want to be alone just yet.'

Quinn sat back in the chair, stifling an impatient sigh. 'Another five minutes then.'

He settled her more comfortably on his lap and arranged the wrap over her bare feet. Very pretty little feet, he noted.

'You must think me a...a blasted nuisance,' she murmured.

'I do.' He smiled at the unladylike term.

'I was t-trying to find a husband, you see.'

He glanced down at the golden head and the profile with its straight little nose and dainty chin. Her eyes were closed, the long lashes fanning out on to her bruised cheek. Her mouth, what he could see of it, was drooping slightly at present, but it looked eminently kissable.

'I do not see that you needed to go to such dangerous lengths for that. There must be hundreds of eligible suitors lining up to offer for you.'

Her hand tightened on his lapel and she snuggled closer. 'That is just it. The eligible ones are not at all interesting.' She said drowsily, 'And much as I want to run my own establishment I *cannot* bring myself to marry a man who bores me.'

'You would rather have one who abuses you?'

He could not keep the anger from his voice, but she did not respond and when he looked down he saw she was sleeping. Quinn put his head back and closed his eyes. He would take her to her room and get Mrs Talbot to put her to bed, but not yet. He had to admit there was something rather pleasant about the way she was nestled against him.

Quinn had no idea how long he slept, but when he opened his eyes the first rays of the dawn sun were shining through the window and glinting on the golden head resting on his shoulder. He groaned.

'Oh, Lord.'

Chapter Three

Serena's eyelids fluttered as she awoke from a deep slumber. She lay still for a moment, allowing the usual morning noises to soothe her, but something was not quite right. The birdsong outside her window was not mixed with the rumble of carriages and her bed—it was comfortable, yes, but the pillow was fatter and the freshly laundered sheets smelled of lavender. Her night-gown, too, did not feel like her usual soft linen and it was so large that it was tangled around her.

She sat up quickly, much to the alarm of the little maid who was tidying a truckle bed in the corner. The girl jumped up and regarded Serena with anxious eyes.

'Oh, mistress, I beg your pardon. Did I wake you?'

Serena gave a slight shake of the head and pulled the voluminous cotton wrap closer about her. There were dark terrors prowling at the edge of her memory but she could not face them just yet. The hangings around her bed had not been drawn and she looked slowly around the room. It was unfamiliar, but comfortably furnished and full of morning sunshine.

'Where am I?'

The question was more to herself than the maid, but the girl bobbed a curtsy.

'Melham Court, m'm. Lord Quinn's Hertfordshire residence.'

Quinn. He had rescued her from… No. She would not think of that. She would think of Lord Quinn, the way he had coaxed her from the bath. The way he had held her. She put a hand to her head. Was it only last night that he had brought her here? She must have spoken aloud, for the little maid bobbed another curtsy.

'Yes, m'm. Shall I call Mrs Talbot?'

'No, no, pray do not disturb her. But I should like something to drink.' Serena smiled at the young maid. 'Could you fetch me something warm. Hot chocolate, perhaps, or coffee?'

'Of course, m'm. I'll do that straight away. But Mrs Talbot did say I was to inform her, as soon as you was awake.'

The maid hurried off and Serena drew up her knees, clasping her arms about them as she finally turned her mind to the events that had brought her here. She touched her neck. Her windpipe felt bruised and it hurt when she swallowed. The shock and fear she had felt at Sir Timothy's attempted seduction was still there, but on top of that she felt remorse and humiliation. She had been foolish in the extreme. Arrogant, too, to think she could play such games without risk.

How worried Henry and Dorothea must be. She glanced at the bell-pull and considered requesting a note should be sent to them immediately, but decided against it. She would be back with them in a few hours, she was sure. Lord Quinn would arrange it.

She rested her chin on her knees and considered her

host. Her rescuer. It was curious that she should have such confidence in a stranger. She had felt nothing but revulsion when Sir Timothy had put his hands on her. She remembered trying to wash away the feel of his touch from her skin, yet she had allowed Quinn to see her completely naked. She had not flinched as he had dried her and dressed her in this ridiculously large wrap. And when she wept he had cradled her in his arms. For such a big man he had been surprisingly gentle and she had clung to him, feeling safe and secure enough to curl up on his lap and fall asleep.

No man had ever held her thus before, not even Papa. In truth, Serena barely remembered her father. Neither could she remember much about her mother. Mama was a shadowy figure, nothing more than swirl of fashionable silks and a trace of perfume who had disappeared from her life completely when Papa had died. Serena had grown up in the care of nannies until she was old enough to be sent to school and after that she only met her half-brothers on rare occasions. She had grown up resilient, self-sufficient and independent. But very much alone.

There was a murmur of voices outside the door and the maid came in, carrying a tray laden with coffee, bread and butter. She was followed by the housekeeper, Mrs Talbot, who had a foaming cloud of lemon and white over her arm. She greeted Serena with a cheerful smile.

'Good morning to you, Miss Russington. I trust you slept well? We have done what we can to clean and repair your clothing. 'tis not perfect, but I think, with your shawl about you, it will do to get you home.'

Home! Serena glanced at the window. The angle of

the sun showed it was much later than she had first thought.

'Oh, heavens, yes.' She waved away the breakfast tray. 'There is no time to lose. I must get up immediately. I did not realise I had slept so long.'

'All in good time, miss.' Gently but firmly, the older lady ushered Serena back into bed and smoothed the bedclothes so that the maid could put the tray down before her. 'Lord Quinn instructed that you should be left to sleep as long as you wished this morning.'

'That is all very well, but—'

The housekeeper put up her hands. 'Lord Quinn insists you break your fast before you go downstairs. And his lordship likes his orders to be obeyed.'

Serena sank back against the pillows. She did not feel up to a battle of wills with anyone, let alone a man to whom she owed so much. Obediently she drank her coffee while Mrs Talbot directed the maid in her duties, tidying the room and building up the fire, before sending her away to wash her hands and fetch up hot water.

'When Meggy comes back she will help you to dress,' she told Serena, when the coffee was drunk and the last crumb eaten. 'Then you are to go down to the library.' She picked up the tray and headed for the door. 'Lord Quinn is waiting there for you.'

Some half-hour later Serena asked Meggy to show her the way to the library. A glance in the looking glass on the dressing table told her the bruise on her cheek was now blue-black, but there was nothing she could do to hide it. However, it was not painful and Serena did her best to ignore it. Mrs Talbot had washed her muslin fichu and Serena crossed it over the bodice of her gown and tied it at the back, so no one would see the repairs, but there were shadowy marks on the petticoats, evidence of her struggle with Sir Timothy. As she descended the stairs, the whisper of her satin skirts taunted her. It was easy enough to replace a gown, but her lost reputation was an altogether different matter.

She had been oblivious to her surroundings last night and had no idea what Melham Court looked like from the outside, but from what she could see inside, it was clearly an old building and everything suggested it was well maintained. The wainscoting and the staircase, with its intricately carved balusters, were polished to a high shine and there was not a speck of dust on the windowsills. Fine paintings covered the walls and exquisite porcelain was displayed on side tables. Serena was in no mood to dwell on her surroundings, but there was an indefinable feeling of calm comfort about the house. Meggy left her in the staircase hall, where a waiting footman escorted her through the great hall, with its lofty vaulted roof, to the library.

Serena's step faltered as the servant opened the door and it was with a definite straightening of the back that she stepped across the threshold. Lord Quinn was standing in the window embrasure, scrutinising a large framed canvas propped against one side of the bay. He did not appear to notice her entry and she walked across the room until she, too, could see the picture. It was a woman, half-naked, sitting on a velvet-covered couch and looking into a mirror held aloft by two red-haired cherubs. The painting glowed with colour, especially the golden sheen of the woman's hair and the deep red velvet drapes that covered the lower half of her body.

She said, 'Is that a Titian?'

'Yes. *Venus with a Mirror.*'

'By the master, or a copy by his students? I believe there are several versions in existence.' He looked at her in surprise and she explained, 'My half-brother made a tour of Italy during the Peace of Amiens. He came back full of admiration for the old masters and talked of them to anyone who would listen.'

Serena stopped. She often encouraged Henry to tell her about art, especially when he summoned her to his study to criticise some aspect of her behaviour. She thought wryly that the situation now was not so very different. Lord Quinn had turned his attention back to the painting.

'Experts are agreed this is by the master.' He beckoned her to come closer. 'Look at the brush strokes. He has given her a most natural complexion and the velvet is so fine one can almost see each thread.'

His enthusiasm was infectious and it distracted her from other, more disturbing thoughts, a dark, shadowy terror she did not want to face. She took another step towards the picture. 'I like the way we see her reflection in the mirror.'

'But look at her eyes,' he said. 'She is not actually looking in the mirror; her gaze is towards someone out of the frame. Her lover perhaps?'

He turned to her for an answer as if it was the most natural thing in the world. Serena felt a blush stealing into her cheeks. She was an unmarried lady, she should not discuss such things with a stranger. His look changed, as if he realised how inappropriate was their conversation and he turned away with something between a cough and a growl.

'I beg your pardon. I should not be talking about

Titian when there are far more important matters to discuss.'

There were indeed. Her spirits sank and she waited to be rebuked for her folly.

'That bruise on your face, for example. Does it hurt?'

She blinked. 'No…that is, only if I touch it.'

He nodded, then turned and walked across to the desk. 'You must be wishing you were at home.'

No. I wish I could run away and hide from the world.

'Of course.'

'I took the liberty of writing to Lord and Lady Hambridge, to assure them that you are safe.' He picked up a letter. 'I sent it at first light and this has just arrived, express. They are on their way to fetch you.'

'Thank you, my lord. You are too kind.' She looked at her hands, twisting themselves together as if trying to wipe away the shame of it all. 'Kinder than I have any right to expect.'

Her voice wobbled and she bowed her head to hide her tears.

'Enough of that, madam. You were served an ill turn by a rogue. *He* is to blame, not you. You behaved foolishly, to be sure, but you have escaped quite lightly, in the circumstances.' She kept her head down and dashed a tear from her cheek. She heard a couple of hasty steps and he was before her, holding out his handkerchief. 'Come now, dry your eyes. Lord and Lady Hambridge will not be much more than an hour. What would you like to do until then?'

Serena wiped away the tears and took a couple of deep breaths. 'I had best return to my room.'

As she handed the handkerchief back to him he caught her fingers and she looked up quickly. His hazel eyes were fixed upon her and she felt the full force of his penetrating gaze.

'If I were a doctor I would prescribe fresh air to put a little colour back into your cheeks.' His brows snapped together. 'There is no need to look like that, Miss Russington. I have no designs upon your virtue, but I would have you look less like a corpse when your brother comes to fetch you.'

His rough manner had its affect. For the first time since this whole sorry business had begun she felt like smiling, if only a little.

'Very well, my lord. I shall take a turn in the gardens. If you will excuse me...'

'Oh, no,' he said. 'The place is a rabbit warren. I will not risk losing you.'

'I must not take any more of your time,' she protested.

'Not at all. I should like to show you the gardens. Now run upstairs and fetch your shawl.'

Quinn escorted his guest out of doors, resigning himself to an hour's tedium. He could have appointed a servant to accompany her, if he was so worried about the woman's well-being, but something had made him speak, and once the words were out there was no going back. He led her out into the cobbled courtyard around which the old house was built. The west front with its central, castellated gatehouse was of sturdy stone, while the other three walls were all half or fully timbered, the upper stories jutted out and a haphazard collection of leaded windows overlooked the yard.

'The building predates the Tudor monarchs, I think?' she said, looking around.

'Yes. It is medieval in origin but there have been alterations, over the centuries.' He pointed out the most notable features. 'Look up there. That room on the first floor was originally the solar, but it was rebuilt later and you can see Henry VIII's emblems carved on the timbers. And over there, the open arcade running along the eastern side is one of the finest of its kind.'

'And the clock face in the gatehouse tower, is that new?'

'Yes. I installed that a few years ago, when we carried out repairs.'

He was reluctant to say too much for fear of boring her, but Serena appeared to be genuinely interested. She asked pertinent questions and he found himself telling her what he knew of the house's history.

'It was built for a wealthy farmer and passed into my own family only two generations back. My ancestors never cared for it,' he told her. 'There are few guest chambers and the reception rooms are small. The house does not lend itself to entertaining.'

'Oh, but surely there is room to dance in the great hall,' she replied. 'It would be a wonderful setting for a ball and guests could always be accommodated at the local inns, could they not?'

'I did not move here to be sociable, Miss Russington.'

She lapsed into silence and he cursed himself for snapping at her. He sensed she had withdrawn from him, even though her fingers still rested on his sleeve. He led her out through the arch saying, as they crossed the bridge, 'There is a moat, too. You may not have noticed it when we drove in last night.'

Damnation, another blunder, to remind her how she came to be here! Nothing for it but to continue.

'The stables, gardens and outhouses are spread over the adjoining land, but the moat surrounds the house and has always defined its limits.'

'Perfect, if you do not wish to be sociable.'

He glanced down quickly, not sure he had heard aright. She was looking around her, but he detected a very slight upward tilt to her mouth. So, she had not quite lost her spirit. The thought cheered him.

'My lord, someone is approaching!' Her hand tightened on his arm and he looked up.

'Devil take it, 'tis Crawshaw, the vicar. And he has seen us.'

Serena watched the stocky figure in cleric's robes hurry towards them, one hand holding his shallow-crowned hat firmly on his head. She pulled her fan from her reticule, spreading it wide as the vicar greeted them.

'Lord Quinn. Well met, sir, well met indeed. I was hoping for a word.'

He stopped before them, beaming and looking from Quinn to Serena, clearly waiting to be presented. Surely even someone as famously rude as Lord Quinn must comply. She kept the fan high, almost hiding her face. Better that Mr Crawshaw should think her shy than he should see that tell-tale bruise.

'Miss Russington is waiting for her guardian to collect her,' explained Lord Quinn, once introductions had been performed. 'We expect him any moment.'

'Then I shall not keep you,' replied the vicar. 'I merely wanted to discuss the repairs to the bell tower. Have you seen the church, ma'am? It is a fine example of the perpendicular Gothic. You must allow Lord Quinn to show it to you before you leave.'

Serena murmured something polite and Quinn dismissed Mr Crawshaw with a promise that he would make a generous donation to the restoration fund.

'Nothing could have been more unfortunate,' he muttered under his breath, when the vicar had gone on his way. 'I beg your pardon, Miss Russington. I hope I have given him the impression that you have only spent the morning here.'

'Is he likely to speak of me?'

'I hope not, but I thought it best to keep to the truth as far as possible.'

'Of course. To be caught out in a lie would be the worst of all worlds,' she replied. 'Let us pray he is too intent upon repairing his bell tower.'

Quinn gave a bark of laughter. 'After what I said to him, I have no doubt he will expect me to pay for the whole.'

'Would you have done that if I had not been here?' She sighed. 'Your silence gives me my answer. I do not know how I am to repay you for all your kindness, my lord.'

'I do not want any recompense, madam, merely to see you safely returned to your guardian.'

'Perhaps I should go indoors until then, lest there are more visitors.'

'If you wish.' He hesitated. 'But the sun is still shining and you have not yet seen the gardens.'

Hell and damnation, Quinn, what are you doing?

He should take her back, leave her with Mrs Talbot until Hambridge arrived. After all, he had put himself out more than enough for the woman already. But when she indicated that she would like to continue their walk, he was not displeased. The day suddenly became a little brighter.

* * *

It was like a dream, thought Serena. To be walking with a stranger, calmly discussing flowers. She felt oddly detached from everything. Until she had climbed into Sir Timothy's carriage yesterday, she had thought herself very much in control of her own life, but she realised now that had been an illusion. Her half-brothers and their wives had always been there to protect her. Even when she had slipped away to flirt with some gentleman, their proximity had given her a modicum of protection.

Putting herself in Sir Timothy's power had changed all that. She had been in real danger. He had intended to rape her, then force her into marriage to gain control of her fortune. She had fought him desperately, prepared to die rather than give in, and the bruises around her throat convinced her that her defiance might well have ended with her death.

Quinn had rescued her, but her life was still in ruins. Dorothea and Henry would insist she went into the country. If the whole affair could be hushed up then after a suitable period she might be allowed to return to society, but she knew she would never be as confident, happy and carefree as she had been one day ago. Things had changed. *She* had changed. No matter how brightly the sun shone everything was dulled by the grey cloud that enveloped her and weighed heavily upon her spirits.

'You are not attending, Miss Russington.'

Lord Quinn's gruff tones brought Serena out of her reverie and she quickly begged pardon.

'I asked what you thought of these roses from China. They bloom every spring, even this year, despite the atrocious weather.'

'Oh. Yes. They are very beautiful.' She glanced up, needing to be truthful. 'I was thinking of my future.'

'No doubt you think it destroyed for ever,' he said. 'Do not believe it. You are feeling very sorry for yourself at present but you will forget this unfortunate episode, in time.'

'I do not think so.' She pulled her arm free to rearrange her shawl.

'Believe me, you will recover. Why should you not, when you have all the advantages of birth, fortune and a family to support you?'

'I never thought myself in any danger until yesterday. Until Sir Timothy b-began to maul me.' Her fingers crept to her throat. 'I thought I was going to die. I shall never forget that.'

'Perhaps not, but you must not let it blight your life.'

His cool assurance annoyed her.

'How dare you tell me what I must or must not do? What do you know about me, about how I feel?' She gave an angry sob, saying wildly, 'There is nothing left for me now. Nothing.'

'Stop that!' He caught her shoulders, pulling her round to face him and giving her a little shake. 'You are what,' he demanded, 'eighteen, nineteen?'

She turned her head away, presenting the undamaged side of her face to him.

'Much older than that.' She sniffed. 'I am almost one-and-twenty.'

'Very well then. You have years of happiness before you, if you wish it, and with such advantages as many can only dream of. How dare you think your life is over, merely because some ignominious creature tried to seduce you? He did not succeed and you are alive, Serena. *Alive*. You should be grateful for that.'

He has lost someone.

She looked up into his eyes and saw the pain behind his anger. Her self-pity faded. She wanted to apologise, to ask him about his past, but even as the words were forming he released her and turned away.

'It is time we returned to the house.' He drew her hand back through his arm. 'Your family will be here soon. It is better that they do not find us wandering out of doors.'

Serena was sitting in the drawing room with Mrs Talbot when Henry and Dorothea arrived. The latticed windows of the panelled room looked out across the gardens, so she did not hear the coach on the drive, but at the sound of voices in the great hall she rose and faced the door.

'Where is she?' Dorothea's shrill voice echoed through the house and an instant later she was in the room, hurrying towards Serena. 'Oh, good heavens, look at your face!'

'It is only a bruise, Dorothea. I have suffered no other hurt, I promise you.'

'Then you have escaped more lightly than you deserve! What on earth possessed you to go off like that? We have been positively *frantic* with worry!'

'Now, now, my dear, do not scold her. We must be thankful that Serena is safe and well.' Henry followed his wife into the room, less anger and more concern in his face.

Dorothea took Serena's hands and gave her a searching look. 'You are sure there is no *irrevocable* harm done?'

'None, Dorothea, you have my word.' Serena glanced at Mrs Talbot, who was moving towards the door.

'If you will excuse me, Miss Russington, I am sure Lord and Lady Hambridge would like a little wine and cake after their journey.'

As the door closed behind the housekeeper, Dorothea rounded on Serena.

'Foolish, *thoughtless* girl, to deceive us in this way! When you did not come home last night I naturally thought I had mistaken the matter and you were staying with the Downings. Then this morning, when Elizabeth and her brother came to ask if you had recovered, I was quite thrown into a panic.' Dorothea sank down on the sofa, pulling out her handkerchief. 'I was so overset there was no keeping from them that you were not at home. The shame of it! It will be months before we will be able to hold our heads up again.'

Henry patted her shoulder. 'There, there, my dear, pray do not distress yourself.' He looked at Serena and took up the tale. 'If it had not been for the fact that you had quite clearly engineered this whole escapade, Serena, we would have called in the Runners immediately. As it is, Lord Quinn's note arrived shortly after the Downings had quit the house.'

'It was very bad of me, Henry, I apologise.'

'Apologies are no good,' snapped Dorothea. 'Your credit with the Downings is quite gone. Oh, they have promised they will not say a word, but I do not doubt they are laughing up their sleeves at us, convinced you made a secret assignation.'

'I did, Dorothea, but everything went horribly wrong.' Serena hung her head. 'I arranged to go to Vauxhall with Sir Timothy Forsbrook.'

'Forsbrook!' cried Henry. 'Then what are you doing at Melham Court?'

They were interrupted by a soft knock on the door and their host came in.

'I could not help overhearing your question, Hambridge,' he said, with all his customary bluntness. 'Perhaps you will allow me to answer for your sister. She is not yet fully recovered from her ordeal.' Gently, he took Serena's arm and guided her back to her chair. 'Forsbrook abducted Miss Russington and brought her to the Swan, just outside Hitchin, where I came upon him, forcing his attentions upon her.'

'The devil he was!' Henry sank down beside his wife.

'I understand his plan was to make sure of her before carrying on to the border, where he would make her his wife.'

'For her fortune, no doubt!' put in Dorothea.

Quinn bowed. 'Precisely, ma'am. When Miss Russington realised his intention, she bravely fought him off, but it left her understandably distressed. There being no suitable female at the Swan, I brought Miss Russington to Melham Court and placed her in the care of my housekeeper.'

The way Quinn relayed the story it all sounded so sensible and straightforward, thought Serena. And perfectly respectable. There was no reason he should tell them that he had helped her, naked, from the bath. That she had spent the night in his arms.

A second knock heralded the return of Mrs Talbot with refreshments. Serena took advantage of the distraction to glance up at Quinn. His smile was brief but reassuring.

When they were alone again, Henry said, 'We are in your debt, my lord, for your assistance to our sister.'

'Although I have to say she brought it on herself,' Dorothea said, 'scheming to go off alone with a man. I have warned her, time and again, what would come of her headstrong ways!'

Quinn shook his head. 'Whatever Miss Russington's behaviour, madam, it is Forsbrook who acted wrongly.'

'I should call him out,' muttered Henry, frowning, 'But I fear that would only make matters worse.'

'I agree,' said Quinn. 'The object now must be to protect Miss Russington's reputation.'

'If it can be done,' said Dorothea, shooting a resentful glance at Serena. 'You know how these things get about.'

Henry was more optimistic. 'Forsbrook will not want it known that his abduction failed. But you mean the Downings, I suppose, my dear, since they are the only other people who know of this. They have agreed to say nothing and I am sure they will keep their word. After all, what do they really know, save that Serena did not go to Vauxhall with them? No, the main thing now is to get Serena back to Bruton Street with all speed. I am sure Lord Quinn will understand if we do not tarry.'

'Of course. The sooner you remove Miss Russington from this house the better.'

Serena had grown used to Quinn's manner, but she saw Henry blink at these terse words and Dorothea positively bridled.

Serena said quickly, 'Then let us not take up any more of Lord Quinn's time. If you have finished your wine, Brother, we will be gone.'

* * *

'Well,' exclaimed Henry, as the carriage rattled out of the courtyard, 'I had heard it said that Rufus Quinn had no social graces and now I have seen it for myself. Why, he virtually threw us out of the house.'

'You said yourself we should not tarry,' Serena reminded him, but she could not help feeling disappointed. Quinn had left it to Henry to escort her to the carriage.

'That may be so, but the fellow was positively curt,' retorted Henry, settling himself back into a corner. 'Heaven knows he must have some good qualities, Serena, but you have to admit he has no manners.'

'Yes, for all his wealth he is odiously rude,' Dorothea agreed. She glanced out of the window, 'And I had expected Melham Court to be much grander. Why, I should be ashamed to receive visitors in such a small house.'

'I do not think Lord Quinn wishes to be sociable,' murmured Serena.

Henry snorted. 'Well, thank goodness he spends so little time in town, because I confess I should find it difficult to be civil to such a man!'

Chapter Four

Serena kept to her room for a full week and even after that she was reluctant to leave the house. Gradually the bruises and the horror of the abduction faded, but her spirits remained low. She had no defence against Dorothea's constant reminders of how badly she had behaved. Even a note from Elizabeth Downing, wishing her well, could not raise her mood. Henry cheerfully assured her that she could go out and about again as if nothing had happened.

'Trust me,' he told her, 'Lord Byron's flight to the Continent and the salacious rumours that have been circulating about him have cast your little scrape into the shade. And now there's speculation that poor Brummell is quite done up. And don't forget Princess Charlotte's recent wedding. The gossipmongers are far too busy to concern themselves with you, Sister.'

Dorothea, who had been listening, gave a little snort of derision. 'You believe that if you will, Henry, but I think such optimism is misplaced.'

It was. Late one afternoon, barely ten days after the thwarted abduction, Serena heard the ominous words that

Lord Hambridge wished to see her in his study. Henry and his wife were deep in conversation when she entered and looked so anxious that she stopped by the door.

'Is something wrong?'

'It is indeed,' exclaimed Dorothea. 'You are undone.'

'Undone?' Serena moved to a chair and perched herself on the edge of it. 'I don't understand.'

'I was taking tea with Lady Grindlesham two days ago when more visitors came in,' Dorothea told her. 'Among them Mr Walsham. He had just returned to London after going north to attend his father's funeral.' She added pointedly, 'He was one of the suitors you rejected, Serena.'

'Yes, I remember. A horrid little man. What of it?'

Dorothea tapped her foot on the floor and glared at her husband, who said solemnly, 'Walsham was on the night mail on May Day. It stopped at the Swan. *He saw you there*, Serena, going up the stairs with a man. He is now making it very clear to everyone that he is exceedingly relieved you rejected his offer.'

Dorothea jumped up and began to pace the room. 'You know what a gossip Walsham is,' she said. 'And a vicious tongue, too. Of course, I told him he must be mistaken, that it could not have been you, but the damage is done. I have just come back from Bond Street, where more than one acquaintance stopped me to ask after you. Lady Mattishall even asked me outright if you had eloped!'

'Oh, dear,' said Serena faintly.

'It is time you were seen out and about,' Henry told her. 'You must drive out with Dorothea, then at least we may stop the rumours that you have run off. And there is one stroke of luck,' he continued. 'Walsham was unable to name the fellow at the Swan. If I had dined at home rather than going to White's that night, we might have said I was escorting you. As it is, we must continue to deny that it was you at Hitchin that night.'

'Which the Downings will not believe,' cut in his wife, still pacing.

'Elizabeth assured me in her letter that they have not said anything,' added Serena.

'Which is quite true,' Henry agreed. 'And in time the rumours will be forgotten.'

'In time!' Dorothea shook her head. 'Serena is very nearly one-and-twenty. By next Season she will be considered an old maid. I vow I am ready to give up on her!'

'Perhaps you should. I know I have disgraced myself, and I am very sorry for it.'

'Well, one thing is plain now, madam.' Dorothea stopped her perambulations and glared at Serena. 'There is no possibility of your marrying well!'

Henry protested mildly, 'Come, come, my dear. Serena still has a considerable fortune. *Someone* will have her.'

Serena winced. 'I will not marry a man merely to save my reputation,' she said. 'I am already resigned to remaining single.'

Dorothea's eyes narrowed. 'Pray do not think we will allow you to set up your own establishment. What would people say about us then?'

'They would most likely say I was an eccentric. And they would pity you most sincerely.'

'It is not to be thought of,' declared Henry. 'Once you come into your own money at five-and-twenty it will be a different matter, but at the moment you are far too young to consider such a thing.'

'Perhaps I could go and live with Russ and Molly at Compton Parva.'

Henry shook his head. 'It will not do. You are known there and I have no doubt they will have heard all about this little episode, even in such an out-of-the-way place. I have written to Russ, assuring him it is all nonsense and that there is no need for him to come to town.'

'No indeed,' agreed Dorothea. 'His concern must be for his wife. I believe the birth was a difficult one and she is not yet recovered. They will not be able to look after Serena.'

Serena's chin went up. 'I do not expect anyone to look after me. I merely need somewhere to live.'

'To hide, more like.'

'Call it that, if you wish, Dorothea.' Serena rose. 'I will drive out with you in the carriage, so that people may see I am in town, but please do not ask me to accompany you to any balls or parties. I do not feel ready to meet anyone just yet. Perhaps you could say I am recuperating,' she suggested. 'That would give you an excuse to ship me off to the country.'

'It would, my dear, if that is really what you want, but let us discuss it again later. Off you go now and change your gown for dinner. We will say no more about it tonight.' Henry waited until Serena had left the room, then he said slowly, 'I do not like it, Dorothea. She has lost her spirit.'

'That can only be a good thing. The girl was growing far too wild.'

'I grant you she was always a little hot to hand, but this new meekness—I cannot be easy. Perhaps we should call the doctor.'

'What, and have him quack her with expensive and

unnecessary medicines? No, leave her be, Henry. I have long considered that she thinks far too highly of herself. This incident with Forsbrook has brought her down to earth. I have no doubt she will recover and, in the meantime, we should seek out a husband for her. With her fortune it should not be impossible to find an acceptable match, despite this scandal.'

'I agree. There are several fellows who would take her, I am sure.'

'Then we should see to it, while she is so biddable.'

Henry shook his head. 'I don't know, Dorothea— would it be right to persuade her to tie the knot when she is not herself? When her spirits return she might regret it.'

His wife cast him an impatient glance. 'That will be her husband's problem, not ours.'

Quinn scooped up the small pile of letters from his desk and glanced at each one. Nothing from Bruton Street.

'Confound it, what do you expect?' he growled to himself as he threw the letters back down.

It was nearly two weeks since Hambridge had carried Serena away from Melham Court, but the fellow was unlikely to write and thank him for his part in rescuing his ward and it would be highly improper for Serena to do so. Discretion was the watchword and it would be foolhardy for any mention of the matter to be committed to paper.

He reached for a pen and began to trim the nib. He should forget all about it. After all, he wanted no thanks for what he had done. But the image of Serena haunted his dreams. Not the cowering figure he had come upon at the Swan, but Serena as he had seen her in the gardens of Grindlesham House, head up, eyes sparkling with indignation. The same eyes that had gazed upon him so trustingly as he coaxed her from her bath.

His hands stilled at the memory. He had subdued the thought at the time, but she had reminded him of a painting he had seen as a very young man: another Titian Venus, but this time the goddess was rising from the sea. Shy, vulnerable and utterly enchanting.

Quinn shifted in his chair. Enough of this. He had no interest in Serena Russington. She had foolishly put herself in danger and he had acted as any gentleman would, nothing more. The Hambridges would look after her and quell any gossip, so there was no point in Quinn worrying about the chit. But he was damned if he could forget her!

He heard voices in the hall and the study door opened.

'Tony!' Quinn jumped up and came around the desk, holding out his hand to his friend. 'I thought you were staying in town for another month at least.'

'That had been my intention. Lottie remains in town—she has engagements that she cannot break, but I confess my curiosity got the better of me.' Sir Anthony Beckford gestured towards his buckskins and glossy Hessians. 'I am on my way now to Prior's Holt, but thought I would stop off and try some of the claret you were boasting of.'

'By all means. Come along to the drawing room and I will have Dunnock fetch some.'

In very little time they were sitting comfortably, a decanter on the small table between them and a glass of ruby-red wine in hand.

Quinn watched in amusement as his friend made a

show of sniffing the wine and taking a sip before nodding appreciatively.

'Excellent. This came in through Bristol, you say? I must put my man on to it.'

'Send him to Averys and they will see to it.' Quinn shot a glance at his friend. 'But you did not come here merely to taste my wine. What is it that has whetted your curiosity?'

'Why you, my friend.' Tony lifted his glass to the light and twisted the stem between his fingers. 'I came to discover for myself if you have taken a mistress.'

The calm atmosphere of the drawing room became suddenly tense. Quinn schooled his expression into one of amusement.

'What an absurd idea. You know I am not in the petticoat line.'

'That is what I thought, but the rumours in town made me wonder.'

Quinn put down his glass. The way his hand had been tightening around it he was afraid he might snap the stem.

'Then perhaps you would be good enough to tell me just what it is that you have heard.'

'I was at White's a couple of nights back and Walsham came in. You may not know him. Something of a mushroom, but with connections enough to give him entrée into most places in town. He strolls up to Hambridge and asks after his sister. Now, in general such a remark would pass unnoticed, but a sudden hush fell over the room, and Hambridge looked so put out there was no ignoring it.' Tony settled himself more comfortably in his chair. 'Walsham did not leave it there, however. He pulls out his snuff box and says, in the coolest way imaginable. "Your good lady told me I was mistaken in thinking Miss Russington was at the Swan and it must be so, because Jack Downing says she cried off from Vauxhall that very same evening, pleading ill health. I trust it is not serious, no one's seen her for well over a week." Well, by this time Hambridge is frowning like a thundercloud. He jumped to his feet, exclaiming that he had no patience with all the tattling busybodies who try to make mischief out of nothing. Then he stalked off. Quite out of character, I thought. He is generally such a dull dog.'

'And this is all?' Quinn refilled their glasses. 'My dear Tony, I am surprised at you, to be taking note of such a trifle.'

'And I should not have thought any more about it, had I not gone to Tattersall's yesterday. You will recall there was a very pretty Arab mare I had my eye on, but that is by the by. I ran into Sir Timothy Forsbrook there, you see. He was selling his greys and mighty cut up about it, too. Blamed it all on a woman who had dashed his hopes. He was in his cups and happy to tell anyone who would listen how the mysterious *Miss R.* had persuaded him to run away with her on May Day, only to abandon him at Hitchin for a much richer prize.' Tony's shoulders lifted a fraction. 'The *richer prize* was not named, of course, but I remembered you had travelled to Melham Court that evening, and would have passed the Swan.' He paused. 'It made me wonder—'

'Hell and damnation!'

At Quinn's violent exclamation Tony's casual manner deserted him and he sat bolt upright.

'Never say that there is any truth in this, Quinn!'

'No. Yes!' Quinn jumped to his feet. 'Has anyone else connected me with this affair?'

'Not yet, although at the clubs last night they were already beginning to link Forsbrook's juicy tale to Walsham's gossip. 'tis commonly believed now that the lady is Serena Russington, Hambridge's ward.'

Cursing softly, Quinn went over to the window. He said over his shoulder, 'I stopped at the Swan on my way home. Forsbrook was there and I…er…removed Miss Russington from his company. She was unharmed, save for a few bruises, but it was already gone midnight so I was obliged to bring her here.' *No need to go into detail, Quinn.* 'I put her into Mrs Talbot's care until the Hambridges could collect her the next day. As for her persuading Forsbrook to elope, I believe it was quite the reverse. He tricked her into accompanying him.'

'Then why hasn't Hambridge called him out?'

'He thought it would cause the sort of scandal he was anxious to avoid.' Quinn's jaw tightened. 'I agreed with him, at the time. I thought Forsbrook would be too embarrassed by what had happened to blab about it. Now I see we were wrong.' He turned back and looked at his friend. 'Well there, at least, I will be able to act!'

'The devil you will. Confound it, Quinn, you are so rarely in town your mere presence there sets the *ton* by the ears. If you come back to call the fellow out, I won't be the only one to remember you live within a stone's throw of Hitchin. No, no, you keep well out of it, my friend. No need to become involved.'

'I am already involved,' Quinn reminded him, a trifle grimly. 'And the devil of it is that Crawshaw met her here, the following morning.'

'The vicar! That's a dashed nuisance.'

'Aye. I had no choice but to introduce him. So far he hasn't said anything, but…' Quinn let the words hang and a brooding silence fell over the room.

At last Tony gave a sigh. 'Well, Crawshaw is a good fellow and not one to gossip. I suppose your servants know the whole?'

'How could they not? I can rely upon Dunnock and Mrs Talbot to be discreet, but some of the younger ones may let it slip.'

'And since most of 'em are related to my own staff, everyone at Prior's Holt knows of your visitor by now. Not to worry. I'll have a word, stop it spreading further if I can. Of course, it would be better coming from Lottie, as mistress of the house, but she's still in town. I'll write to her, tell her to do what she can to squash any rumours she hears.'

'You are both very good, but I fear it may be too late for that.'

'Well, there is no need to involve yourself further,' said Tony with finality. 'You know as well as I that once gossip starts it must run its course, and if Hambridge is wise he will remove his sister from town until this has all died down.' He rose. 'Now, I had best be getting on to Prior's Holt or they will not have time to find me a decent dinner.'

'If that is the case then you can come back here and take pot luck with me,' said Quinn, accompanying him out of the house.

Once his friend had driven away Quinn returned to his study, but the letters he had planned to deal with that morning remained unopened. Instead he sat in his chair for a full half-hour, staring into space and thinking over all Tony had told him.

* * *

'Smile, Serena. And sit up straight. Remember this is for your benefit.'

Dorothea's hissed whisper was cut short as she turned to greet Lady Drycroft, whose carriage had drawn up alongside their own. It was the third day running that Dorothea had taken Serena out at the fashionable hour and the May sunshine had encouraged even greater crowds than usual to throng Hyde Park. Progress around the gravelled drives was little faster than a walk.

It was a nightmare, thought Serena. To be smiling, calmly exchanging greetings, when all she wanted was to hide from the world. It was her own fault, she had compromised herself by running off with a man and Dorothea and Henry were doing their best to mend matters. All that was expected of Serena was that she appear in public and act as if nothing had happened.

Two weeks ago, she would not have doubted her ability to ride the storm. But she was not the same confident lady who had set out to meet Sir Timothy Forsbrook. She had lost her self-assurance and no longer felt any interest in what was happening to her. However, it was easier to try to please Dorothea than oppose her, so she smiled and replied politely to the barbed comments of the spiteful. At the same time she discounted her friends' kind words, knowing she had brought this fate upon herself. Her face ached with smiling. All she really wanted to do was to take to her bed. To go to sleep and never wake up.

They returned to Bruton Street an hour later and entered the house just as Henry was crossing the hall. He waited while they discarded their bonnets and spencers, then ushered them into the drawing room.

'How was your drive around the Ring today?'

'Humiliating,' replied Dorothea. 'We received only the coolest of nods from several matrons, including Lady Mattishall. The Duchess of Bonsall cut us altogether! No one believes Serena has been ill. I have had to suffer innumerable sly remarks.'

'They will come to believe it, if you persevere. They *have* to believe it,' Henry added, his teeth clenched. He shrugged off his anxiety and said more cheerfully, 'Now that Serena is out and about again this little setback will soon be forgotten.'

'Little setback?' Dorothea retorted. 'Have you not noticed how few invitations we have received recently?' She waved towards the mantelpiece, which was usually crowded with cards. 'And even when I do go out, I am teased about it constantly.'

Serena thought that if Dorothea had not been so cool to those she considered inferior, then society might have been a little more sympathetic, but she said nothing. It did not seem worth the effort.

'Well, we must bear it for a few more weeks,' Henry replied. 'Then you can leave town for the summer. What say you to hiring a house at Worthing? You and Serena can travel ahead and I will join you as soon as Parliament rises.'

'Worthing! What is the good of that, when everyone of note will be in Brighton?'

'That is just the point, Dorothea,' Henry explained patiently. 'By the time you meet your acquaintances again, other scandals will have arisen to eclipse Serena's disgrace. Poor Brummell, for one, the wolves are already circling his door. And who knows,' he added hopefully, 'you might by then have found a husband for her.'

'You forget, Henry, I do not want a husband.'

Serena's quiet words brought a cry of exasperation from Dorothea.

'You see,' she cried, turning to her husband. 'You see what I have to put up with? If ever there was such an ungrateful wretch. Oh, go up to your room, girl, and change for dinner. Henry, where are you going?'

'I am also going up to change, my dear,' said her long-suffering husband. 'I am engaged to dine at White's tonight, so you and Serena must excuse me.'

Serena quietly followed Henry out of the room, wishing that she, too, could escape what promised to be a depressing meal in the company of her sister-in-law.

'Well, now, Miss Serena, 'tis a beautiful morning.'

Serena winced at Polly's cheerful greeting. She heard the rattle of crockery and dragged herself up in bed so that her maid could place the tray across her lap.

'Will you be joining my lady for breakfast today, ma'am?'

Polly had asked the same question every morning since Serena had returned from Melham Court and Serena's reply never varied.

'Not today, Polly. A cup of tea will suffice.'

The maid's eyes moved to the plate of bread and butter lying on the tray, but she had given up trying to persuade her mistress to eat anything in the mornings. She left Serena to drink her tea while she bustled about the room, collecting together the clean chemise, stockings and gown that her mistress would wear that day.

'Lady Hambridge is expecting visitors this morning, Miss Serena, and she has asked that you wear the powder-blue muslin.'

'Visitors?'

'Miss Althea—Lady Newbold, I *should* say, miss. She is bringing Master Arthur to visit his grandmama.'

'Oh, Lord.'

Serena closed her eyes. Althea was Henry and Dorothea's only child. She was the same age as Serena but had already been married for two years and provided her husband with a lusty heir. Dorothea was understandably proud of her daughter's achievements, as she constantly reminded Serena. There was no doubt that Althea would want to hear every horrid detail of this latest scrape, while Serena would be expected to play the doting aunt to little Arthur who, in her opinion, was developing into a bad-tempered child.

She gave a little sigh. 'Pray give my apologies and say I have the headache.'

'I will, miss,' said Polly, shaking out the blue muslin. 'But not if you are going to mope around in your room all day. We'll get you dressed and you can stroll in the gardens.' The maid met Serena's questioning eyes with a determined look in her own. 'Are we agreed, miss?'

The sun shone down on Serena's bare head and the bright day lifted her spirits sufficiently for her to think Polly had been right to press her into going out of doors. She allowed her shawl to slip off her shoulders so she could feel the sun's comforting warmth on her skin. The black cloud that enveloped her spirits was still there, but it had thinned a little.

The crunch of footsteps on the gravel path behind her made her turn.

'Lord Quinn!' Her pulse quickened. Embarrassment, she thought, given the circumstances of their previous meeting.

He came towards her, his large frame blocking the sun. 'The butler told me you were taking the air.'

'And my sister?' She looked past him, expecting to see Dorothea hurrying along behind.

'Lady Hambridge has a guest, so I said not to bother her. I would find you myself.'

Serena imagined the servants falling back before him, if not cowed by his sheer size, then dominated by the force of his personality.

'Are you come to town to buy more artwork, my lord?'

'No, I came to see how you go on.'

He stopped, towering over her, the brim of his hat shadowing his face. He looked serious, which was an advantage, since it saved her the trouble of smiling.

'As you see, sir.'

'You are very pale. I had expected you to have fully recovered your looks by now.'

'You say what everyone else is thinking, my lord. Which is why I am in the garden today.'

'Then let us walk.'

'The path is not wide enough.'

'It is if you take my arm.'

Serena hesitated, then slipped her hand on to his sleeve and they strolled on.

'This is a very small garden, compared to your own grounds at Melham Court.'

'It is sufficient to give you an airing,' he replied. 'You have been indoors too long and have lost your bloom.' She winced and he said quickly, 'Forgive me, I am not in the habit of making pretty speeches.'

A wry smile flickered within her. 'I am becoming accustomed to it, my lord. It does not offend me.'

'It doesn't?' He stopped and looked down at her. 'My friends tell me I can be brutal.'

There was a shadow of concern in his hazel eyes. It disconcerted her and she looked away.

'You tell the truth. I appreciate that.'

They had completed a full circuit of the walled garden before Lord Quinn spoke again.

'I believe there has been some talk.'

'Yes. I was recognised, at the inn. My brother has denied it, of course, but to little effect.'

'And your keeping to the house has not helped.'

'No.' She touched her cheek. 'But it was agreed I should not be seen abroad until the bruises had died down.'

'Were they very painful?'

'No more than I deserve.'

The words were a whisper, but he heard them.

'Forsbrook is the villain here, Serena, not you.' He drew a breath, as if reining in his anger, and laid his free hand over her fingers, where they rested on his arm. 'You will come about, my dear.'

The change in tone brought a sudden constriction to her throat. She fought it down and with it the desire to tell him that she did not want to *come about*.

She said, 'My brother and his wife are doing their best to make sure of it. I have started going out in the carriage. They think it is very necessary that I am seen.' She bit her lip. 'You may not know, Sir Timothy set it about that the plan to elope was mine.'

'Yes, I had heard,' he growled. 'Hambridge has denied it, of course.'

'Yes, and I hear that Sir Timothy has left town now.'

'I know.' She looked up quickly and he added, 'I, er, persuaded him.'

Serena caught the dangerous note in his voice and decided it would not be wise to ask the means of his persuasion.

'That was kind of you, but the damage is done, I fear.' Serena thought of Dorothea, sitting with her daughter in the drawing room. She said lightly, 'My reputation is ruined. My sister-in-law says no one will marry me now.'

'I will, Serena. I will marry you.'

Chapter Five

There, he had said it. Quinn felt the little hand on his sleeve tremble.

'It…it is not your place to offer for me,' she said, her voice constricted. 'None of this is your fault. You should not be punished for another's wickedness.'

'You have a very low opinion of yourself, my dear, if you think it would be a punishment to marry you.'

'Pray do not joke with me, my lord.'

'I do not. I say nothing but the truth.'

She shook her head. 'I thank you for your kind offer, Lord Quinn, but I cannot accept.'

'Why not?'

'Because you have no reason to marry me.'

A hiss of exasperation escaped him. 'Serena, you spent the night in my house.'

'It was an act of kindness. You rescued me.'

'That is beside the point. I took you to Melham Court. Mrs Talbot prepared a bed for you, but my entire household is aware you were in my room until dawn. My neighbour was in town and heard the gossip about what occurred at Hitchin and he is already drawing his own conclusions. It is only a matter of time before it becomes public knowledge.'

She waved distractedly. 'But you do not *want* to marry me!'

He caught her hands and turned her to face him. 'I am one-and-thirty and I must marry one day. It may as well be you as anyone.'

A laugh escaped her. 'When you put it so prettily, my lord, how can I refuse?'

'Precisely.' He smiled. 'I think we shall deal very well together, Serena. You are not unintelligent, you will not expect us to live in each other's pockets and there is plenty to keep you occupied. I have several properties, some are let, but there is more than one that requires a mistress. Of course, if you would rather not trouble yourself with such things there are housekeepers—'

'No, no, my lord, I like to be busy and would happily run your houses. That is, if I should accept your offer.'

'Then what say you, Serena—will you be my wife?' He saw the troubled look in her eyes and turned away, fixing his attention on a bee hovering around a nearby rose bush. He cleared his throat. 'If you are worried about the…er…other duties of a wife, I give you my word I will not force myself upon you. We will have separate bedchambers, and I shall respect your wishes on that aspect of our marriage. I shall not touch you without your consent. Until you ask it of me.'

The image flashed into his mind of Serena rising from the bath, her hair curling wildly from the steam and the water running from her naked body. Could he do this? Could he share a house with this woman and not take her to his bed? Easily, he told himself. This was a marriage of expedience, to save his reputation as much as Serena's. The affections of neither party were engaged.

So why did he feel such disappointment at her next words?

'I am very grateful of the honour you do me, Lord Quinn, but I cannot accept your offer.' She withdrew her hands from his clasp. 'It is not right that you should suffer for the rest of your life on account of my folly.'

'Suffer? Madam, I do not consider marriage to you a cause of misery. I should count myself honoured to have secured your hand.' She looked up, her dark, liquid eyes shadowed with doubt. He said, 'I am not the marrying kind, Serena, but I *am* a target for the tricks and stratagems of every matchmaking mother in town. I have even been pursued into Hertfordshire, upon occasion. I soon learned that being civil has little effect on determined parents or their daughters.'

'So you became the rudest man in town,' she murmured, a faint smile replacing the frown in her eyes.

'Oh, I was already that,' he told her. 'I do not suffer fools gladly and my manner of plain speaking is not to everyone's taste, but many females are willing to overlook that, to secure a rich husband. There is a novel out at present which is very popular—you may have read it. It begins by asserting that every single man of large fortune must be in want of a wife.'

'Yes, I know it. But it is love that triumphs in the end. You may yet fall in love, my lord.'

'No, I assure you that will not happen.' Quinn paused. 'I was engaged, once, but the lady died.'

'I am very sorry.'

He waved a hand, as if to deflect her sympathy. 'It was a long time ago. The past is gone. We cannot change it.'

'No, but it can haunt us.' She twisted her hands together. 'Perhaps you remember my mother…no?' She gave a little smile. 'Then it is only right you know, so you may reconsider offering for me. She caused quite a scandal some dozen years ago when she ran off and married a rich Italian. My father had not been dead many months.' She gave a little shrug. 'I barely remember her. The thing is…' She paused again. 'I have been told that I am very like her, in looks. And now that I have created a scandal, they will say I am like her in other ways, too.'

'I do not believe that.'

She flushed. 'No, I do not *think* it is true.'

'Then let us waste no more time on it.' He waved an impatient hand. 'Consider this, instead. In marrying me you would gain the protection of my name.'

'And *you* would have protection from unscrupulous husband-hunters.'

'Exactly, madam. So, Serena, what is your answer?'

Quinn thought he should leave, give her time to consider the matter. He was about to suggest as much when a maid came hurrying towards them.

'Miss Russington, the mistress has asked that you come to the drawing room. Immediately.'

Serena looked at Polly, who shifted uncomfortably from one foot to the other.

'I beg your pardon, ma'am.' She cast a nervous look towards Lord Quinn. 'I told her ladyship that you was in the gardens and she said I was to fetch you at once, no excuses.' Polly dragged in a deep breath, as if steeling herself to continue. 'She said, ma'am, that if you're well enough to walk in the gardens then you're well enough to join her and Lady Newbold, and to look after Master Arthur.'

'And who the devil might these people be?' demanded Lord Quinn.

Serena explained. 'Lady Newbold is my niece, Lady Hambridge's daughter. Arthur is her son, a grossly indulged infant who cries all the time. Possibly because he is overfed,' she added thoughtfully. 'Dorothea will want me to amuse him so she and Althea can talk uninterrupted.'

'Very much like a spinster aunt with nothing better to do,' Quinn muttered.

He had voiced her own thoughts and Serena could not quite stifle a sigh.

'Perhaps you should let me accompany you,' he suggested. 'We could inform Lady Hambridge and her daughter that the situation has changed.' He was regarding her steadily. 'Well, madam, what do you say. Will you accept my hand in marriage?'

Polly gave a little squeak but Serena ignored it. Could she do this? Could she marry a man she barely knew? She considered the alternative. Months, possibly years of enduring Dorothea's constant jibes. She and Henry did not really want Serena in their house. Russ and Molly had their own family now. No one needed her. No one wanted her.

She took a breath. 'Yes, Lord Quinn. Yes, I will marry you.'

'Well, I must say, Sister, I never expected to see you settled so well!'

Henry was beaming down at her, but Serena felt none

of his delight. It was her wedding day, but the sense of detachment, of sleepwalking through each day, had intensified during the past two weeks. It was as if she was merely an observer, watching a story played out before her. It was not that Serena was unhappy, rather that nothing seemed to touch her.

Dorothea's shock when Lord Quinn had announced he and Serena were to be married had soon turned to rapture. There had been a brief battle of wills when it was announced they were to be married by special licence in Bruton Street; Lady Hambridge had wanted a big wedding, perhaps in Hanover Square, where they might invite the world to see that Serena was not ruined at all but, on the contrary, making a splendid alliance. However, Dorothea was no match for Lord Quinn, who told her bluntly that the ceremony would be a private one.

'It will take place here, madam. Or, if you prefer, at Melham Court, with no one but yourselves and my neighbour. Make your choice.'

Dorothea had bridled at that, but Henry had quietly pointed out that, as Serena's guardian, he felt obliged to stand the expense of her wedding. This hit the right note with his spouse, for the considering look she threw at Serena said clearly that she was in favour of spending as little as possible upon her ungrateful sister-in-law.

Serena herself was silent throughout this interchange. Quinn had asked her earlier, and in private, if she wished her wedding to be a grand affair and she had been emphatic in her denial. She could summon no enthusiasm at all for her forthcoming nuptials. She allowed Dorothea to decide upon her bridal clothes and made no demur when she was informed that, apart from her brother and sister-in-law, the only witnesses to the ceremony would be Lord and Lady Newbold, and Quinn's neighbours, the Beckfords.

When Quinn had suggested she should invite a friend to support her, Serena had declined. She had lost touch with her friends from the various schools she had attended and since then Miss Downing had become her closest friend. In normal circumstances she would have wanted Elizabeth present, but Serena was too ashamed of the way she had deceived the Downings to invite them. So now here she was on her wedding day, in the drawing room of Bruton Street with only a handful of guests around her and feeling more alone than ever.

Quinn appeared at her side. 'You are very pale, Serena. Are you feeling faint? Would you like to sit down?'

'Tush, man, of course she does not wish to sit!' replied Henry. 'Serena never faints. She has more energy than the rest of us put together.'

'Then you must excuse a new husband for being over-protective.' Quinn took her hand and pulled it on to his arm, holding it there in a warm clasp. 'If you will excuse us, Hambridge.'

He led her away, muttering under his breath. 'Damned, insensitive fellow. Does he not know you at all?'

Surprise pierced the grey cloak of indifference wrapped about Serena.

Not as well as you, apparently, my lord.

She said, mildly, 'He and Dorothea have their own concerns. Pray do not be too critical of them. They have always done their duty by me.'

'And your other brother has not even made the effort to attend.'

'Now there you are being unjust,' she protested, roused briefly from her lethargy. 'I explained to you that Russ has a new daughter. I wrote to him, expressly forbidding him to leave Molly and the baby at such a time.'

She did not add that it had been necessary to hint at a whirlwind romance between herself and Quinn, to stop Russ posting south.

'I confess I should have liked them here,' she murmured.

'Then we shall call on them as soon as they are receiving visitors.'

'Thank you, my lord, you are very kind.'

He turned to face her. 'I am nothing of the sort. It is my duty now to attend to your comfort, Serena.'

Again, she felt a little kick of pleasure that he should think well of her, when she was so undeserving. She glanced up to find him regarding her, a faint smile in his eyes.

'The spirited lady who upbraided me in the Grindleshams' rose garden would expect nothing less of her husband.'

A stronger sensation jolted her, making her pulse race and the nerve ends tingle throughout her body.

She shook her head, her cheeks burning. 'How can you even refer to that meeting, knowing how foolishly, how *shamefully* I behaved? The creature I was then is quite, quite dead, my lord.'

'Oh, I hope not.' Her eyes flew to his face. Had she heard him correctly? He flicked her cheek with a careless finger. 'Never mind that now. I see my neighbours are eager to congratulate us. Come along.'

He led her towards Sir Anthony and Lady Beckford,

who were smiling and nodding at them from the far side of the room. Serena had only been introduced to them that morning, but now Sir Anthony reached out for her hands and lifted one then the other to his lips.

'Lady Quinn, may I offer you my congratulations?'

'Nonsense, it is Quinn who is to be congratulated upon winning himself such a lovely bride.' Lady Beckford bustled her husband out of the way and kissed Serena's cheek. 'You cannot know how delighted I am to have you as a neighbour, my dear. I hope we will be welcoming you to Prior's Holt very soon.'

'Thank you, my lady.'

'No, no, we shall not stand on ceremony—you must call me Lottie and I shall call you Serena, if I may? I am sure we shall spend many a happy hour closeted together and complaining about our husbands!'

Sir Anthony protested at that, trying to look severe and telling his wife to behave, but Lottie was irrepressible. She slid one arm about Serena.

'One always needs a close friend with whom one can grumble without it being taken seriously. Tony, Quinn and his lady must dine with us as soon as possible after the honeymoon. Where are you taking her, Quinn? Now the horrid war is over will you go abroad—Italy, perhaps?' She paused and looked from Serena to Quinn and back again. 'You *are* going away, are you not?'

'Lottie, pray do not be so inquisitive.' Tony frowned at his wife. 'It is none of our business.'

'It is no secret,' said Quinn. 'We spend tonight at Melham Court and tomorrow we set off to tour my estates. Serena must decide which, if any, she wishes to use.'

'But I thought most of them are let,' said Lottie.

'They are, but that is a minor problem, if Serena takes a fancy to one of them.'

Tears stung the back of Serena's eyes at Quinn's concern for her wishes.

Dorothea came up, smiling graciously at everyone. 'Serena, my dear, we have prepared a wedding breakfast for our guests, if you and Lord Quinn would like to lead the way to the dining room?'

He held out his arm. 'Well, madam wife, shall we go in?'

Quinn tasted nothing of the light repast laid out for him. Serena, too, he noticed only picked at her food in silence. Thank heaven Tony and Lottie were present to make polite conversation with their hosts and the Newbolds.

Lady Hambridge might have been denied her grand ceremony, but when the time came for Quinn and his bride to leave, she insisted they wait while the servants were marshalled to line the hall for their departure. All the guests spilled out on to the flagway to see them off and Dorothea even went so far as to embrace Serena.

'I hope you realise your good fortune, madam. Lord Quinn has saved you from shame and disgrace. I pray he will not live to regret it.'

Her words were softly spoken but Quinn heard them. He saw the flush on Serena's cheek and a flash of irritation ran through him. What a dragon the woman was, to say such a thing to a bride on her wedding day! For Serena's sake he took polite leave of her family but exchanged warmer farewells with Lottie and Tony before handing his bride into the waiting chaise. As the door closed upon them and they rattled away along the

street, he sat back with a sigh. Then he turned his head
to look at his new wife, sitting quietly beside him, hands
folded in her lap.

'Well, Serena?'

She gave him a little smile. 'I am very grateful to
you, my lord.'

His brows snapped together. 'Confound it, madam, I
do not *want* your gratitude.' She flinched, distress shadowing her dark eyes, and he cursed his harsh tongue and
hasty temper. He said more gently, 'I beg your pardon,
I was not always such a brute, but I have lived alone
for too long and have forgotten my manners. They will
improve, you have my word upon it.'

She was looking down at her hands and he noticed
how tightly they were clenched together.

'I only hope you will not regret marrying me, sir.'

*Damn Lady Hambridge for putting that thought in
her head!*

'We agreed this marriage was to the advantage of
both of us, did we not, madam?'

'Yes, but—'

He put his fingers to her lips. 'Hush now. We shall
deal extremely well together, my dear, trust me.'

Serena's heart skipped a beat. The gesture was gentle, even affectionate, and he was smiling at her, his
hazel eyes warm.

'I do.' She said again, more strongly, 'I do trust you,
my lord.'

'Good.'

His fingers slid from her lips and he cupped her
cheek. It was an intimate gesture and for an instant she
wanted to press against his palm and absorb some of

his strength. Her eyelids drooped as something stirred, deep inside: pleasure, anticipation. Desire. She wanted to chase the fleeting sensation, explore and enjoy it, but all too soon it was gone, replaced by a dark and undefined feeling of terror.

Her eyes flew open. Suddenly the air within the carriage was charged with menace. She was back in the candlelit bedroom at the Swan, with Sir Timothy bearing down on her, his hands around her neck. Serena could not help herself, she recoiled, shuddering. Immediately Quinn's hand dropped. He turned away from her to look out of the window, pointing at an inn sign as it flashed into view.

'Ah. We are passing Old Mother Red Cap's. So we are not yet at Highgate. Plenty of time to sleep, if you wish. It has been a busy morning.'

Quinn's tone was conversational and Serena's panic subsided. He settled back in his corner and closed his eyes and she drew in a deep, steadying breath. He had told her he would not force his attentions upon her and he was keeping his word. She felt a sudden rush of gratitude. Rufus Quinn might be known as the rudest man in London, but to her he had shown nothing but kindness.

The steady rocking of the carriage was soothing, but Serena was too on edge to sleep. However, she no longer dreaded their arrival at Melham Court. There would inevitably be some gossip, for the servants knew of her previous visit, but for the first time she thought that with Quinn's support it would not be so very bad.

In another example of his thoughtfulness, he had ordered the coachman to avoid Hitchin. The new route was slightly longer and the road a little rougher, but

Serena was glad they would not pass the Swan and revive those terrifying memories.

She was not sure if Quinn was really sleeping, but he kept to his corner with his eyes closed until they were on the final approach to Melham Court, when he sat up and stretched.

'The house should be in sight by now,' he told her, glancing out of the window. He gave a little bark of laughter. 'And my people have gone out of their way to welcome you. Look.'

Leaning forward, Serena peered through the glass as the carriage bowled around the last, sweeping curve and she saw that the bridge and the arch of the gatehouse had been decorated with flowers and gaily coloured ribbons which fluttered in the breeze.

The team did not check as they rattled across the bridge and through the arch into the courtyard, where the servants were all waiting to greet them. Serena spotted Meggy, the serving girl who had looked after her on her first visit, and also Polly, who was now her full-time maid. Henry had agreed to Polly leaving his employ and she had travelled to Melham Court earlier that morning, along with Serena's baggage.

Unlike the staff of Hambridge House, who had lined the hall in solemn silence to see them off, Lord Quinn's servants were milling around the courtyard, laughing and cheering as the carriage came to a halt. More ribbons and flowers adorned the courtyard, hanging from the upper windows and forming a decorative arch around the open door, where the housekeeper and butler were waiting. Quinn jumped down and turned back to give Serena his hand.

'Welcome to your new home, Lady Quinn.'

Serena had made up her mind that, however hard it might be, she would look cheerful upon her arrival at Melham Court, but in the event it was no effort at all. The delight of the servants was infectious and, with her hand tucked snugly into the crook of Quinn's arm, she went with him into the house. The butler and Mrs Talbot fell back before them and there was no doubting that their smiles and words of welcome were genuine.

The newlyweds were ushered into the drawing room where Mrs Talbot bustled about them, pointing out the cakes and wine on a side table for their delectation and asking in the same breath if Lady Quinn would like to rest before taking refreshments.

Serena smiled. 'My lord's carriage is so comfortable I am not at all fatigued, I assure you. A little wine would be very welcome, I think.'

She untied the strings of her cloak and immediately Quinn was behind her, lifting it from her shoulders. He handed it to Mrs Talbot to take away before going across to the table to pour two glasses of wine.

'You were anxious about your reception here, I believe.' He handed her a glass. 'I hope this relieves your mind. Believe me, it is none of my doing.'

'I *am* reassured, thank you.' She took a sip of the wine. It was rich and fruity, and would no doubt make her light-headed if she drank too much of it. She put it down on the mantelshelf. 'I hope the welcome will be as warm at all your houses.'

'At the first of them it will be, I am sure of it, because we travel to my hunting lodge in Leicestershire. As to the properties which are let, Johnson, my steward, has written to request that we may call, but I have made it clear we will be staying at local hostelries. In the main they are very good and we shall not be uncomfortable.' He emptied his glass and went back to the table to put it down. 'I told Johnson to bespeak separate bedchambers for us at every stop. And here, too, you have your own rooms.'

Quinn's broad back was towards her and Serena had no indication of his mood. The thought that he was happy with the arrangement, that he did not want her, was strangely dispiriting, even though the idea of consummating their marriage filled her with a blind panic.

She said carefully, 'If that is your wish, my lord.'

'No, but it is yours, I believe.'

His blunt honesty disarmed her and she hung her head. She was staring at the floor when his feet appeared within her view. He put his fingers beneath her chin and tilted it up until she was looking into his face. She felt dwarfed by his presence. He towered over her, blocking her view of everything save his broad shoulders in their covering of superfine broadcloth.

He was so close that she could see the exquisite tailoring of his coat and appreciate the fine linen of his shirt and neckcloth. She thought she could even detect the fresh smell of clean linen and a hint of spicy soap on his skin. When she had first seen him this morning his brown hair had been brushed back, but now it hung over his brow, too long to be fashionable but giving his rugged features a boyish look.

'I told you I should not press you,' he said, holding her gaze. 'You shall come to me when *you* are ready and not before.'

She gave a tremulous smile and did not move as he slowly lowered his head towards her. She froze, waiting for the black, blinding terror, but it did not come. His fingers pushed her chin a little higher and, nervously, she ran her tongue over her lips. His head was too close now for her eyes to focus and she closed them. She felt his mouth brush hers, fleeting and light as a butterfly. It was over in an instant, but the sensations that shot through her body startled her. A white heat that made her want to grab him and drag his mouth back to hers. To lose herself in his kiss.

Slowly her eyes opened. Quinn had raised his head but he was watching her, his gaze more intense, as if he was looking into her soul. When he removed his hand from her chin she felt unsteady, as if she was standing on the edge of a cliff, ready to topple. Quickly she took a step back.

'I... I should change for dinner.' Another step, but instead of feeling safer as she moved away she felt the panic growing. She fluttered a hand. 'N-no need to ring for the housekeeper, I will find her, or someone...'

And with that she turned and fled.

Quinn did not move until she was gone. Then he raised one fist and placed the back of it against his mouth. He could still taste her sweetness, still feel the soft cushion of her lips against his. She had not shuddered. Had not pulled away from him.

'Well,' he said to the empty room. 'That's progress, I suppose.'

It was late July before Quinn brought Serena back to Hertfordshire. Within days of their return, Charlotte Beckford sent them an invitation to dine at Prior's Holt.

'I hope you do not object that you are the only guests,' said Lottie, when she welcomed them into the elegant drawing room. 'After such a long time traipsing around the country I thought you might like a quiet little dinner.'

'Yes, thank you.' Serena perched on the edge of a sofa. 'We dined with several of Quinn's tenants during our travels, but it was all rather formal. They were very much aware that he is their landlord.'

'And did you visit *all* your estates, even Northumberland?' asked Tony. 'That must have been a gruelling schedule.'

'No.' Quinn carried two glasses of wine over to the sofa and took a seat beside Serena. 'We only went as far north as Leicester before going to Devon, then on to Sussex, where we took the opportunity to stop a few nights in Worthing.'

'Worthing!' Tony exclaimed. 'What in heaven's name took you there?'

'You forget, my dear,' said Lottie, a laugh trembling in her voice. 'The Hambridges were going to Worthing directly after the wedding and with Redlands being only ten miles away, it would have looked odd if they had *not* called in.'

'Aye, it would,' Quinn agreed. 'They are there with the Newbolds.'

Serena did not miss the horrified look that passed between Tony and his wife.

'And, you stayed with them?'

Quinn shook his head. 'I had already contacted an old friend who was delighted to put us up. I do not think my wife was too unhappy with the arrangement.'

He glanced at Serena, his eyes warm with amusement, and she could not but smile in response. The days spent in Sussex had been the most interesting and enjoyable of the whole tour. Redlands, Quinn's Sussex property, was a grand Palladian mansion, much used for entertaining by Quinn's parents, but he had leased it to a rich nabob who had returned from India with a large fortune and ambitions to match. Ten minutes in his tenant's company had shown Serena why Quinn had advised they refuse the invitation to stay at the house and instead they had been the guests of Dr Young and his wife, Eliza.

It was not long before Serena realised that her husband's friend was the celebrated polymath, Thomas Young. The doctor was quite delighted when Serena told him she knew of his work on decipherment of Egyptian hieroglyphs, and more specifically the Rosetta Stone, and when the gentlemen joined the ladies in the drawing room each evening their discussions ranged widely, from medicine, physics and Egyptology to Dr Young's thoughts on tuning musical instruments and his abhorrence of slavery.

'A visit to Henry and Dorothea was unavoidable, since we were in the area,' Serena said now, 'but I was very glad we were not obliged to stay with them.'

'Aye,' added Quinn, with feeling. 'One dinner in their company was quite sufficient. However, Serena assures me her other brother, Russ, is a very different character. He and his family live in the north. Yorkshire, I believe. We will visit them on our way to the Northumberland house. I want to show Serena the coalmines.'

'Coal!' Lottie pulled a face.

'They are very lucrative, even if they are not beautiful,' remarked Tony, laughing at his wife's look of distaste. 'However, visiting properties ranging from Devon to Leicestershire and Sussex in six weeks is no mean feat. You must be completely fatigued, Lady Quinn.'

That had been the point of it, thought Serena. Travelling the breadth of the country, driving about each of the estates, meeting tenants, talking to stewards and local villagers. There had been no time or energy for dalliance. Her husband had been attentive and friendly, dinners had been companionable enough, but every night Serena left Quinn alone with his brandy and retired to her room. Mostly she fell into a deep, dreamless sleep of exhaustion, but some nights her slumbers were disturbed by dark, terrifying nightmares: Sir Timothy ripping her clothes, pressing hot, brandy-fumed kisses upon her, dragging her back from the window when she shrieked for someone to help her.

'Scream if you wish,' he had jeered, throwing her down on the bed. 'Do you think anyone can hear you? Do you think anyone *cares*?'

'And what did you think of the other houses, Lady Quinn?' Serena jumped as Lady Beckford addressed her. 'Are you going to turn out any of the tenants?'

'Lottie!'

'What have I said?' She raised her brows at her husband. 'Is that not what Quinn told us he would do, if Serena wanted to live in one of them?'

Quinn laughed. 'I did, but you need not fear for my tenants just yet. We have the hunting lodge in Leicestershire and my wife tells me she is not enamoured of any of the other properties.'

'They are all very fine,' put in Serena, 'but most are very large. I prefer Melham Court and I agree with

Quinn—it is better that the properties are occupied rather than standing empty for most of the year.'

'Well I for one am very relieved to hear it,' Lottie told her. 'I think we are going to be very good friends, Serena!'

Chapter Six

Lottie repeated this sentiment when the two ladies retired to the drawing room after dinner.

'Tony will be glad not to lose Quinn's company. They have been friends for ever, you know, and went to the same school. It might even be said they grew up together.'

'Oh?' Serena was puzzled. 'I thought Quinn's family preferred houses where they might entertain in style.'

'They did.' Lottie sat down on the sofa and patted the seat, inviting Serena to join her. 'However, they left Quinn in Hertfordshire for most of the year, until he was old enough to go to school.'

'Ah, poor boy!'

'Quite.' Lottie's cheerful face showed uncharacteristic disapproval. 'Fortunately, Tony's family is an ancient one and Lord and Lady Quinn considered him a suitable companion, so Quinn spent a great deal of his time here at Prior's Holt.'

Serena shifted in her seat. 'Perhaps you should not be telling me this, if your husband told you in confidence.'

'No, no, my family lived nearby, you see, and most

of it is common knowledge locally. But if you would rather not hear any more—'

'On the contrary,' Serena assured her. 'I would like to know as much as possible. Everything. It might help me to be a better wife.' She flushed. 'You are aware that the circumstances of our marriage are somewhat… unusual.'

Lottie gave her a speaking look and reached across to squeeze her hand.

She continued, 'Quinn received a great deal more affection here than from his own parents. It came as no surprise when he offered for Tony's sister.'

'Ah.' Quinn's words came back to Serena. 'She died, I believe?'

'Yes. Poor Barbara. Such a lively girl. She was barely a year younger than Quinn and they were inseparable. They wanted to marry once she reached eighteen but Quinn's parents refused to countenance a match. They had selected a viscount's daughter for his bride. Quinn stood firm, though. He and Barbara were engaged as soon as he reached his majority.' She spread her hands and gave a loud sigh. 'Barbara went off to town to purchase her bride clothes and contracted a fever while she was there. She was dead within the month. Poor Quinn—he loved her so much. He has hated London ever since and rarely goes into society.'

Lottie paused and Serena could think of nothing to say to fill the silence. She knew what it was like to be brought up by nannies and tutors, and her heart went out to the lonely child Quinn had been. And then how devastating to lose the love of his life so cruelly.

'But that is all changed now.' Lottie gave herself a little shake, throwing off the melancholy thoughts.

'We always hoped Quinn would find someone else to make him happy.'

'You mistake,' stammered Serena. 'It is n-not a love match.'

'Not yet, but you are so beautiful I have no doubt he will soon fall in love with you,' replied Lottie comfortably. 'Tell me, is there any indication that you might be in an *interesting state*? Oh, now I have made you blush! Pray forgive me, Serena. I should not be asking such questions, should I? Tony is always chiding me for being far too forward.'

'No, no, I am not offended, but, no, I am n-not with child…'

Lottie reached out and caught her hands. 'Do not worry, my dear, there is plenty of time. Your marriage is very young yet.'

Serena murmured her agreement and sought for a way to turn the conversation away from her marriage.

'Do you have children, Lady Beckford?'

'Call me Lottie, my dear, I pray you.' She smiled, but a shadow passed across her face. 'Alas, no. I suffered an illness in the early years of our marriage, you see, which has left my heart weak. We have consulted the best doctors in the land but they are all agreed that it would be unwise for me to bear a child.'

'Oh, I am sorry.'

'Do not be. Tony and I came to terms with the fact long ago and have a very happy life, I assure you.' She gave Serena a quick, mischievous look. 'And I hope you will make us godparents to your own children, that we may spoil them quite shamelessly!'

Serena wondered what Lottie would say if she knew that the marriage was not even consummated, but she summoned up a laugh, determined her new friend should not suspect there was anything amiss. However, it was with relief that she heard the door open and the gentlemen came in, putting an end to further confidences.

Quinn followed his host into the drawing room and his eyes went immediately to Serena. He thought how good it was to hear her laugh, but when he drew closer he saw that the merriment did not reach her eyes and he was surprised how much that disturbed him. How much he wanted to make her happy.

He gave her a small, reassuring smile and lowered himself into a chair near the empty fireplace, where he could watch her. There was no doubt she was beautiful, with her golden curls, chocolate-coloured eyes and her serene smile, but she had a distant, detached air and he was haunted by the memory of the first time he had seen her, full of energy, her eyes sparking fire at him.

'What say you, Quinn?' Tony's voice jolted him back to the present.

'I beg your pardon, what was that?'

'You know we always hold a ball every summer, but this year Lottie deliberately delayed until you returned, because she wants to introduce your new bride to the neighbourhood. It will not be a very large affair, mainly local families, although we have invited some of our friends from town, those who have not gone off to Brighton for the summer.'

From across the room Lottie wagged her finger at Quinn. 'You have refused my invitations thus far, my lord, but you cannot do so this time.'

'Indeed, I cannot. If my wife wishes to attend then we shall do so.' He looked a question at Serena.

'Of course. We are delighted to accept.'

Was he the only one to notice the lack of enthusiasm in her response? She wanted company no more than he. In that, at least, they were in accord.

The drive back to Melham Court was accomplished in silence. It was impossible to pierce the darkness, but Serena was aware of Quinn's abstraction. Prior's Holt was the home of his lost love. Did visiting there remind him of Barbara? She could not ask him such a question, but she longed to reach out for his hand, to comfort him and take comfort in return. Instead they remained in their separate corners for the journey.

'It has been a tiring evening,' Quinn remarked as he handed her out of the carriage. 'Shall I escort you directly to your room?'

'Yes, thank you.' As they made their way up the stairs she asked him a question that had been teasing her. 'Would you rather we did not go to Lady Beckford's ball?'

'By no means. You know I am not fond of such events, but I think it is necessary that we go to this, do not you?'

'Why yes, I do.' She risked a tiny smile. 'I have no doubt your neighbours will be agog to see your new bride.'

'They will indeed.' They had reached the door of her chamber and he stopped. 'We shall at some point be obliged to hold something similar here, but this will relieve you of the necessity of planning anything of that nature just yet.'

'Oh?' Her head came up. 'Do you think I could not do it?'

'I am sure you could, but I would like you to take your time to settle into your new home.'

He raised her hand to his lips, murmured goodnight and walked away, leaving Serena to enter her chamber where she found Polly dozing in a chair.

'Oh, lawks, my lady, I beg your pardon. I tried so hard to stay awake.'

She waved away the maid's apologies. 'I see no reason why you should not rest while you wait for me.'

Polly bustled around, helping her into her nightgown, and Serena allowed her thoughts to wander. She was disappointed at the little spurt of anger that had caused her to challenge Quinn like that, for she had resolved to maintain an attitude of quiet obedience towards her husband. After all, he had rescued her from a shameful escapade and deserved nothing less than a conformable wife, as Dorothea had pointed out to her constantly in the days leading up to the wedding.

It was your wilfulness that brought you to this pass, Serena. You must curb that headstrong nature of yours. No man wants to be married to a termagant!

'Would you like me to stay and brush out your curls, ma'am?'

'Thank you, Polly, but I can do that. Off you go to bed now.'

When the maid had gone, Serena sat at her dressing table and pulled the brush slowly through her hair. Day and night her sister-in-law's words ran through her head, a never-ending litany. Since the wedding she had tried to be a model wife and Quinn appeared quite content.

Certainly, he had made no physical demands upon her. Apart from that one kiss, on their wedding day.

It was seared in her memory, the feel of his lips on hers, the sudden scorching desire that had shocked her to the core. She had run away from him then and he had made no effort to detain her, or to kiss her again. He was unfailingly polite and considerate, but it appeared that Quinn did not want her, termagant or no.

A week later they were back at Prior's Holt for the Beckfords' ball. It was their first formal engagement and a little shiver ran down Serena's back as the liveried servant announced them. Lord and Lady Quinn. There was no going back now.

Quinn put his hand over her fingers, where they rested on his arm.

'Nervous?'

She glanced up at him. She had prepared carefully for the evening, choosing to wear once more the gown she had worn on her wedding day. The cream muslin was decorated at the neck, sleeves and hem with delicately embroidered apricot flowers and a tracery of leaves, all enhanced by silver thread work. She had allowed Polly to nestle matching roses among her curls and had put on the diamond ear drops and necklace that Quinn had given her as a wedding gift. In looks at least she hoped she would not disappoint.

'I trust I shall not let you down, my lord.'

He squeezed her hand. 'You could never do that, Serena.'

She straightened her shoulders and raised her head. She had little interest in what anyone thought of her, but this was Quinn's neighbourhood and she wanted to make a good impression, for his sake.

Lottie came forward to greet them, Tony only a step behind. Serena was enveloped in a warm, scented embrace before her hostess carried her away, bent upon introducing the new bride to as many people as possible before the dancing began.

'I am so glad you did not come fashionably late,' she said, linking arms with Serena. 'The dancing will not commence for an hour yet, so we have plenty of time for introductions. You will be acquainted with most of our guests from town, I am sure. Indeed, one is a close friend of yours, I believe. But our near neighbours are all impatient to meet you.'

'Should we not wait for my husband?' asked Serena, hanging back.

Lottie gave a little laugh. 'You must not worry about Quinn. He is the most unsociable man I know and would not enjoy doing the pretty. Much better to leave him with Tony. Now, let me see, who shall be first? Let us begin with Sir Grinwald and Lady Brook, the local magistrate and his wife...'

Time passed in a whirl of new names and faces for Serena. She was aware that behind the polite greetings and questions, Lottie's guests were all very curious. As Sir Grinwald put it, most improperly, they wanted to know what had made the old dog put his head in the parson's mousetrap at last. For the first time she was grateful that Dorothea had insisted she should be well versed in the social graces. Now that training came to her aid. She smiled and talked, responding to compliments and turning off sly questions about married life with an elegant riposte.

Everyone was charming, but Serena was not fooled. Quinn's immediate neighbours were genuinely welcoming, but she detected a coolness in those who mixed more in London society. They had heard the rumours and were reserving judgement upon the new Lady Quinn.

There was only one awkward moment. Lottie was glancing about her, wondering who next should be presented to the new bride, when Serena spotted Mrs Downing across the room, accompanied by her son and daughter. Shock held her motionless, then she recalled Lottie's words about the guests here tonight: *one is a close friend of yours*. She meant Elizabeth, of course.

How wrong Lottie was to think they could still be friends, thought Serena, wretchedly. She was not aware of holding her breath, until Lottie tugged her arm and led her off to introduce her to an elderly couple who were near neighbours. It was only then she realised how relieved she was that she need not face the Downings. Not yet.

'Well, it is going very well,' announced Lottie at last. 'Now let us go through to the ballroom, for that scraping of fiddles tells me the musicians are ready to strike up. To whom shall we allow the honour of the first dance with you, I wonder?'

'No one.' Quinn appeared, his large frame blocking their way. 'You have done quite enough for now, Lottie. I have come to claim my bride for the first two dances.'

His manner brooked no argument and with no more than a half-hearted pout, their hostess stood aside.

'Very well, my lord, I suppose you may do so, if you wish.'

'I do wish it.' He held out his hand to Serena. 'Come along, madam.'

Lottie's eyes widened at his peremptory tone and she shot one final, mischievous glance at Serena before walking away.

'Was I impolite?' he muttered, as he escorted Serena on to the dance floor.

'Exceedingly,' she responded. 'But I am very glad you came for me. My head is spinning from so many introductions. It will be a relief to dance with you.'

'You may quickly change your mind on that,' he warned her. 'I am sadly out of practice.'

But when the dance started Serena discovered that her husband was an excellent dancer. For such a big man he was very light on his feet and moved through the dance with the lithe grace of a wild animal. Not a bear at all, she thought. A big cat. Powerful. Agile. Dangerous.

As he clasped her hand for the promenade she missed her step and immediately his hold tightened, steadying her. She looked up to convey her thanks, but all thought of gratitude faded under the blaze of possession she saw in his eyes. For an instant the heaviness that constantly overlaid her spirits was pierced, like sunshine breaking through rainclouds.

The carefree girl she had been would have revelled in that look. The old Serena would have agreed to accompany him on any adventure, stand shoulder to shoulder with him to face any danger. No. She dragged her eyes away. That wilful creature was no more. She would be a good wife who would cause him no trouble.

Who would have thought a dance could be so pleasurable? As Quinn turned, circled and promenaded with

Serena he knew he had never enjoyed a dance more. True, his partner was extremely beautiful and at least half the men in the room envied him his place with her, but that did not matter. If they had been alone in the ballroom he would have been just as happy. He felt an overriding urge to protect her and when she stumbled he was ready, his grip sure, supporting her. Even such a small service gave him a rush of pleasure, heightened by the grateful look she threw at him. It was a fleeting glance and disappointment stabbed him when she looked away.

The two dances were over all too soon and even as they left the floor Lottie was waiting for them, Serena's next partner at her side. At least it was Atherton, Quinn thought grimly. Fifty, if he was a day, and happily married. Quinn made his way to the card room, knowing that if he remained in the ballroom he would be obliged to dance, and how could he give his attention to his partner while Serena was dancing with another man?

However, he soon discovered that even cards could not hold his attention. The music was audible from the card room and when he heard a new tune he wondered who was now dancing with Serena. Was it another elderly neighbour, or some young buck intent upon flirtation?

'Come along, my lord, we are waiting for you.'

The jovial voice of a fellow player cut through Quinn's thoughts and he selected his discard. It was quickly swept up by his neighbour, who gave a triumphant cry and displayed his winning hand. Quinn felt a touch on his shoulder and looked round to find Tony beside him.

'Not like you to make such an error.'

'No.' Quinn threw in his hand and rose from the table. 'I am playing abominably tonight. Let us return to the ballroom. I want to see how my wife does.'

'Serena is doing very well, my friend, trust me.'

'I should still like to see for myself.'

'No doubt you intend to stand, brooding, at the side of the room and watch her like a lovesick moonling?' Tony laughed. 'Lottie would never allow that.'

'Is it any wonder I never attend these dashed events?' muttered Quinn, scowling.

Tony grinned. 'You will have to accustom yourself to this sort of thing, now you are married. Unless you are prepared to dance with one or other of the ladies present, you had best come to the library with me, out of the way.' When Quinn hesitated he added quietly, 'You may safely leave Lottie to look after your wife, old friend.'

They went across the hall to the study, where a decanter and glasses stood on the desk.

'This is my bolthole,' explained Tony. 'I always find time to slip away here for a while. Of course, I must not be absent for too long or I shall incur Lottie's wrath, but one is rarely missed for the odd half-hour. Sit down and I will bring you a glass of wine. I had it fetched from Averys in Bristol, as you suggested. I believe it was worth the longer journey.'

Two wing chairs flanked the empty hearth. Quinn lowered himself into one and for a while silence reigned.

'So, my friend, what is your opinion of married life?'

Quinn studied his glass. 'It is not uncomfortable. Serena and I find we have much in common.'

'I am glad to hear it. And when do you go to town?'

'We do not.'

'Oh? You are still recovering perhaps from your

jauntering all over the country. But once you are rested you will be hiring a house in town, I am sure.'

'We have no plans to visit London.' Quinn glanced up. 'That surprises you? I do not see why it should. Neither Serena nor I wish for society. You are aware of the circumstances of our marriage, the rumours and gossip. I would not ask my wife to face that.'

Tony hesitated, 'It might be better to face it now than have people say your wife is in hiding.'

Quinn frowned. 'They would not dare.'

'Not in your presence, certainly, but there are rumours about why you married her.' Tony coughed. 'Some might think you are ashamed of your bride.'

'Ashamed! No, indeed, quite the contrary. Serena is not only beautiful but intelligent, too, and well educated.' He sat forward, grinning. 'If you could have seen her at Worthing, Tony, when we were staying with the Youngs. She is well read and has an enquiring mind. She knows enough about Egyptology to put some pertinent questions to Thomas. He was most impressed and has invited us to attend his next lectures.'

'That will mean going to London.'

'Yes, but we will not stay more than a night or two, as I have done in the past. We need not go into society.'

'You would turn Serena into a recluse like yourself.' Tony's countenance was unusually solemn. 'We were not acquainted with Serena when she was Miss Russington, but one saw her everywhere and could not fail to notice her. Oh, it was nothing detrimental, my friend, so you need not show hackle! She had a reputation as a cheerful, spirited young lady who could be relied upon to bring life to the dullest party. Lottie tells me her admirers swore she could light up a room.'

'Could she?' Quinn thought of the first time he had seen Serena, fire in her eyes and an angry flush upon her cheek. Had that fire been extinguished, or was it merely damped down?

'Her family kept her pretty well hedged about, of course,' Tony continued. 'But that is understandable, given her history.'

'They stifled her,' said Quinn. 'If Hambridge and his wife had not tried to clip her wings she would not have felt it necessary to give them the slip.'

'But that is just it, my friend. She may not have intended any harm, but there is no denying she did go off unescorted.'

'Marriage should have reinstated her.'

'I'm afraid not.' Tony fixed his eyes on Quinn. 'It has only given credence to Forsbrook's claim that she left him when a more attractive proposition presented itself.'

Quinn jumped to his feet, cursing roundly. He strode up and down the room, his brow furrowed.

'I had hoped that particular story had been forgotten.'

'It might have been, if Forsbrook wasn't back in town and presenting himself as the injured party. The thing is,' Tony went on slowly, 'there are some who say that Serena is following in her mother's footsteps.'

'The devil they are! Then I must deal with Forsbrook once and for all!'

'Call him out? That would only add fuel to the fire.'

Quinn stopped pacing and ran a hand over his face. 'Then what do you suggest I do to protect my wife?'

'It strikes me that you have two options. You could keep Serena from town and make a pleasant enough life for yourself in the provinces.'

'As you said earlier, turn her into a recluse, like myself.' Quinn met his friend's eyes steadily. 'And the second option?'

'Take her to London, face down the gossips. Serena has been used to town life—parties, concerts, the theatre, debating societies—you, too, once enjoyed those things.' He grinned suddenly. 'Not so much the parties, perhaps, where you were surrounded by flatterers and matchmaking mamas, but the rest of it.' Tony pushed himself out of his chair and stood before Quinn, one hand resting on his shoulder. 'You have shut yourself away since Barbara died. Society is not all bad, my friend. Perhaps it is time you started living again.' He glanced at the ormolu clock on the mantelshelf as it chimed the half-hour. 'Our guests will be going into supper shortly. We should join our wives.'

Since when had dancing become a chore? Serena kept her smile in place as she went down the dance with her latest partner. Sir Grinwald was not only the local magistrate but also one of Quinn's closest neighbours. He was a kindly gentleman and she could not blame him if she was not enjoying herself. She could not blame any of her partners. It was just that she did not *feel* anything tonight.

No, she corrected herself, that was not quite true. She had felt something when she danced with Quinn. A certain *frisson*, a little thrill of excitement.

The sort of thing I was seeking in a husband.

The thought brought a little flush of remorse to her cheeks as she recalled how reckless she had been. But no more. In future she would be the very model of decorum. The music ended and Sir Grinwald led her off the floor to where his wife was waiting.

'I must find Lady Beckford,' said Serena. 'She seems determined that I should dance all evening.'

'And why not?' declared Lady Brook, beaming at her. 'You young things have so much energy.'

Serena merely smiled. Such kind people would be hurt if they knew how little she wanted to be here. She turned away, her smile faltering as she found herself face to face with Miss Elizabeth Downing.

Chapter Seven

'Please, do not run away.' Elizabeth touched her arm. 'I was looking for you, to find out how you go on. I have been worried about you.'

Serena hung her head. 'How can you, after the way I tricked you and your family?'

'We are friends.' Elizabeth stepped closer, saying quietly, 'And as a friend, tell me, if you will, and truthfully. Did you mean to elope with Sir Timothy that night?'

'No.' Serena sighed. 'I agreed to go with him to Vauxhall, but instead—'

'I thought as much,' said Elizabeth, relief warming her voice. 'I have heard his scandalous hints but I did not think even you would take such a step.'

Even you!

Serena closed her eyes as a wave of mortification washed over her. 'Oh, Lizzie, can you ever forgive me?'

'It is already done. Mama, too, is anxious to speak to you.' Elizabeth took her arm. 'Come along, she is waiting for us across the room.'

'Oh, no, I cannot face her.'

'Of course you can.'

Elizabeth tightened her grip. Mrs Downing was standing with a group of fashionable matrons and as the girls approached she turned to greet them, holding out her hands to Serena and drawing her forward to kiss her cheek. There was no mistaking the looks of surprise that passed between the other ladies as they witnessed such obvious affection. Mrs Downing cut short Serena's whispered apologies and drew the girls away from the interested stares of her companions.

'Enough of that now, my dear,' she said, squeezing Serena's arm. 'I was put out at first, but a little reflection convinced me it was a girlish prank that went horribly wrong.'

'It was,' muttered Serena, shuddering.

'But it is all over now,' Mrs Downing continued. 'You have come out of it remarkably well, when all is said and done. I, for one, am very pleased for you.'

'Thank you, ma'am.' Serena looked about her. 'And your son, is he here this evening?' She swallowed. 'Is he very angry with me?'

'Oh, yes, he's here somewhere,' replied Elizabeth cheerfully. 'He was outraged at first, of course, but he has got over that.'

'He is far too staid for you, my dear,' replied Jack's fond mama. 'I never thought it a good match.'

Serena blinked. 'But Dorothea said it was your dearest wish.'

'It might well have been Lady Hambridge's dearest wish,' retorted Mrs Downing drily. 'I am sure she was only too eager to see you settled. Well, she should be delighted that you have married so well.'

Serena thought of the letter she had received that morning from her sister-in-law.

'Dorothea is mortified by all the gossip. She and my brother have extended their stay at Worthing.'

A shadow of annoyance crossed Mrs Downing's kindly face. 'She would have done better to remain in town and deny it, especially now. Running away only gives credence to the rumours. Really, the woman is most—' Mrs Downing closed her lips firmly upon whatever utterance she had been about to make.

Serena sighed. 'You cannot deny I have given her a great deal of trouble, ma'am.'

Mrs Downing patted her hands. 'You are not the first young lady to be taken in by a rake, my dear. You acted recklessly, but that is all in the past now. You may believe that your true friends will support you.' She looked past Serena and smiled. 'There you are, my lord. Pray accept our felicitations upon your marriage.'

Serena looked up to find Quinn at her side.

'Thank you.' He nodded, unsmiling, before addressing her. 'I have come to take you to supper. Lady Beckford has reserved seats for us at her table. If you will excuse us, ma'am?'

'By all means,' replied Mrs Downing graciously. 'And you will be very welcome in Wardour Street, when you bring your bride to town. I hope we may expect to see you there soon, my lord?'

'As to that, we have not yet made any plans,' replied Quinn, pulling Serena's hand on to his arm. As he led her away he muttered, 'It is very warm here tonight, even with the doors leading to the terrace opened wide, and August has only just begun. London will be white-hot, but I will take you there if you wish it.'

The possibility of meeting Sir Timothy made her

shudder, but Serena knew a good wife deferred to her husband in all things.

She said in a colourless voice, 'I have no preference either way, my lord. It is for you to decide.'

Tony's words in the library came back to Quinn. Was this the same woman who could be relied upon to bring life to any party? Now she walked beside him, eyes lowered, a picture of meek obedience. The light had gone out of Serena.

Sitting between Quinn and their host at supper did much to restore Serena's spirits and afterwards Sir Anthony demanded the honour of standing up with her when dancing recommenced. Quinn would have followed, but he was waylaid by one of his neighbours who wanted the opportunity to discuss a shared boundary. He gave Serena a brief, wry smile and turned aside, leaving Tony to escort Serena to the ballroom.

As they emerged from the supper room a stocky, sober-looking young man stepped in front of them.

'Ah, Downing,' Tony greeted him jovially. 'Come to beg me to give up my partner, is that it?'

Jack Downing made a very proper bow. 'It is indeed, sir. If Lady Quinn will do me the honour?'

'With pleasure.' Serena smiled, glad to accept this olive branch. 'If Sir Anthony does not object?'

'Well, of course I object to giving you up, but you will be wanting to dance with your old friend, I've no doubt.' Laughing, Tony strolled off, leaving Serena to take Jack's arm.

Throughout the dance she tried to converse, but by the time they made their bows and parted she was weary of the effort. Really, why had he asked her to dance if he was intent upon being morose and silent? She wondered if he was jealous, but she quickly dismissed the idea. Jack Downing had considered her an eligible match, but his feelings had never been engaged, she was sure of it, and from the little Elizabeth had said, the scandal had cured him of any slight fancy he might have had for her.

Quinn watched his wife going down the dance, pleased that the rift with the Downings was mended. He had heard that Jack Downing was one of Serena's admirers and that Lady Hambridge had been in favour of the match, but to his mind it would never have worked. The fellow looked like a dull dog, too starched up to appeal to Serena.

And is a surly recluse any more appealing?

Thrusting aside the unwelcome thought, Quinn turned away. He headed for Tony's study again, but even there he could not settle and after a while he went back to watch the dancing. Serena was now partnered by another neighbour, but her pleasure seemed muted, her smile a little strained. He would not be surprised if she was fatigued by the noise and the heat. Perhaps she was ready to leave. He resolved to ask her as soon as the dance ended.

The crowded, candlelit room was very warm and the air would be fresher out of doors. Quinn stepped outside and moved away from the house to look at the gardens, bathed in moonlight. He had spent many happy days here, as a boy and a young man, enjoying the company of Anthony and his sister. For once the memories of Barbara did not tear at him and he could face them with affection. Perhaps, at last, he could put his grief behind him and appreciate the time they had had together. Perhaps he could move on.

A group of guests strolled out on to the terrace, their chatter preceding them. They were strangers, presumably Tony and Lottie's acquaintances from town. No matter, there was plenty of room. The terrace ran the length of the house and it was an easy matter for Quinn to ignore them, until a voice caught his attention.

'Oh, yes. I have known her since her come-out. You are surprised, I suppose, that I have not cut her acquaintance, considering her scandalous behaviour.'

Quinn frowned. The speaker had his back to him, too busy addressing the little crowd gathered about him to notice anyone else on the terrace, but at that moment he turned slightly and Quinn recognised Jack Downing. Someone spoke, too low for Quinn to make out the words, and Downing laughed.

'So true. A lady can never be too careful of her reputation. I consider myself fortunate to have escaped her wiles. But she has changed.' The sneering tone was even more pronounced. 'She is but a shadow of her former self. She has lost her sparkle, her youth is completely cut up.' An exaggerated sigh was followed by a short, derisive laugh. 'Not so long ago, Serena Russington was considered a veritable diamond in society, but now... now she is no more than a drab country housewife.'

Two steps took Quinn to the group. He caught Downing's arm and swung him around. The look of shock on the younger man's face was almost comical, although Quinn was in too much of a rage to think so.

'L-Lord Quinn, I—'

Quinn cut him short.

'Do you think it gentlemanly to disparage a lady?' he snarled, dragging Downing away from the group.

'I intended n-no harm,' Downing stammered as Quinn towered over him, menace in every line of his body. 'I beg your pardon!'

The music had ended and the group on the terrace was hushed save for a frightened squeak from one of the ladies as they watched Downing retreat. Quinn followed, blinded by rage.

'Pardon be damned,' he ground out. 'I'll teach you to—'

'Quinn!' Tony grabbed his arm as he was about to launch himself at the snivelling figure in front of him. 'Damn it, man, come away. You cannot start a brawl in my house!'

Quinn tried to shake him off. 'Can I not?'

'For heaven's sake, man, the fellow has apologised.'

'Indeed, indeed, I have, sir,' gabbled Downing. 'It was ungentlemanly conduct, I admit it. If you wish for satisfaction, my lord—'

'Of course he doesn't,' Beckford snapped.

'Oh, yes, I do! Confound it, Tony, let me go!'

His friend's response was to cling tighter while he addressed Downing.

'Get out of here, for heaven's sake. Leave my house forthwith and be grateful that you do so with your skin intact!'

Downing hesitated, then he gave a stiff little bow and strode off, his friends following him. The red mist was receding and Quinn let out a ragged breath.

'You may release me now, Tony. I shall not go after the wretch.'

'I take it he said something about your wife.'

'Aye.'

Quinn's anger had reduced to a simmer, with a dull ache of regret that he had allowed himself to be roused to such a fury. After all, what had the fellow said that was not true? His wife was retiring to the point of non-existence. It was not Serena's true self, he was damned sure of it. But he was even less sure he wanted a wife who was wilful, headstrong and high-spirited. Marriage had already overturned his quiet life. He rubbed a hand over his eyes.

'What the hell have I done?'

Tony squeezed his arm. 'Nothing that cannot be mended, I hope,' he said, misunderstanding. 'That young pup will think twice before insulting a lady again. Come along. Let us go inside.'

Serena was at her dressing table, submitting patiently to Polly's administrations upon her hair. Part of her wanted to crawl back into bed, but that was impossible. Ever since their return to Melham Court, the neighbours had been calling upon the new bride and Serena allowed herself to be dressed each morning in a new gown, ready to welcome all visitors. She had no doubt that there would be even more callers today, following last night's ball at Prior's Holt.

They would be sure to ask if Lady Quinn had enjoyed herself. At least there she might tell the truth. Dancing had improved her spirits and there had been no shortage of partners. Even Jack Downing had danced with her, although the family had left early and she had not had a chance to take her leave of them.

And then there was Quinn. He had seemed distracted when she sought him out at the end of the evening and barely spoke to her in the carriage. She had wanted to ask if she had offended him, but instead she remarked how much she had enjoyed the evening and expressed the hope that he, too, had found some pleasure in the society.

'It was interesting,' he had replied, his tone discouraging further conversation.

Nor had he made any effort to detain her when they arrived at the house and Serena had retired to her solitary bed. As she had done every night of her marriage.

That information was not something she could share with anyone, she thought, swallowing a sigh. But at least there was a glimmer of light. The nightmares had all but stopped.

'There, madam. We are done.' The maid put down the hairbrush and comb.

'Thank you, Polly.'

Serena rose and made her way to the door. She did not pause as she passed the long glass, knowing what her reflection would show. A plain muslin gown made high to the neck, the prim image enhanced by the lace cap pinned over her curls. The very model of wifely decorum.

Quinn pushed away his plate. He had no appetite for breakfast, having spent a restless night wondering if marrying Serena had been a disastrous mistake, and not only for himself. Serena was an extraordinary woman. Had marriage to him turned her into something less than ordinary?

A drab, country housewife.

Jack Downing's words had gnawed away at Quinn all through the dark night and he had been relieved when dawn came and he could leave his bed. But even an early morning gallop had not helped. He could not outrun his thoughts and had returned to breakfast as restless and discontented as ever.

Serena came in and he greeted her with a gruff good morning. She looked pale and a little unhappy, which only added to the guilty irritation brewing within him. He watched her cross to the table, her eyes downcast. The plum-coloured muslin did not suit her. It made her skin look grey, while the matching cap concealed the crowning glory that was her hair. He closed his lips tightly against the angry words that rose to his tongue. Is this what she thought a wife should look like? Or was it the result of Forsbrook's attack? Was she trying to keep him at bay with her dowdy appearance?

Suddenly it was all too much. He was incapable of making polite conversation over the teacups and had to get out before he said something to hurt her. His chair scraped back and with a muttered 'excuse me' he strode away.

Serena watched in dismay as Quinn hurled himself out of the room and after a brief, inward struggle she went after him. She had to run, but she was in time to see him disappear into the library, closing the door behind him with a definite snap. Without stopping to think she followed him into the room.

He was standing at a window, staring out. Serena closed the door and stood with her back pressed against it, one hand on the handle, ready for flight.

'My lord, is something amiss?'

'Go away, Serena.'

She was accustomed by now to his gruff tone. Instead of obeying him she walked closer.

'Perhaps I could help.'

'Yes, you can.' He swung about, scowling at her. 'You can go and change out of that damned ugly gown. It does you no favours. In fact, with the exception of the gown you wore last night, you have worn nothing remotely flattering since we married!'

She reeled back as if he had struck her. 'They are perfectly suitable. Dorothea would not have chosen them else…'

'Do you mean to tell me Lady Hambridge had the ordering of your wedding trousseau? Ha! That explains a great deal.'

'She said I should be appropriately dressed.'

'Did she? Those gowns are only appropriate for a matron in her dotage,' he said brutally.

Serena pulled her head up. 'Dorothea wanted me to look respectable.'

'Respectable—you look positively nun-like!' He took her shoulders and gave her a little shake. 'I want you to dress for what you are, Serena, a beautiful young woman. These clothes are more suited to a fifty-year-old.' His eyes moved to her hair. 'And as for that monstrosity—'

Before she could protest he tore off the cap, pulling with it the pins that had so artfully confined her curls, and she felt the heavy, silken weight tumble about her shoulders. A blaze of fury ripped through Serena. Her breast heaved and she glared at him, but as their eyes locked another sensation cut through her rage. Something altogether more dangerous. Desire.

She realised now that it had been curling within her since last evening, growing, spreading into every pore, every nerve-end. Now, at last, the barriers between them were down. She wanted him to reach out and pull her into his arms. She was almost quivering with longing, even though her limbs would not move. Invisible bonds were wrapped about her, keeping her still and mute.

Kiss me. Kiss me now!

Hope flared when his eyes darkened. There was naked lust in his glance and her heart began to thud so hard against her ribs he must surely hear it. She waited, breathless, for him to close the gap between them, to drag her into an embrace, yet even as he reached out for her she could not help herself. She flinched.

The effect was like a dowsing in ice-cold water. His hand dropped and he stepped back, dragging his eyes away from her.

'Forgive me,' he said, his voice ragged. 'That was not worthy of a gentleman.'

He turned on his heel and walked away, leaving Serena to stare after him, not sure whether she most wanted to laugh or cry with frustration.

Chapter Eight

Quinn brought the axe down, splitting the log cleanly in half. He picked up another and placed it on the block. His muscles screamed at him to stop but he couldn't. He had to keep working, to keep at bay the burning desire. It had almost consumed him this morning, when he had pulled off that damned mobcap and Serena's hair had tumbled free, a sunlit waterfall rippling down over her shoulders. She had been incandescent then, angry, raging, but gloriously alive. He had wanted to carry her off to his bed and make love to her, slowly, thoroughly, and then to watch her sleeping with that golden cloud of hair spread over the pillow.

Confound it, put such things from your mind or you will go mad!

He had given Serena his word that he would keep his distance, but every time he saw her it became more difficult. At first, his overriding thought had been to protect her, but now she was recovering and the glimpses of her fiery spirit were testing his self-control to the limit. Her passionate nature called to him, like some kindred spirit. He longed to meet fire with fire, but even the slightest hint of desire brought back her fear. Witness how she had recoiled from him in the library.

Perhaps she was wise to dress like a nun, to remind him that he must not touch her. He swung the axe again and again. The pile of firewood was growing, but when he glanced at the newly split logs even they reminded him of Serena's fair hair, gleaming in the sun. He wanted her, but he was damned if he knew how to proceed.

'Good morning, my lady. 'tis a sunny day for a change. Last night's rain has cleared the air and not before time.'

Serena slowly sat up in her bed and reached for the cup her maid had placed on the bedside table. Despite Polly's cheerful words, she felt only discontent as she gazed out of the window at the clear blue sky.

It was seven days since the Beckfords' ball. Six since Quinn had torn the cap from her head and at the same time ripped all pretence from her soul. In the past week neither of them had mentioned that incident, save one oblique reference when Quinn told her he was no judge of female attire and had no wish to dictate to her.

He had said, 'You must wear whatsoever you deem fitting for your station. Whatever makes you comfortable.'

Serena had thanked him politely, but although she continued to wear the dresses Dorothea had purchased for her, she never again donned any of the caps. Quinn was perfectly correct about the gowns and she bitterly regretted allowing her sister-in-law to dictate to her, but she was loath to go to the considerable expense of replacing them, when Quinn had as good as told her that he had no interest in what she wore.

She gazed now at the pale pink muslin that Polly had fetched from the linen press. She remembered Dorothea trying to force the same colour upon her during her first Season. She had protested violently on that occasion and, fortunately, Russ and Molly had supported her, allowing her to wear the brighter, jewel-like colours she preferred. The discontent turned into irritation and she waved a hand at the maid.

'Take that dress away and dispose of it, Polly. Bring me something else to wear.'

'Yes, m'm.'

It was a tiny act of rebellion, but Serena felt a little better for it.

Half an hour later she made her way to the breakfast room, checking in the doorway when she saw Quinn was sitting at the table. For the past week he had been out of the house by the time she came downstairs.

'Oh—good morning, my lord. I did not expect to see you.'

'I wanted to speak to you.' He rose and pulled out a chair for her. When she was seated he remained behind her. 'That gown is another of Lady Hambridge's choosing, I suppose.'

'It is, my lord.' She managed to speak coolly, although her spine tingled, knowing he was so close.

'Olive green and plain as a Quaker. Designed to blend into the shadows.' When she did not reply he went on, 'Is that a style and a colour you would choose for yourself?' He gave a little bark of laughter. 'Your silence tells me it is not. I have given you *carte blanche* to spend what you like on clothes, Serena.'

He had returned to his seat opposite and she flushed slightly, not meeting his eyes. 'I know, my lord. You are very good and I shall do so, in time.'

She risked one swift glance from under her lashes, bracing herself for his reply. He looked as if he would speak but thought better of it. Instead he reached for the coffee pot and filled her cup.

'What are you doing today?'

'I must speak to Mrs Talbot, and to Cook about tonight's dinner.'

'And are you free once you have seen them?'

'Lady Brook promised to call this morning.'

'Good lord, is she visiting you again today? The knocker has not stopped this past se'ennight.'

Serena's tension eased at the familiar, brusque tone. They were on safer ground now. She knew that despite his grumbling, Quinn was not displeased his neighbours were so attentive.

'Since the ball.' She nodded. 'It is very gratifying.'

'I dare say. What is Lady Brook's excuse today?'

'When I saw her yesterday she promised me a receipt for making apple tart the French way. She swears it is superior to any other method.'

Quinn stared at her across the breakfast table. 'Good God. Are you so at a loss for entertainment that you must resort to *baking*?'

'By no means. I shall accept gratefully and pass it on to Cook.'

'I am glad to hear it.' He refilled his own coffee cup. 'Are you very bored here, Serena?'

She looked up, startled. 'N-no, not at all. My days

are always full. I go through the menus with Cook and discuss household matters with Mrs Talbot. Then there are flowers to cut for the house—'

'Those are your household duties,' he interrupted her. 'What do you do for *pleasure*?'

She felt a little flutter of unease and said carefully, 'There are morning calls to be paid and received.'

'Yes, when you discuss the best way to cook apples. How stimulating!'

His tone was scathing and she bridled. 'And you enjoy the benefits of such conversations when you sit down to your dinner!'

His eyes widened in surprise, but there was something more gleaming in them. Something that set her pulse racing. She quickly looked away.

'I do indeed. I beg your pardon.' His tone was perfectly polite, amused, even, but she dared not look at him again. Instead she finished her bread and butter and pushed aside her plate.

'Are you done?'

'Yes.'

His lip curled. 'That is barely enough to keep a bird alive.'

'It is all I want.'

'Very well. Then run upstairs and fetch your shawl. I wish to show you something. Outside.'

'Now? I have arranged to see Mrs Talbot.'

'Send word that you will see her later.'

She could not help it. She stiffened at his autocratic tone, her brows rising. Quinn met her affronted gaze with narrowed eyes, then with a slight nod he threw down his napkin and stood, saying with exaggerated civility, 'Perhaps, my lady, you would be so good as to oblige me in this. I would very much appreciate your company.'

The change in manner brought the heat to her cheeks. 'Of course, my lord.'

'Good.' He walked to the door and held it open for her. 'I shall wait for you in the hall.'

Silently she left the table and walked to the door. As she passed him she glanced up. There was the glimmer of a smile in his eyes and her lips curved up a little in response. Really, she thought, he might be quite charming if he put his mind to it. The idea persisted only as long as it took her to cross the hall, for as she ascended the stairs he called after her.

'Five minutes. And do not keep me waiting!'

Slightly more than five minutes later Serena made her way back to the hall. Perhaps it was the sunshine streaming through the house, but the lethargy that had made her limbs feel so heavy and slow these past few weeks had eased and she ran lightly down the stairs, one hand on the rail the other clutching a thin silk shawl she hoped would be sufficient to keep off any light breeze.

As she descended the last flight she saw Quinn. He was staring out of the open door, his hands clasped behind his back. Not for the first time she thought how well he looked in country dress, his legs encased in buckskins and glossy top boots. A dark brown frock coat was stretched across his broad shoulders and the light flooding in through the open door brought out a tawny glint in his mane of light brown hair, reminding her of the big cats she had seen at the Exeter Exchange. But those animals had been caged, safely behind bars.

Quinn, on the other hand was here, just feet away from her.

And he is your husband.

Serena slowed as she reached the last few stairs, trying to understand the welter of emotions flooding through her. She wanted to flee, although she knew not where. At that moment Quinn turned towards her and the world steadied when he met her eyes. She trusted him to take care of her.

'Well, my lord, I am here.' She summoned up a smile as she crossed the hall.

'Yes.'

He took the shawl from her and draped it about her shoulders as they made their way out of the house. In the enclosed courtyard the summer sun was hot and bright and Serena stopped, blinking.

'Where are we going, sir, is it far?'

'No. Only to the stables.'

He pulled her fingers on to his arm and they set off again, not through the gatehouse as she had expected, but via a small enclosed passage opposite, where a solid oak door led to a small footbridge across the moat and directly into the new stable block.

'My grandfather had this entrance added to the house when he rebuilt the stables some fifty years ago. It made it quicker for the servants to summon his carriage.'

Serena nodded. Her old self would have explored every nook and cranny of her new home as soon as possible. Instead she had allowed Mrs Talbot to show her around Melham Court, going only to those rooms the housekeeper considered it necessary for the lady of the house to visit. Now she felt the first stirrings of curiosity to see more.

The stables were far more modern than the main house but equally well maintained. Not a weed was to be seen in the yard, where the cobbles were being swept by a couple of young stable hands under the watchful eye of Bourne, the head groom. The boys did not stop their work but Bourne gave a respectful nod in their direction.

'Morning, m'lord. M'lady.'

Serena acknowledged his greeting, then looked up at her companion.

'I have not been here before,' she remarked. 'I should very much like to look around, if I may?'

'Of course, I will show you.' Quinn turned to Bourne, who was waiting expectantly. 'We shall be back in, say, ten minutes.'

'Very good, m'lord.'

Quinn took Serena through the nearest double doors, into the carriage house. From there they progressed through the harness room and on via a feed store to the looseboxes and stalls. There were several men and boys in the stables, grooming the horses, mucking out the stalls or cleaning the carriages. Quinn presented every one of them to Serena as they made their way through the building.

'I am impressed,' she told him, when they had reached the end of the tour. 'You appear to know everyone and everything that goes on here.'

'A good master takes an interest in his staff. I look after them and they work hard for me.' He gave a short laugh. 'I admit I have rarely seen so many of them working at any one time. I suspect they were eager for a glimpse of their new mistress.'

'It was remiss of me not to come before.'

'Nonsense. My parents rarely came to the stables. I doubt my mother even knew the way here.'

He said no more, but Serena marvelled that he should have grown up to be such a considerate master if his parents were so indifferent. They had reached the loose boxes, in one of which was a powerful black horse.

'My favourite hack, Neptune.' Quinn introduced him. 'French-bred. He's an ugly brute, but strong. He can carry me all morning without tiring.'

Serena reached up one hand to scratch the long, bony nose. 'It must be difficult to find a mount that is up to your weight.'

He grunted. 'Luckily I don't aspire to cut a figure in Hyde Park.'

'Nor I.'

'But you do ride?' he asked her, a slight frown in his eyes. 'You and Lottie were talking of it at supper the other evening.'

'Why yes, but not in town,' she replied. 'That is, I was used to do so when I was living with Molly and Russ, but Henry prefers his carriage and Dorothea does not ride at all. They would not countenance my going out without them, even in the most respectable party.'

She could not keep the note of regret from her voice and felt slightly aggrieved when she saw that Quinn's brow had cleared. Perhaps he, like Dorothea, considered riding to be an unladylike activity.

She said, a little coldly, 'Thank you for taking the time to show me over your stables, my lord, but perhaps you would like to tell me why you wanted me to accompany you?'

'I should indeed.' He took her arm. 'Come along.'

The sunlight was blinding as they stepped into the

yard and Serena was momentarily dazzled, but as her vision cleared she saw that Bourne was walking a dapple-grey horse around the yard.

'There. The mare is what I wanted to show you.'

'She is a beauty,' said Serena, as Bourne brought the horse closer. 'Is she a new addition to your stable?'

'My tiger fetched her yesterday. She answers to the name of Crystal. Irish-bred and used to a lady's saddle.'

It took a moment for his words to register with Serena.

'You…you mean she is for *me*?'

'If you want her. Perhaps I should have discussed it with you first, but when Bourne told me yesterday morning that Lord Hackleby was selling off his horses I rode over to Pirton to see if there was anything in his stable suitable for a lady. If I had had more notice you might have come with me, but you had already arranged to call upon the Brooks.'

The groom brought the mare to a stand before them. Serena slowly put out her hand and ran it along the glossy neck, murmuring quietly to the animal.

'Hackleby bought her for his late wife, who was an enthusiastic rider,' Quinn told her. 'He says the mare is very well mannered, if handled properly. He also said she is fast and strong, can go for miles and will jump anything. Since Lady Hackleby died last winter the horse has been exercised by a groom. Clem put her through her paces and thinks she is a little out of condition, but with regular use would soon return to form. We have the lady's saddle, too, which I hope will fit you well enough until we can have one made for you.' He cleared his throat. 'Of course, if you would rather choose your own mount, we need not keep her.'

'No, no, she is perfect for me. She sounds as if she

has spirit, too, which is just what I like.' She glanced up at him. 'How did you know?'

'I did not expect anything less of you.'

She could not resist returning his smile.

'Not that I can take all the credit for it,' he continued. 'I wrote to Hambridge some weeks ago, asking him what sort of horse would suit you. His reply was that I should find you something steady. An old animal, perhaps. One that could be relied upon not to bolt with you.'

'A slug, in fact!' she replied tartly.

'Exactly.' His lips twitched. 'However, he also informed me that you had always been quite heedless of your own safety and had regularly flouted his advice regarding which of his horses were suitable for you. From that I gathered that a safe, steady mount was the last thing you would want.'

Serena's heart swelled. She knew an impulse to throw her arms about Quinn—well, as far as they would go around him. Such a display would shock the servants and might well give Quinn a disgust of her. Instead she tucked her arm into his.

'How can I ever thank you, my lord?'

Quinn nodded to Bourne to take the mare away and turned to escort Serena back to the house.

'By riding out with me as soon as Lady Brook has gone today. That is, if you have a riding habit?'

'I do, somewhere. It will be in one of the trunks we brought from Bruton Street. I am afraid it is not in the latest style.' She hesitated, then said haltingly, 'Dorothea did not include a new habit in my wedding *trousseau*.'

'No doubt she disapproves of ladies riding.'

Serena chuckled. 'She does.'

'It is of a piece with her taste in gowns.' He bent a

searching look upon her. 'Tell me truthfully, my dear, do you like *any* of the clothes she bought for you?'

She sobered and looked away. 'It was a difficult time. Dorothea acted as she thought best.'

Quinn held back a snort of derision and refrained from giving his opinion of Serena's sister-in-law.

He said decisively, 'I shall ask Lottie to recommend her favourite modistes and we will have them come here to fit you out with more suitable gowns.'

'The ones I have are perfectly suitable, my lord.'

'Aye, for an ageing dowager,' he retorted, then stopped. 'They are not the style you would have chosen for yourself, are they?' he asked again and put his hands on her shoulders, 'Tell me truthfully, Serena.'

'No.' She looked away, but he could see the distress in her face. 'But my judgement is not to be trusted. Not for the world would I want to disgrace you, my lord.'

Something contracted, hard as iron, around his heart. Without thinking he drew her into his arms. Immediately she stiffened. It was like holding a block of wood, was his first thought, quickly followed by the realisation that it was terror holding her motionless. Carefully he released her, knowing one wrong word and she would run from him. He pulled her hand back on to his arm and continued to walk.

'You could never disgrace me, Serena.'

He was looking straight ahead, but from the corner of his eye he saw her hand come up and dash away a tear.

When they reached the house, Serena excused herself and went up to her room to divest herself of her shawl and tidy her hair. Her head was still full of Dorothea's shrill tones, telling her how fortunate she was and how little she deserved it, but deep, deep inside was a faint glimmer of happiness.

She sat through Lady Brook's visit with outward calm, all the time wondering if Polly had managed to find her old riding habit. She had not needed it at all this year so perhaps it was gone. That thought pierced the blanket of indifference that was wrapped about Serena and she realised with something of a shock how much she wanted to ride the beautiful dapple-grey Quinn had bought for her. Something bubbled up inside. Something she had not felt for months. Joyful anticipation.

Quinn paced the hall. Lady Brook had left the house twenty minutes ago and Dunnock had informed him that my lady had gone directly upstairs to change. How long would that take her? he wondered. Fashionable ladies were notorious for taking an age over their *toilette*. Perhaps he had been over-eager in sending word to the stables. Then he heard a soft, melodious voice behind him.

'I trust I have not kept you waiting, my lord.'

He turned and the breath caught in his throat. Serena had paused, halfway down the stairs, one daintily gloved hand on the rail, the other holding her leather crop and the gathered skirts. A single glance told him that although the riding habit was not new, it was the work of a master. The soft wool jacket fitted snugly, the masculine tailoring and military frogging only serving to accentuate her womanly curves. Beneath her chin was a snowy cravat, tied with a simple knot. Her golden curls were tamed by a matching and very mannish beaver hat with a small brim.

The ensemble was both fetching and eye-catching. The bold colour suited her, too. It was the colour of young, rain-washed evergreens and it enhanced the creamy tones of her skin. It was the sort of outfit worn by a confident young woman, one who did not give a jot what the world thought of her. The woman Serena had once been. Now he read uncertainty in her brown eyes and smiled to reassure her.

'Not at all—you are in good time,' he said. 'I have ordered the horses to be brought to the door and they are not yet here.'

'Oh, good. I would not have had them standing in this sun.' She sounded relieved and was more forthcoming than he had ever known her. 'Polly found my habit you see. Fortunately, it still fits, even if it is a little sun-bleached in places. That is what comes of wearing it out of doors in all weathers, I suppose.'

She chattered away as she descended the last few stairs but Quinn was not attending, distracted by her dainty feet, encased in half-boots of soft kid. Strange, how arousing the glimpse of a shapely ankle could be.

'I hope you do not think it too shabby for our outing, my lord.'

'Hmm?' Her soft voice caught his attention. She was regarding him anxiously and he profoundly hoped his face gave no indication of his wandering thoughts. He cleared his throat. 'No, no, you look quite delightful,' he told her, further alarming himself with such a candid reply. He swung round towards the open door, his ears picking up the sound of hooves on the gravel. 'Shall we go?'

Serena's cheeks flamed. Silently she accompanied Quinn out to the drive, where Bourne was waiting with the dapple-grey and Quinn's diminutive tiger was hold-

ing on to Neptune. At the sight of his master, the powerful black horse threw up his head, almost lifting Clem
from his feet and causing that worthy to remonstrate vo-
ciferously, chastising the animal in colourful language
that made Serena stifle a giggle. It dispelled much of
the awkwardness she had felt at Quinn's unexpected
compliment.

'That's enough, Clem,' barked Quinn, but there was
no mistaking the quiver of laughter in his voice. 'You
had best walk Neptune around again while I attend to
my lady.'

Serena looked at the mare and felt a ripple of excitement. This was no docile hack, but a large, spirited animal that would need all her skill to master. The
meekness and deference she considered so necessary
in her role as Quinn's wife had no place here.

With Bourne holding the mare's head, Quinn threw
Serena up into the saddle and remained close until she
was securely seated. She did her best to ignore the
strong hands that brushed her skirts as he checked the
girth and the stirrup, but she felt strangely bereft when
he pronounced himself satisfied and stepped away. She
buried the thought. She must give her attention to con-
trolling the mare.

'Thank you, my lord.' She gathered up the reins
and nodded to the groom. 'You may release her now,
Bourne, I have her.'

'Are you sure, my lady? She's very fresh. And 'tis a
while since she's had a lady on 'er back.'

'And it is a while since I have been on a horse,' replied Serena, smiling. 'We shall soon grow accustomed
to one another. Let her go.'

Free of the groom's hand on her halter, the mare

threw up her head, but Serena was ready. She turned the animal, murmuring soothingly as Crystal pranced and sidled.

'There,' she said, finally coming to a stand again and running one hand along the glossy neck, 'We understand one another already, do we not?' Quinn was still standing, watching her. She read the approval in his face and her confidence grew even more. 'Well, my lord, will you mount up now? I should like to see just what this lady can do.'

The sound of hooves on the cobbles echoed around the courtyard as Quinn led the way out through the arch. They crossed the bridge and turned on to the path leading into the park. The lad waiting to open the gate for them gave a cheeky grin as he tugged his forelock and Serena could not but smile at him. The day was bright, the sun was warm on her back and suddenly, *suddenly* it was good to be alive. How long had it been since she felt like this?

'Well,' said Quinn. 'Shall we put your mare through her paces?'

She turned her smiling face towards him. 'By all means, my lord!'

Quinn touched his heels to Neptune's sides, marvelling at the change in his wife. Gone was the anxious, hesitant creature who had descended the stairs in her faded habit. Serena on horseback positively glowed with life and assurance. They cantered together through the park, heading for the dense woods that covered the rising ground in the distance. Quinn kept a steady pace, frequently glancing across at his companion. She looked completely at her ease. Very much like her name, he thought. Serene.

He drew rein, bringing Neptune to a walk. 'You ride very well. Is the saddle comfortable for you?'

'Perfectly, thank you, my lord.' She looked about her. 'From the height of the gate and the walls, I suppose this was once a deer park.'

'Yes, we still have red and fallow deer but they prefer the higher ground to the north. In Queen Elizabeth's time the park was double the size, but some of the land was sold off about a century ago and it was remodelled. That was when the avenues of beech, sycamore and lime were planted. They make good rides.' He pointed. 'That avenue leads to an ancient viewing tower, where visitors to Melham could watch the hunt. You can just see the top of it.'

She followed his outstretched finger with a steady, considering stare and he said, 'We could gallop there, if you wish.'

The look she threw at him was full of laughter and mischief. 'You have read my mind, my lord!'

She touched her heel to the mare's flank and set off, her skirts billowing around her.

'Whoa, Neptune.' He held the black in check, enjoying the view of Serena galloping away along the wide avenue. 'By God, she is a bruising rider.'

It needed no more than a word from Quinn for Neptune to leap forward in pursuit. For all his horse's strength, he wondered briefly if he had allowed Serena too much of a start. However, by the time they crested the rising ground Neptune had drawn level and they raced neck and neck towards the stone tower. It reared up before them, massive as a cliff face.

'Pull up,' shouted Quinn as they thundered towards it. 'Pull up, for God's sake!'

For one searing moment he thought Crystal had bolted and would crash into the tower, then he heard Serena laugh and at the very last moment she swung the mare away. The avenue had once extended past the tower to the very edge of Melham land, but it had been allowed to fall into disuse, and no more than a hundred yards beyond the tower was a mass of unkempt bushes and trees.

Quinn brought Neptune to a plunging halt and watched as Serena slowed the mare and brought her back towards him. He was torn between admiration of her skill and blazing anger at her reckless behaviour. She was smiling, her cheeks glowing from the exercise and her eyes sparkling. She had never looked so beautiful.

By heaven, if this is the real Serena then she will lead me a merry dance.

He said with a calm he was far from feeling, 'A trifle foolhardy, don't you think, to ride like that on a horse you do not know, over unknown ground?'

She looked a little conscience-stricken, but her eyes were still shining, which pleased him.

'I beg your pardon. I had not realised just how much I missed riding.' She glanced up at the tower. 'What a grand edifice. Can we go inside?'

'Of course.'

He jumped down and tied Neptune's reins to a bush. When he turned back, Serena had already dismounted and was following suit with the mare. He was disappointed that she had not waited for him to help her down. He would have liked the excuse to hold her in his arms.

* * *

Serena took her time fastening Crystal's reins to a branch. The heady exhilaration was fading and she was regretting her recklessness. Not that Quinn was angry with her, quite the opposite, but even now she felt the panic rising when she recalled the glow of admiration in his eyes. It was so confusing, because she really did want him to admire her, to *desire* her. When he smiled at her she wanted nothing more than to melt into his embrace and yet she could not overcome the black, chilling terror at the thought of being in any man's arms.

She wished she had not dismounted, for now he would have to help her up into the saddle again and that would mean standing close to him, breathing in his scent, the mix of soap and leather and spices that was so strangely intoxicating. She was afraid she might do something rash, like throw her arms about his neck and beg him to kiss her.

Such an action was fraught with danger. She could not be certain that he would want to kiss her and if he did, she might recoil, as she had done before. That would make him angry or, even worse, leave him wounded and unhappy. Then there was Dorothea's assertion that such forward behaviour in a wife would disgust any decent man and Serena had no doubt her husband was a good man.

Quinn was standing by the tower's bleached oak door. 'Well, shall we go in?'

'Is it not locked?' she asked, walking over to him.

'Of course, although it is doubtful if anyone would ever stray this far into the park.' He reached up to a small crevice between two of the stone blocks and pulled out a large iron key. 'So now you are one of the privileged few who know the secret.'

The smile that accompanied his words caused a sudden fluttering inside Serena, as if someone had opened a sack full of butterflies. She dragged her eyes away from his mouth and fixed them on the oak door, but even the sight of him turning the key in the lock made her tremble as she imagined those same fingers on her bare skin.

The door opened and she gave a nervous laugh. 'I expected it to creak, like something from a Gothic novel.'

'The tower is well maintained.'

He stood back to let her precede him into the gloom. The only light came from the open door and a small window set high up in the walls. 'This area was only ever used for storage. The main chamber is above us.' He glanced down at her. 'You are shivering. Are you afraid?'

She could not speak of it, the sudden terrifying memory that had assailed her. Cruel hands around her throat and blackness so deep it made her tremble. She said instead, 'It is very dark, after the bright sunshine.'

'Let me guide you, I will go first.'

He took her hand and drew her towards the stone steps built against the far wall. The terror faded as quickly as it had come. There was something comforting about the way Quinn's huge, warm hand enclosed her fingers. He would protect her from anything and anyone who threatened harm.

But he cannot protect you from yourself, Serena.

The steps opened directly into the main chamber, which boasted windows on all four sides. A large fireplace was built across one corner, with another set of stairs in the opposite corner, leading upwards.

'On inclement days, guests could watch the hunt from here,' Quinn told her.

He was still holding her hand and she was far too aware of him. She was torn between wanting to cling tighter and running for her life.

'It is a lovely, light room,' she said at last. She gently freed her fingers and walked from one window to the next. 'And the views are spectacular. One cannot quite see over the rise to Melham but there are wonderful views over the park.' Turning back, she looked about the room, anywhere rather than at Quinn. 'If it was furnished with a table and chairs, and a thick carpet over the flags, one might dine here very comfortably. A small party, of course, just a few friends. Or it would make a wonderful retreat from the world,' she went on, her imagination taking flight. 'Somewhere one might read in peace and solitude. Or sketch, perhaps.'

Her thoughts ran on. What a wonderful place this would be for a young boy to act out his adventures. His own little kingdom. A castle, perhaps, or a ship at sea.

'I suppose you are right,' said Quinn, coming to stand beside her. 'I never spent much time in here.'

She turned towards him. 'Did you ever play here? It would make a fine lair.'

'When I was a child this place was forbidden. I only remember being chased away from it. I suppose the adults were afraid we might come upon them indulging in an illicit liaison.'

'Your parents' guests?'

'Not only guests,' he said bitterly. 'My parents used

it, too, on the rare occasions they were here. Although not together. Never together.'

The bleakness in his eyes was chilling. She wanted to reach out to him, to kiss away the pain, but what right had she? He might turn away. He might reject her.

For all that she could not resist laying a hand gently on his arm. 'May we go up to the roof?'

Her words seemed to bring Quinn back from a dark place. She watched as he almost physically shrugged off his memories.

He did not take her hand this time and she followed him up the stairs to where another solid oak door opened outwards on to a flagged walkway. The wind gusted around them, but Serena barely noticed it as she slowly made her way around the parapet, drinking in the view. From here she could see the church and the village. Closer, just visible over the hill on the southern side, was the stone and timber square of Melham Court with its red-tiled roof and the tall brick chimneys reaching towards the sky. In the other direction, the woods stretched away into the distance, a thick bubbling blanket in a dozen shades of green.

'Look.' Quinn put one hand on her shoulder, the other stretching out towards a grassy knoll. 'Red deer.'

A small herd were grazing peacefully, watched over by a lordly stag.

Serena gave a small sigh. 'How privileged we are, to be able to stand here and see such beauty.'

'Indeed.'

There was something in the way he spoke the word, his voice slow and deep, that set Serena's body tingling. His hand still rested lightly on her shoulder and she held her breath, imagining his fingers tightening their hold, turning her about so that he might kiss her.

Her stomach swooped at the thought. She wanted it to happen. She wanted it so badly she was tempted to turn and drag his head down towards her. She fought against it. Her forward behaviour had already brought her to the point of ruin once and she was terrified that it would repel Quinn. She must keep quite still and savour the intimacy of standing thus, with her husband. The effort proved too much. She shivered and Quinn's hand dropped.

'Is it too cold for you? We should go inside.'

'No, I am not cold.' The moment had gone, disappearing like smoke. She sighed. 'But perhaps we should be getting back.'

The scene on the rooftop replayed itself over and over in Quinn's head as they made their way from the tower. He was enjoying showing Serena his world—her world now, too. When she had remarked on the view he had wanted to take her in his arms and tell her that she enhanced its beauty but he had hesitated. Soft words and compliments were not his style. And besides, she did not want his advances. Even his hand on her shoulder had made her shudder. Now she was standing beside him as he locked the door and replaced the key in its hiding place. She looked sad and he wanted desperately to make her smile again.

As they walked back to the horses he said, 'It is time we made use of the tower. I shall have the chimney swept and then you shall furnish it. There is plenty of spare furniture in the house, ask Mrs Talbot to show you. But if nothing suits then you must buy more.'

'How would you wish it furnished?'

'That is for you to decide. It can be your own private tower, where you may retire whenever you wish to be alone. Read, draw, whatever you wish to do. No one shall intrude upon you there.'

'Th-thank you.'

He threw her up into the saddle and when she was secure he untied the reins and handed them to her.

'Melham Court is your home now, Serena. I want you to be happy here. The tower shall be your retreat from the world.'

With that he turned to mount Neptune. There. He had said it. He had given her permission to shut herself away from the world. From him.

They rode directly to the stable yard, where the grooms were waiting to run to the horses' heads. Once again Serena dismounted before Quinn could help her, but she did not refuse his arm for the short walk back to the house.

'Thank you for buying Crystal, Quinn. She is perfect. I enjoyed our ride together.'

'And I.' He glanced back at the clock as they entered the main courtyard. 'I had not realised it was so late. There is barely an hour until dinner.'

'That should be sufficient,' she told him. 'I gave orders before we left that we would need hot water upon our return. I am learning to be a good housewife, you see, my lord.'

Her shy smile lifted his spirits as he led her into the hall. He thought she would make directly for the stairs, but she stopped.

'I have been thinking about the tower,' she said, stripping off her gloves. 'With your permission, sir,

I would like it to be a little parlour, with comfortable chairs where we may sit, if we wish, but I should also like to add a dining table. We might dine alone, or invite friends to join us. Perhaps in the summer, when we might go up on to the roof after dinner and watch the sun setting. The views are too special to be kept for us alone. I should like to share them. To share the happiness they bring.'

Where we may sit!

A glow of pleasure warmed Quinn's heart at her words, but he said carefully, 'An admirable idea, my dear, but are you sure that is what you wish?'

'It is.' She glanced up at him. 'I should like to replace the memories you have of the tower with happier ones, my lord.'

And with that she turned and hurried away, leaving Quinn to stare after her.

Chapter Nine

'Well, madam, if you don't like any of these, what *will* you wear tonight?'

Serena looked at the gowns spread over the bed. She was still glowing from the glorious afternoon spent riding with Quinn, although the happiness was fading a little now. Quinn was right about her wardrobe. Dorothea had called her dresses decorous. The old Serena would have said they were uniformly *dull*.

How had it come to this? she wondered. Her sister-in-law had disposed of all her lovely gowns and turned her into a dowd. Anger roiled inside her. At Dorothea, a little, but mainly at herself for allowing it.

'Do we have any of my old gowns, Polly, besides my riding habit?'

'No, ma'am. Lady Hambridge took them all away, saying you would not be needing them.'

Sighing, Serena returned to the selection of gowns in front of her and picked out the charcoal grey with its cream embroidery. It was severe but at least it did not make her look sallow. And she might leave off the bertha, the cape-like lace collar and ruff that covered the low neckline.

'And on your hair, madam? Will it be the matching cap?' Polly added, coaxingly, 'The lace edging is very fine.'

'It is indeed,' agreed Serena. 'I remember Dorothea telling me how expensive it was.'

Polly looked relieved. 'Well then, madam, will you wear it?'

Quinn came downstairs in good time for dinner. In fact, he knew he was early, for the long case clock in the great hall had only just begun to chime the hour. The ride that afternoon had sharpened his appetite and he hoped Serena would not keep him waiting. Not that she had ever done so yet, he thought, a reluctant smile tugging at his lips. She was not one of those fashionable beauties who lost track of time while sitting at their dressing table.

The smile grew as he entered the drawing room to see his wife was already there, gazing out of the window at the gardens, which were bathed in evening sunlight on the far side of the moat. She had her back to him but he was struck by the pleasing image she presented. Her curls were swept up on her head, enhancing the graceful line of her neck above the dark gown. Desire stirred and it positively leapt when she turned around and he saw the tantalising amount of satin-smooth skin exposed by the low décolletage. His gaze lingered on the creamy swell of her breasts. By heaven, he had not expected to lust after his own wife.

Quinn dragged his eyes away. Serena was a wife in name only and would remain so until she chose to change that.

He kept his eyes firmly on her face as she came towards him, but it did nothing to lessen the attraction. The afternoon's exertion had brought more colour to her cheeks. There was even the suggestion of a sparkle in her eyes.

'Good evening, my lord. I have chosen the least nun-like of my gowns. I hope you do not disapprove?'

His eyes narrowed. Was she *teasing* him? That explained the sparkle.

'Only the colour, my dear. It is quite funereal. Mayhap Lady Hambridge anticipated you would drive me to an early grave.'

She laughed at that. 'Mayhap she did. Dunnock tells me dinner can be served as soon as we wish, so shall we go in? We have only ourselves to please, after all.'

'By all means.' He gave her a searching look as he offered her his arm. 'Are you a mind-reader, too, Serena? Did you know I am decidedly sharp-set this evening?'

She shook her head, flushing. 'By no means, but I confess that I am very hungry, too.'

They sat down to dinner very much in harmony, and the accord lasted throughout the evening. Conversation had always flowed easily between them but this evening it was even more pleasurable. Quinn did not linger over his brandy, preferring his wife's company, but when he returned to the drawing room he found her a trifle preoccupied.

He knew what it was, of course. He had seen the nervous shadow flicker across her eyes when he looked at her. She knew he desired her but, confound it, had he not given his word he would not rush her? He wanted to remind her, but was afraid it would destroy the easy camaraderie they had been enjoying. So instead they talked of horses and riding, of his plans for the estate and tomorrow's dinner with Tony and Charlotte.

He said, trying for a light-hearted note, 'We must soon invite more than just the Beckfords to our table.'

'It will be expected, my lord, now you have a wife.'

There it was again. The faintest tremor on that last word. He glanced at the clock.

'It is nearing eleven. You must be fatigued after so much time out of doors today.'

Serena longed to tell him she was not at all tired. She wanted to say how much she enjoyed his company, to stay and converse with him into the early hours, and then to have him invite her to his bed. But Quinn was already rising from his seat, clearly anxious for her to go. Earlier she thought she had seen admiration in his eyes and perhaps a hint of desire, too. But not enough.

'Yes of course.' She rose and shook out her skirts while Quinn opened the door for her. 'Goodnight, my lord.'

He caught her hand as she went to pass him, obliging her to stop. He lifted her fingers to his lips, the veriest touch, but it sent fiery darts racing through her blood. Her eyes flew to his face.

He smiled. 'Goodnight, Serena. Sleep well.'

She hurried up the stairs. Sleep! How could she *sleep* when he had roused in her an indefinable yearning for she knew not what? When she reached the landing she slowed. She was not being honest. She knew exactly what she wanted. She wanted Quinn to sweep her off her feet and take her to bed. Just the thought of it set her spine tingling. But he had told her he would not force himself upon her. When they consummated their marriage, it would be her decision. Did that mean going to his room?

A shimmer of anxiety ran through her. Such wanton behaviour would go against everything she had been told a husband wanted in a wife. The argument went back and forth in her mind as she made her way to her bedchamber. Dorothea had been at pains to tell her how a wife should behave, but until that fateful night at Hitchin Serena had always scorned her sister-in-law's advice. Why, then, was she inclined to believe her now?

The answer was clear: she had no confidence in her own judgement. She was prepared to believe her sister-in-law knew best, just as she had been willing for her to dictate what clothes she should wear. Serena stopped at her door, her fingers clasped about the handle. Quinn did not approve Dorothea's choice of clothes. He had told her as much and now, as the heavy gloom of depression was beginning to lift from her spirits, she could see how wrong they were for her. How was Quinn to know what she wanted, unless she told him?

It was midnight and Quinn could not sleep. After tossing and turning until his bed was hot and uncomfortable, he sat up and reached for the tinderbox. The restlessness had been growing all day and riding out with Serena had only enhanced it. Instead of sleeping, all he could see in his mind's eye was Serena galloping through the avenue. Serena smiling up at him, her countenance flushed and alive with the pleasure of the ride. Serena at dinner, her golden curls piled high and that creamy skin glowing in the candlelight.

Once the candle was burning steadily, he sat for a moment, head bowed and his fingers clutching at his

hair. He tried to breathe deeply, but the air felt thick
and heavy in his lungs. Throwing aside the covers he
jumped out of bed and walked, naked, to the window.
He threw up the sash. The night was still, silent, but at
least air flowed in, cooling his heated skin. A sliver of
moon was reflected in the water of the moat and, together with the pinpricks of starlight, threw a blue-grey
light over the surrounding land.

It was a view Quinn loved, but tonight he saw nothing, his thoughts turned inward, to the desire that
burned so fiercely within him. It was not his custom
to dredge up memories of Barbara but he did so now,
trying to recall if he had felt this way about her. They
had been young and very much in love, but indulging
in anything more than a chaste kiss had been unthinkable. Ironic, then, that now he was married and even a
kiss was out of the question.

His sharp ears picked up a noise outside his door.
He eased the window closed, listening. There it
was again, a definite padding of feet in the corri-
dor. Frowning, he scooped up his dressing gown and
shrugged himself into it. Who on earth was abroad
in the house at this time of night? He would stake his
life that it was not Shere. The valet's step was firm
and steady. What he could hear was definitely stealthy.
Furtive. Intruders, perhaps. He moved quietly towards
the door, but now there was nothing but silence. He
held his breath as his ears strained for the faintest
sound. Then he heard it. The creak of the floorboard
directly outside his room.

For a third time, Serena hesitated in the dark cor-
ridor. When had she become so indecisive? She must

either carry out her plan or scurry back to her room
and admit she was a coward. Screwing up her courage, she stepped up to Quinn's door, only to recoil as it
flew open and Quinn's black shape filled the opening.

'Serena!'

Her hand was still clenched, ready to knock, and he
caught it in his own. There was no going back now. He
drew her into the bedchamber, a room the same size
as her own, but whereas Serena's chamber was decorated in soft shades of yellow, the master bedroom
was much darker and furnished with heavy mahogany
pieces. A single candle burned, enough light to see the
garish pattern on his silk banyan. He had loosely knotted the belt to hold it in place, but her heart, already
thudding, jumped erratically when her eyes wandered
to the alarming amount of bare chest on display.

'Why are you here?'

Her throat was too dry to speak. It was impossible
to drag her eyes away from the muscled contours of his
breast and the smattering of fine hairs that shadowed it.

'Serena?'

His finger beneath her chin obliged her to look up.
He was smiling at her and she desperately wanted to
smile back, but her nerves were too stretched. But she
must speak. She must say something.

'I, um, I wanted to see you.'

'I am flattered.'

His hand dropped but his eyes were still upon her,
warm and reassuring. If she kept looking at him, if she
did not think about the black frame of the bed loom-
ing in the shadows behind him, the threatening darkness might not terrify her. She ran her tongue nervously
across her dry lips.

'I am your w-wife, Quinn. It is time we...' The thunder of her heart was so loud she could not concentrate. 'We...'

Gently, he drew her closer, his huge frame blocking out the light. She turned her face up to him, wanting his kiss, wanting to feel safe. She would close her eyes and surrender to the desire that was slowly unfurling deep inside her. He lowered his head and her eyelids fluttered as his lips brushed hers. It was gentle, the merest touch, but the jolt of awareness took her by surprise and she jumped.

Immediately Quinn released her. Behind him she saw the huge bed, it loomed over them, throwing deep shadows on to the ceiling. The blackness of the canopy drew her eyes and held her gaze. She was transported back to the inn, trapped, powerless. Suffocating.

Don't let me go, Quinn. Hold me. Hold me!

The words screamed in her head, but she could not give voice to them and, worst of all, when she did manage to shift her eyes back to him, Quinn was looking at her in bewilderment. If only she could speak, explain, but fear held her mute and mixed with the dreadful terror that filled her head was Dorothea's voice, dripping with scorn.

He is too good for you. You do not deserve him. You will only disappoint him.

'Serena. What is it?'

Quinn put out his hand and she quickly stepped back.

'I c-cannot.' Her hands clutched at her wrap, pulling it tight beneath her chin. 'I thought I could, but... forgive me.'

And with a sob, she fled.

* * *

The morning sun streamed into Serena's bedchamber. She was sitting at her dressing table, staring at her wan face in the glass. After what had happened last night, how could she face Quinn? She had already asked Polly to bring her breakfast upstairs, to delay leaving her room, but the bread and butter remained untouched on the tray. Perhaps she should go back to bed and have Polly say that she was not well. A coward's way out, she knew, but it would buy her a little more time.

There was a light knock at the door and she turned as Quinn entered. Her heart sank. Would he dismiss Polly and demand an explanation for what had occurred last night? Instead he met her nervous gaze with a smile.

'Good morning, madam. It is such a glorious day that I thought we might ride out.' He spoke cheerfully and she wondered if last night had been nothing but a dream, but only for a moment. Quinn glanced towards Polly. 'Fetch my lady's riding habit, if you please.'

As the maid hurried off into the dressing room, Serena turned back to her glass and picked up the hairbrush.

'I am not sure I have the time to ride this morning,' she said, trying to keep the rising panic from her voice. 'I must see Cook. Surely you have not forgotten the Beckfords are dining with us again?'

'No, I have not forgotten. Nor have I forgotten that you agreed the menu yesterday. There is nothing that cannot wait until we have had our ride.' He came over and stood behind her, resting his hands lightly on her shoulders. If he noticed how she froze he did not show it. 'A little fresh air will do you good, Serena. I shall have the horses brought to the door in half an hour. Is that long enough for you to make yourself ready?'

His tone was perfectly amicable and his reflection showed he was smiling, but there was something in his eyes that told her he would not accept a refusal.

'Perfectly, my lord.'

'Good girl.' She felt the pressure of his fingers on her shoulders and he dropped a quick kiss upon her head before leaving the room. Even her heightened senses could detect no censure in him, only calm reassurance. When she was alone her shoulders sagged. Dorothea was right. She did not deserve such a man.

Once they were mounted, Quinn dismissed the grooms and escorted Serena into the park. She was on edge, last night's encounter hanging over her like a cloud, but a gallop across the springy turf did much to calm her. Quinn led the way to the northern boundary, drawing rein in a small stand of trees on the high ground and pointing out to her the fallow deer grazing in the sheltered valley below them. The scene was so peaceful and Serena felt the last of the tension draining away. A sigh of contentment escaped her and she was aware of Quinn's sudden, questioning glance.

'You have a delightful home, my lord.'

'It is your home, too, Serena.'

'Yes, of course.'

She felt the flush on her cheek, a sudden prickle of guilt, but Quinn was staring out across the park.

'This is one of my favourite spots,' he remarked. 'Look, over there is the tower, where we were standing yesterday.'

'Yes, I see it.'

She followed his pointing finger, but her thoughts were fixed on what had occurred last night. It had been such a good day and they had been in accord. Until the end, when she had ruined everything.

'My lord, about last night.'

His hand came up. He said, not looking at her, 'You do not need to say anything, Serena.'

'But I do.' She kept her own gaze straight ahead, her hands resting together on her leg and Crystal's reins held lightly in her fingers. Somehow it was easier to talk thus. 'I panicked. Suddenly I could think of nothing but that night. At Hitchin.'

'The memories will fade in time, believe me. I am sorry if you think I am rushing you.'

'No, no, it is not your fault at all. You have been most patient with me.' She drew a breath. 'I rarely have nightmares now and I thought... I wanted to prove I could be a...a good wife, but the memory was too strong, it blotted out everything else. After all your kindness.'

She stopped, her voice suspended, and he reached across, his large hand enveloping both of hers.

'Then we must make new memories. Happy ones to replace your terrors. Are we agreed?'

'Yes.' She raised her head and gave him a tremulous smile. 'Yes, indeed that is what we must do. So perhaps we should continue exploring the park, if you have time, my lord?'

He released her hands, flicking her cheek with one careless finger.

'All the time in the world for you, Serena.'

That surprised a shaky laugh from her. 'Why, sir, was that a compliment?'

'Aye, by Gad, I think it was. Whatever is happening to me?' He scowled, but beneath his brows there was a definite gleam of amusement in his hazel eyes. 'I shall have to insist upon your silence, madam, or I shall be losing my reputation as the rudest man in England!'

The drawing room was empty when Quinn walked in later that day. He glanced around him, a slight smile of appreciation curving the corners of his mouth. Everything was in readiness for the evening. The panelling glowed and the air was redolent with beeswax, decanters and glasses had been placed on a side table, and the empty fireplace was filled with a colourful arrangement of summer flowers. That must be Serena's idea, he thought, for it was not something he had seen in the house before.

Serena. He threw himself down in a chair, the smile growing. The morning's ride had somehow turned into a day's excursion. Neither of them had been in any hurry to curtail their outing and when they had finished exploring the park, he had taken her out into the surrounding countryside, where they had stopped to refresh themselves at an inn at the very limit of the Quinn estates.

The Bird in Hand was a small hostelry, more used to catering for local farmers and tradesmen, but Lord Quinn was well known and the landlady had hastily tidied her own parlour for their use and provided them with lamb pie and a rich fruitcake, washed down by a very palatable ale. The landlady had been mortified that she had nothing save coffee that was suitable for a lady to drink, but Serena had immediately assured her a glass of small beer would suit her very well.

The new Lady Quinn had put her hosts at their ease. There was nothing high in her manner, she had shown no reluctance to converse with them and when those locals gathered in the taproom expressed a desire to give a toast to my lord and his lady, she had suggested a fresh barrel of ale should be tapped and the reckoning sent to Melham Court.

The smile turned into a full grin. Nothing was more guaranteed to endear her to the neighbourhood and they had ridden away from the Bird in Hand to the huzzahs and cheers of the assembled company. It was difficult to describe the warm glow of pride he had felt for his bride at that moment.

'Sir Anthony and Lady Beckford, my lord.'

Dunnock's announcement interrupted Quinn's reverie and he rose to meet his dinner guests. Lottie did not stand on ceremony, she clasped his hands when he welcomed her, tugging him down so she might kiss his cheek.

'Are we unpardonably late, Quinn? Tony would insist on changing his coat before we set out.'

'Only because *you*, madam wife, complained the other was too shabby to wear out again, even for a cosy dinner with friends,' drawled Tony, following his wife into the room.

Lottie dismissed the accusation with an airy wave. 'We should give our friends no less respect than anyone else. In fact, we should give them more. Which is why you had to wear your good coat and I had to buy a new gown.'

'I am flattered,' murmured Quinn. 'As to being late… You are nothing of the kind. As you see, Serena is not yet downstairs. We went out riding today and were a little late returning.'

'Riding?' Lottie fixed him with her bright, inquisitive gaze as he escorted her to a chair. 'I did not think you had anything suitable for a lady in your stables.'

'I did not. I fetched a mare over from Pirton earlier this week.'

'From Hackleby's stables?' asked Tony. 'I had heard he was disposing of his cattle.'

'Aye, he doesn't ride much these days and decided it was time to sell almost everything.'

He broke off as the door opened. Serena stood in the doorway, a shy smile trembling on her mouth.

'I do beg your pardon that I was not here to greet you.'

Quinn crossed the floor and took her hand.

'A bride's prerogative, my dear.' He led her forward. 'And we agreed this would be an informal affair, did we not?'

'We did indeed,' cried Lottie, patting the seat beside her. 'Come and join me on the sofa, Serena, and tell me all about your ride today. Quinn says he has purchased a horse for you.'

'Yes,' replied Serena, making herself comfortable beside her friend. 'A beautiful dapple-grey mare.'

'I remember seeing Lady Hackleby out on her in the early part of last year,' exclaimed Lottie. 'That was before her illness. But, heavens, my dear, the creature did not look to be a quiet ride—nor an easy one. Why, she must be fifteen hands at least!'

Serena laughed at that. 'It is true. And she is quite a handful, but I like that. My lord could not have chosen anything better for me.'

Quinn felt a rush of pleasure at her words. He met her eyes for one smiling moment as he crossed to the side table to pour wine for his guests, then Tony was asking Serena what she thought of the park.

'I like it very much,' she responded. 'We rode to the tower. Do you know it?'

'The building at the end of the beech avenue? Yes, I have seen it when I have been riding here,' remarked Tony, taking a glass of wine from Quinn. 'Never been inside, though.'

Quinn smiled slightly. 'My wife has plans to hold dinners there.'

'Very small ones,' added Serena, when Lottie exclaimed in delight at the prospect. 'It will not hold more than half a dozen. More formal dinners will have to be held here.'

'I cannot recall any formal dinners at Melham Court,' remarked Lottie.

'No, my parents only entertained their closest friends here. And as a bachelor I have never felt inclined to host anything of that nature.'

'No, you have never been very hospitable, have you, Quinn?' Lottie wagged her finger at him. 'That must change now, sir!'

Serena shook her head. 'We may hold the occasional party here, but in the main we intend to live very quietly.'

Lottie said drily, 'You will have little choice, my dear, if you intend to rely upon neighbours to fill your table.' She looked up at Tony's muttered admonition and spread her hands. 'What have I said that is not true? There are not above a dozen families here to dine with.

For our ball you know we relied upon acquaintances making the journey from town.'

'Including the Downings,' added Serena. 'I am very grateful to you for that.'

Tony shifted in his seat and looked at Quinn. It was a fleeting glance, but Serena wondered what she had said to cause the look of consternation. Before she could ask, Dunnock entered.

'Ah, dinner is ready.' Quinn rose. 'Shall we go in?'

When the meal was over, Serena carried Lottie off to the drawing room, leaving the gentlemen to enjoy a glass of brandy. They remained in companionable silence for a while, Tony speaking only to compliment his host on the excellence of his wines.

He pushed his glass towards Quinn. 'You will need to restock your cellar, if you plan to entertain more.'

'Serena told you herself that she wishes to live quietly.'

'Yes, I heard that, but I am not sure I believe it.' He sat back, warming his refilled glass between his hands. 'Your wife is a society creature, my friend––it is in her blood, the way she converses, the quickness of her mind. She thrives on company. Mrs Downing said as much at the ball and I agree with her. How long do you think she will be happy, shut away in a quiet backwater?'

Quinn frowned. 'Serena is free to go to town whenever she wishes. She only has to tell me.'

'But will she, knowing that gossip will be rife? You should take her to London, Quinn. Show the *ton* that you are not ashamed of your wife.'

'Of course I am not ashamed of her!' The frown

deepened to a scowl as he recalled Jack Downing's disparaging remarks. He said curtly, 'I will not force her to go to town until she is ready.'

'She will never be ready if you keep her hidden away here, my friend.'

Quinn drained his glass and pushed back his chair. 'Shall we join the ladies?'

Chapter Ten

The golden glow of the evening sun had been replaced by candlelight by the time Quinn and Tony returned to the drawing room, although the long doors to the terrace were thrown wide to allow in the balmy night air. The gentlemen's quiet entrance went unnoticed and they both remained by the door, unwilling to cause a distraction. Serena was at the piano, playing a sonata, while Lottie sat beside her, turning the pages. Quinn had not seen Serena play before, although he had occasionally heard the melodic strains of the piano filtering through the house, but Serena always left the instrument as soon as he appeared.

He stood now, entranced by the performance, until the final note died away.

'Bravo, my lady.' Tony applauded enthusiastically.

'She is very good, isn't she?' said Lottie. 'I could never play Scarlatti.'

'That is because you will not take the trouble to practise,' retorted her fond spouse. 'But Quinn here is an excellent pianist. Has he played for you, Serena?'

'Not yet, but I had guessed he was musical because

this is such a beautiful instrument.' She ran her hands over the keys. 'It is kept in tune, too. Do you do that yourself, my lord?'

'No. Houston's send someone out from town to do it.'

Lottie said mischievously, 'I think the two of you should play a duet for us.'

Serena quickly vacated her seat at the piano, blushing and shaking her head.

'Perhaps we shall,' said Quinn, 'when we have had the opportunity to practise together.'

Serena said hastily, 'Lottie, you were telling me about the new Italian songs you have purchased. Perhaps you would sing one of them?' She glanced at the clock. 'We have time, before I order the tea tray.'

'Yes indeed,' declared Tony. 'Since you made me send for the sheet music, at vast expense, may I say, I should like to see what we get for our money!'

Knowing that Tony would not deny his wife anything, Quinn laughed at that.

'Yes, come along, Lottie,' he said, taking Serena's arm and drawing her down on the sofa beside him. 'It is your turn to entertain us.'

Serena tried to concentrate on the singing, but all she could think of was Quinn sitting beside her. He was at his ease, one arm along the back of the sofa. Surely it was mere imagination that she could feel the heat of it on her spine. If she were to relax just a little, she was sure she would feel his hand against her shoulders. The thought was strangely exciting, but frightening, too. After last night, would he think she was teasing him? He might be offended. He might even move away and that was the last thing she wanted.

Serena remained rigidly upright, fixing her attention upon Lottie's performance and trying to forget how close Quinn was, his muscular thigh almost touching hers, his fingers only inches from her back. She thought she would be pleased when the song was over, but when it ended and Quinn sat up to applaud she found herself wishing she had taken advantage of the situation, had settled herself against her husband and enjoyed a moment of closeness with him. He might even have welcomed it. If only she had made the attempt, but now the moment was gone and all that was left was regret, bitter as gall. Nothing of this showed in her face, however, as she went over to the bell to ring for tea, but she was aware of Quinn's eyes upon her and could not help wondering if he, too, was regretting the lost opportunity.

Conversation was desultory while Serena prepared and served tea to her guests. When Sir Anthony came over to take his cup from her, he remarked cheerfully that he hoped she had not found her first dinner party at Melham Court too onerous.

'Not at all,' she told him, smiling. 'It has been a pleasure.'

'And for me, also,' declared Lottie. 'It is the first time I have ever dined here.'

'Truly?' Serena's brows lifted in surprise.

'As a bachelor I could not invite respectable females to dine here,' explained Quinn.

'Not that he invited *any* females to dine here,' Tony added hastily.

Quinn was grinning and Serena felt emboldened to reply.

'No, he told me he had not moved here to be sociable.'

'Which makes this quite an occasion,' added Lottie. She threw her husband a triumphant glance. 'And therefore merited my buying a new gown!'

'Not that you ever require an excuse,' said Tony.

The loving smile he gave his wife sent a tiny dart through Serena. It felt very like jealousy. Not that it was Sir Anthony she wanted to look at her in quite that way, of course. She glanced from Lottie's canary-yellow gown to her own grey skirts.

'When I looked at my wardrobe this evening I realised that it is all a little…sober. I must remedy that with all speed. Is there a reliable local seamstress, ma'am, or should I look to town?'

'Oh, it must be London, without question,' replied Lottie. 'There is not enough business here to provide a living for a good seamstress.'

'Then I shall send to town in the morning—'

'No need for that,' Quinn interrupted her. 'I shall take you there myself.'

Serena was so surprised that she almost dropped her teacup. She carefully lowered it back into its saucer before turning a questioning glance at her husband. He met her eyes with a smile.

'I think it is time I showed off my wife to the world.'

'Did you mean what you said last night, about going to town?'

Serena and Quinn were at breakfast and, with servants in attendance, she asked the question with as casual an air as she could manage.

'Of course. Johnson is already looking for a suitable house for us. You need any number of gowns and it will be much more convenient than having dozens of seamstresses coming to Melham Court. Mrs Talbot must remain here, of course, but we will take Dunnock with us and he will ensure we are comfortable. Many families will have removed from London by now, but I hope there will be sufficient amusements to entertain us.' Quinn paused to select a bread roll from the proffered basket and waited for the footman to withdraw before he continued. 'We must face society sooner or later, Serena.'

She flushed. 'You mean I must face up to the scandal I have caused.'

'Yes, but you will not be alone. I shall be with you.'

She glanced towards the door, to make sure they could not be overheard.

'I have seen the newspaper reports. I know what they are saying of me. That I, that I—'

'That you eloped with your lover, but forsook him when a wealthier catch appeared. The wealthier catch being myself, although names were not spelled out.'

Her head dropped. 'Yes.'

'Do not be too downcast. Newspapers are notorious for giving too much space to gossip and speculation and not enough to serious matters, such as the riots in East Anglia and the atrocious weather, which will cause food shortages throughout the country.'

'That will affect us all, will it not?' she asked him, momentarily diverted. 'What will you do if your tenants have a bad harvest?'

'I can forgo the rents, although I can do nothing about the rise in the price of bread.'

'But perhaps you should be here, if there is likely to be unrest?'

'Johnson has been my steward and secretary for

years, he knows my ways and can deal with everything in my absence. We will leave at the end of the week, if that is convenient to you?'

'Perfectly, my lord.'

She could not keep the doubtful note from her voice. Quinn pushed back his chair and came to stand behind her, resting his hands lightly on her shoulders.

'We will face down the gossips, never fear.' He gave a short laugh. 'The newspapers are currently speculating on the end of the world, following reports of the earthquake in Scotland! There can be no interest in our little scandal.'

'I devoutly hope you are right, sir.'

Lord Quinn's travelling coach bowled into London on a rainy late-August day, when the sky was dark with lowering grey clouds. There had been little for Serena to do regarding the arrangements. Quinn's excellent steward had found three houses that were available for the summer and Quinn had suggested they take the most fashionable and expensive.

'There is only one detail you might not approve,' he had explained, when they went over the details together. 'There is a connecting door between our bedchambers. However, you have my word I shall never come into your room unless I am invited. You will have to trust me on that point, Serena.'

Serena had agreed to it because she knew enough of Quinn now to believe he would keep his word. However, as they pulled up at the steps of the elegant town house in Berkeley Square, she experienced a little shimmer of apprehension, although it had little to do with the sleeping arrangements. She would much rather be in a quiet street than in such a busy square. Gunter's tea shop was situated close by and it was a popular destination for the *ton*, who could even order ices to be brought to them in their carriages. There would be a constant stream of the rich and fashionable walking or driving past their door.

Quinn gave her fingers a squeeze as he helped her down from the carriage.

'Head up and smile,' he murmured, pulling her hand on to his arm. 'If we are going to cause a stir, then we are well placed here to give everyone something to talk about.'

One of Serena's first tasks was to write to her sister-in-law. Dorothea replied by return, making it plain that the seaside was proving so beneficial to little Arthur's health that she would not be cutting short her visit. However, a note to Elizabeth Downing was followed up almost immediately by Mrs Downing and her daughter calling in person and they left Serena in no doubt of their continued friendship.

This was comforting, but since neither Serena nor Quinn had made efforts to contact anyone else in London, she expected her arrival in the capital to pass almost unnoticed. However, during those first weeks, while she was still, in Quinn's words, *making herself fit to be seen*, a steady trickle of calling cards appeared at the house and the invitation cards lining the mantelpiece grew apace.

Not that Serena had much opportunity to dwell upon the number of invitations. She spent her days visiting warehouses, where she picked out ells of exquisite materials which were then taken to the modistes to be made up into gowns for every occasion. There were also trips to milliners, glovemakers, shoemakers and anyone else who could provide the accessories so essential to a lady of fashion.

Quinn had ordered that Serena was to have the finest of everything and no expense was to be spared. He even accompanied her on some of her outings, including an early call he insisted that she pay to Mrs Bell, to choose a new walking dress. When that celebrated seamstress suggested a pastel blue twill for Lady Quinn he was quick to reject it.

'No, no, such washed-out shades drain her of colour,' he barked. 'Try that one.' He pointed to a bolt of rich turquoise cloth on a high shelf.

Serena's eye had already been drawn to the material but she had allowed herself to be persuaded to look at the pale pinks and blues that Mrs Bell assured her were all the rage. Quinn's brusque intervention made the seamstress bridle a little, but she was too sensible to take umbrage at the interference of such a wealthy customer. However, when Serena stood before the looking glass with a length of the material draped across her shoulder, Mrs Bell was the first to admit that it was the perfect colour for my lady.

'It is merino wool, madam, although not at all heavy. It will make up beautifully into the military style that you have requested.' She stood behind Serena, gazing over her shoulder into the mirror. 'We shall add epaulettes, frogging and braid, and I suggest half-boots of kid, dyed to match. You will need a shirt of the finest cambric, of course, and a cravat. And on your head, we should have something simple, I think, such as a small round hat of moss silk. What say you to that, my lord?

If you prefer we might have a jockey cap, or a silk cap and ostrich feathers…'

'As though you were suddenly the foremost connoisseur of female attire,' Serena told him as he escorted her back to their carriage. She giggled. 'I do not know how I kept my countenance when you told her you knew nothing of such things.'

'It is the truth,' he replied. 'I leave such details to you to decide.' As he handed her into the coach he added darkly, 'As long as the result does not make you look like a dowd.'

'I shall do my best to make sure of that, my lord. But I think you may be assured that Mrs Bell will do her best to please.'

'Good.' He paused in the doorway, one booted foot on the step. 'Now, what are your plans for the rest of the day? Do you wish to visit more warehouses? Or mayhap you wish to go to Bond Street. If that is the case I shall send you back to Berkeley Square to collect your maid. I, on the other hand, believe I deserve a reward for spending the morning discussing frills and furbelows.'

'You do indeed.' Serena smiled, wondering which of the clubs he would visit. She was therefore surprised at his next words.

'I thought I might look in at Somerset House. The Royal Academy. Perhaps you might like to come with me.'

Quinn was busy rubbing at a mark on his boot and not looking at her, so she had no clue as to what he wished her to say.

'I would like that very much.'

'Excellent.' Quinn threw up a word to the driver and

climbed into the carriage. 'I thought you might enjoy it—I remember your interest in the Titian.'

Serena turned to gaze out of the window as a tell-tale flush burned her cheeks. She had not forgotten her first morning at Melham Court, coming downstairs in her ruined gown and feeling more than a little shy. They had discussed the Venus and he had conversed with her as an equal. He had made her forget, for a short while, her disastrous situation.

A sigh escaped her. 'I fear you have paid a high price for your kindness to me that night, my lord.'

To her surprise he smiled. 'I think it might cost me a grand tour. Now the war is over we could travel extensively on the Continent. Would you like that, Serena?' He raised his brows. 'What have I said to make you look so shocked? We rub along quite well together, do we not? And if you dare to tell me you do not deserve such kindness then I shall box your ears!'

That made her laugh. 'Then I shall say nothing of the kind. Instead I will tell you that I should like nothing better than to make the grand tour.' Her laughter died. 'I wish we were doing so now, rather than being in town.'

'I am sure you do, but there are some in London who are determined to destroy your reputation and I will not allow that.'

He looked so fierce that she clasped her hands before her. 'You will not challenge anyone to a duel?'

'Not if it can be helped.' It was not the assurance she was hoping for and she bit her lip. 'Well?' he prompted her. 'You had best tell me what is on your mind.'

She looked down at her fingers, writhing together in her lap.

'You are not renowned for your good temper. If you should become angry, you might forget yourself.'

Quinn stared at her, swallowing the sharp retort that would have demonstrated the truth of her words.

'Are you afraid I shall embarrass you, madam?'

'No, never that,' she replied quickly. 'But I know how you abhor town. You do not like society and you are forcing yourself to endure it for my sake.' She fixed him with a look, her dark eyes full of concern. 'If we are to quell the gossip, you will be obliged to squire me to all sorts of parties, most of them full of tiresome people vying for the notice of the *ton*.' Her shoulders lifted in a faint shrug. 'I have no illusions about the fashionable world, Quinn. Hostesses will be so grateful to have you in their house that they will fawn over you in the most embarrassing way. Sycophants will latch on to you because you are wealthy and you will hate it. How will you bear it without losing your temper with them all?'

I will bear it because you are there.

Where the devil had that thought come from? Quinn harrumphed and shifted uncomfortably in his corner.

'My temper is not so ill controlled as you think, madam. Have I ever given you cause to fear me?'

Her face softened. 'Oh, no, you have always been the kindest of men to me. And for so little reward, too.'

He saw the pain in her eyes. She was recalling how she recoiled from his touch. He wanted to reach out, to enfold her in his arms and tell her it did not matter, that everything would come right, in time. But she would flinch from his embrace and he could not bear that. He kept his hands by his sides and looked out of the window as the carriage slowed.

'Ah. Somerset House. Let us go in.'

* * *

The first weeks in London passed in a whirl of activity for Serena. There was little time to rest. When she was not buying clothes or being fitted for another new gown, Quinn took her out and about with him. She enjoyed these excursions, not only to the Royal Academy and the theatre, but also to small, select gatherings of artists, musicians and authors. It was a world away from the glittering ballrooms of the *ton*. The talk was all of art or literature or even politics and Serena loved it.

'I especially like the fact that my opinion is respected, even if they cannot agree with it,' she told Quinn as he escorted her home late one night. She glanced up at him. 'Do they know who you are?'

He laughed. 'But of course.'

'And yet, no one entreats you to sponsor them, or seeks out your support.'

'Because I have made it plain I will not tolerate that. If I choose to become patron to a young artist, or to donate to some worthy cause, that is my affair. I go there for the company and the conversation.'

'Very different from the Drycrofts' ball, which we are engaged to attend tomorrow,' said Serena. 'Our first official engagement. Are you sure we must do this?'

'I thought you wished to go.'

She sighed. 'I was resigned to the fact that we must do so. But I have had word from Lizzie Downing that she has a slight chill and will not be attending, and now...'

He reached out and caught her hand, holding it warm and safe in his own.

'Do you wish to withdraw from the lists, Serena?'

'Why, yes, if you must know. We might live retired until our situation is completely forgotten. Heaven knows there is enough calamity in the world that no one will remember one little scandal in a year's time.'

His grip on her fingers tightened. 'The danger is that by then Forsbrook and the other vicious scandalmongers will have set in stone their version of what happened and it will be a hundred times more difficult to persuade everyone of the truth.'

She sighed. 'Is that so very important?'

'Yes, confound it!' He turned towards her, pulling her close, so that the street lamps and flaring torches illuminated their faces. 'You are made for pleasure, Serena. For laughter and balls and assemblies and dancing until dawn. If you retire to the country it should be because it is what *you* want, not because you have been driven away.'

Serena felt the breath catch in her throat at his fierce determination. He was willing to do this for her sake! At that moment the carriage swung around a corner, throwing her off balance, and she quickly placed her free hand on his chest to steady herself.

'You are a good man, Rufus Quinn.'

Their faces were only inches apart and the devil danced in his eyes. Serena held her breath, waiting for him to pull her close and kiss her. Instead his mouth twisted.

'I am here to show to the world that my wife is beyond reproach,' he said gruffly.

He released her and drew back into the corner, into the shadows. Serena crossed her arms, hugging herself, but it was nowhere near as comforting as having Quinn hold her.

Chapter Eleven

The Drycrofts' reception rooms were filling up when Quinn and Serena arrived, fashionably late. Serena was already acquainted with Lady Drycroft, a plump, kindly soul but an inveterate chatterbox. She was beaming as they came up the stairs towards her.

'Serena—Lady Quinn, I *should* say, how delightful you look, my dear, that watered silk is charming, quite charming, and the colour! What do they call that, my love, old rose? Yes, I thought so. My dear, I have never seen you looking so well. And how is your dear brother? No, not Lord Hambridge, for dear Dorothea writes to me regularly and I know they are going on very well in Worthing. No, I mean the other one. Russington. *Such* a rogue, but a charming one. And his lady, how is she? She has recently been brought to bed, I hear. Do give her my regards when you write.'

The purple ostrich feathers in her turban nodded as she turned to Quinn, eyeing him a little warily as he bowed over her hand.

'How delightful that you could join us, my lord.' Serena did not miss the doubtful note in the lady's voice. 'I do hope you will enjoy our little soirée. My husband has set up cards in the small salon over there, if that is your pleasure. Not that you are obliged to leave the ballroom, of course. After all, dancing is the reason for a ball, is it not?' She gave a nervous little laugh. 'No, no, you are not to be thinking for one moment that we are wishing you otherwhere. You will want to dance with your wife, which is quite natural, and another gentleman is always welcome, is that not so, Lady Quinn?'

She continued to chatter, offering to come now and introduce Serena to new partners if his lordship wished to go off and play cards, or indeed to present suitable dancing partners to Lord Quinn, if that was his desire. Serena's lips twitched when she glanced at her husband. His features were schooled into a look of indifference, but she was sufficiently well acquainted with him now to recognise the impatience, nay, horror, growing within him as he listened to his hostess. However, he said nothing and Serena took pity upon him. As soon as their hostess drew breath she broke in.

'Thank you, ma'am, but there is no need for you to quit your post, for I see more guests arriving. I know we must appear very unfashionable, but I would much rather have Lord Quinn with me on my first social outing in town since…since my marriage. If you will excuse us, we shall go and find our way about.'

With a smile she led Quinn away.

'What a gabster,' he muttered. 'I do not know how Drycroft can tolerate such a chatterbox.'

'I believe he spends a deal of time at his club,' Serena murmured.

'No doubt he sleeps there, too. If I had to face such

a chinwagger over breakfast, I would cheerfully throttle her!'

She choked back a laugh. 'No, no, she is perfectly good-natured and I am sure if she knew her chatter irritated you she would be quiet.'

'I would not wager on it,' he muttered darkly.

He led her into the ballroom where the first dances had just ended. A liveried servant announced them in stentorian accents and the chatter died quite away as all eyes turned towards the door.

Serena recognised many of the guests. Hostesses who had welcomed her, gentlemen she had danced with, debutantes and their mothers who had been eager to count the popular Miss Russington among their friends. Now their faces displayed either disapproval or curiosity. Even those matrons she had seen at the Beckfords' ball regarded her with more open hostility than they had shown in Hertfordshire. One young lady, Beatrice Pinhoe, smiled at Serena, until her mother nudged her and muttered something that made Beatrice flush and drop the hand she had raised in greeting.

Only pride prevented Serena from turning and running from the room. Pride and Quinn's presence beside her. His elbow was pressing her arm tight against him, so that she was unable to remove her hand from his sleeve. Not that she wished to do so. She was grateful for his support, it wrapped about her like a shield and gave her the strength to keep her smile in place, to raise her head a little higher and meet the cold stares with at least the appearance of complaisance.

A portly gentleman with bushy side whiskers and claret-coloured cheeks pushed his way through the crowd. He came towards them, saying jovially, 'Quinn, my lady. This is a surprise. Didn't expect to see you here, my lord. Thought you'd be at Melham, delighting in that Titian you stole from under my nose!'

'Instead I am delighting in the company of my new bride,' replied Quinn calmly. 'My dear, let me present the Earl of Dineley to you.'

Quinn's voice and the faint squeeze he gave her fingers dragged Serena's attention away from the censorious looks and she managed to curtsy without wobbling. The momentary hush that had fallen over the room ended. People were chattering again and attention had moved back towards the dance floor, where the musicians were tuning up for another country dance.

'Delightful, quite delightful,' declared Lord Dineley, taking her hand. 'I am very glad now that I decided not to leave town just yet.' He winked at Quinn. 'If I had a nabbed me a beautiful young wife I, too, would want to show her off. In fact, I have a mind to claim her for the next dance—'

His grip on her fingers tightened. Panic flared as Serena wondered how she could refuse without offending the Earl. In the past she would easily have dealt with the situation. Indeed, she had done so dozens of times, but now her brain refused to work.

Quinn rescued her, saying coolly, 'In that case, Dineley, I should be obliged to call you out. I mean to dance with my wife myself.'

'What? Oh, quite. Quite so, sir.'

The Earl's face registered surprise and disappointment but he gave in with good grace and stepped aside. With a nod, Quinn led Serena towards the dance floor.

Relief made her want to giggle. She murmured, 'I

did not expect such aplomb from you, my lord. I am all astonishment.'

'Did you think I would relinquish you to that old roué? We are here to *restore* your reputation, madam, not destroy it completely.'

Serena winced inwardly as they took up their places in the set. She wanted to cry at his harsh words. Instead she kept her head up and her smile in place as the dance began. She skipped forward, put her hand out to her partner.

'Forgive me,' he muttered, pulling her closer. 'It seems my new-found aplomb does not extend to those I hold most dear.'

Serena's step faltered and only by the most strenuous effort did she keep dancing. Had he really said that? Had she heard him correctly? A swift glance up at his unsmiling countenance gave her no clue, but all the same she felt the nerves ease. As they progressed through the familiar movements her smile became genuine and she began to enjoy herself.

Quinn danced the first two dances with his wife, after which the Grindleshams came up to congratulate them upon their marriage and Lord Grindlesham carried Serena off to dance with him. Quinn would have preferred to remain as a spectator, but he knew his duty and solicited Lady Grindlesham to join him on the dance floor. That seemed to give the lead to other couples to approach and although Quinn did not dance again he had the felicity of seeing Serena stand up for every dance.

When supper was announced he was waiting to escort her downstairs. Her eyes sparkled as she left the

dance floor on the arm of her partner and there was
a becoming flush to her cheek. Quinn's jaw clenched
when he saw how the young cub was gazing at Serena
and he was obliged to curb his impatience while she
thanked the fellow prettily before turning to accompany Quinn out of the ballroom.

'You appear to be enjoying yourself,' he remarked.

'Yes. Yes, I am.'

'And your last partner looked particularly enamoured.' Something dark and uncomfortable stirred
within him. 'No doubt he wanted to take you down
to supper.'

'He did, of course, but your dreadful scowls frightened him away.'

She was twinkling up at him and the darkness evaporated like smoke.

By the time the carriage carried them back to Berkeley Square Serena was exhausted, but happier than she
had expected to be. After the initial reserve, very few of
the Drycrofts' guests had kept their distance. She was
cynical enough to know that much of this was due to
her new position as the bride of one of the richest men
in London. They might disapprove of the new Lady
Quinn, but they would not cut her acquaintance.

She glanced across the darkened carriage to where
she could just make out the black shadow that was
Quinn. His renowned incivility had not been evident
this evening. She had witnessed first-hand the way some
of the guests had fawned over him and would have for-
given him for uttering a sharp set-down. Even when he
had been subjected to the inane chatter of ladies who

were even more loquacious than their hostess, he had endured it calmly.

'Thank you, my lord.'

The black shape in the corner shifted.

'For what?'

'Oh, for escorting me to the ball, for looking out for me all evening and especially for keeping your temper, when even I found some of the company tiresome in the extreme.'

'Did you?' He sounded surprised. 'You never showed it.'

'Ah, but I had you beside me for most of the evening, ready to carry me away before I could give vent to my impatience. I am only sorry that you did not enjoy yourself.'

'Actually, I *did* enjoy it.'

'What,' she teased him, 'all that toadying and silly chatter?'

'No, not that, of course not. But I took pleasure in some of the company.' She saw the flash of white teeth as he grinned. 'Whenever I wished to escape I could always say I needed to find you. Also, I admit that I enjoyed the music. And dancing with you.' He stretched out his hand. 'We make a good team, I think.'

Smiling, she put her hand into his. 'I am glad you think so, my lord.'

The carriage slowed and Serena recognised the elegant portal of their London house. Quinn handed her out and escorted her into the hall. He gave his hat and gloves to the butler and turned to remove the cloak from Serena's shoulders. His touch through the thin silk set her nerve ends tingling. Little arrows of heat pierced her body, pooling somewhere deep inside. She wanted to lean against him, to turn and put her arms around him, but Dunnock was hovering nearby and such a display would shock the poor man to the core.

Quinn walked with her to the stairs, his hand resting lightly against her back. She hoped he would escort her up to her room. She hoped he would kiss her. Perhaps it was dancing together, or the wine she had drunk, but every fibre of her body ached for his touch. The thought brought on a little quiver of excitement, of pleasurable anticipation that at last she might truly become his wife. She watched silently as he took one of the bedroom candles from the table and lit it.

'You must be tired.' He handed her the candle. 'Goodnight, my dear.'

With a flicker of a smile and a nod, he turned and strode away to the drawing room.

'Damn, damn, damn.'

Quinn shut the drawing room door and leaned against it. He closed his eyes, but all he could see was Serena looking more beautiful than he had ever seen her, with her eyes sparkling and the flawless skin of her shoulders rising from the deep dusk-pink silk gown. Serena dancing at the ball, talking with her acquaintances. Laughing with her partners. Laughing up at *him*.

By heaven, how much he wanted her, but he had given her his word that he would not make love to her until she was ready. When that lecher Dineley had leered at Serena he had seen the panic in her eyes. The woman she had once been would have laughed it off, sent the fellow on his way, but she had lost her confidence and he had stepped in, carrying her off to dance with him, and thereafter he had kept an eye on her, making sure she danced only with gentlemen who could be trusted not to go beyond the line of what was pleasing.

And his efforts had been rewarded. By the end of the evening she had regained much of her sparkle and self-assurance. That pleased him but it had also roused his desire. He shook his head. Much as he wanted to make love to Serena, he dared not rush her.

Exhaling, he pushed himself away from the door and crossed to the side table to pour himself a brandy. Upstairs was his wife, the most desirable woman in London. And he could not have her.

The shadows flickered alarmingly as Serena climbed the stairs and halfway up she stopped, blinking to keep the tears from filling her eyes. The evening had been such a pleasure, she and Quinn had been getting on well, but then, when she wanted him to sweep her up and carry her off to his bed, he had walked away!

'Odious, *odious* creature, how dare he do that?'

How was he to know what you wanted?

She glanced up into the darkness of the landing above her, then down towards the drawing-room door. Dare she do this?

She breathed deeply, trying to calm her nerves and steady the hand that was carrying the candle, then she turned and went back down the stairs. Dunnock had retired back to the nether regions and the hall was deserted. Serena left her bedroom candlestick on the side table and crossed to the drawing room.

Quinn was lounging in an armchair beside the empty fireplace, his eyes fixed upon the brandy glass cradled in one large hand. The draught of the opening door caused the candles in the room to flicker. Quinn glanced up and Serena found herself subjected to a brooding stare. Not only her body, but her mind froze.

'I am not tired,' she managed to say at last, then cringed inwardly. She sounded more like a petulant schoolgirl than a seductress.

Quinn's brows went up a fraction.

'I am pleased to hear it.' He pushed himself out of the chair. 'Would you care to sit down?'

Well, at least he had not thrown her out. Yet. She closed the door and moved to a sofa, grateful for all those years of deportment training that allowed her to glide across a room even when her legs felt like jelly.

He glanced at the assortment of decanters and glasses arranged on a side table.

'May I pour you a glass of something. Ratafia, perhaps. Or claret?'

'Brandy.' Sir Timothy had tried to intoxicate her with red wine and she wanted no reminders of that now. 'I will drink a little brandy, if you please.'

'Very well.'

Quinn poured out a small measure and carried it across to her. He looked wary but intrigued and after handing her the glass he sat down beside her, his large frame filling the satin-covered space. He touched his glass against hers, then settled himself back into the corner, turning slightly so that he might look at her, his free hand resting along the back of the sofa.

A stillness settled over the room, broken only by the occasional flicker of a candle and the rhythmic tick, tick of the French ormolu mantel clock. Serena took a sip from her glass, remembering far-off days when she had smuggled brandy into the school for a midnight feast with her friends. She needed to find a little of that daring spirit now, for Quinn seemed determined to wait for her to break the silence.

'I enjoyed this evening, my lord,' she said, running her tongue over her dry lips. 'I did not want it to end. Not the dancing,' she added hastily. 'I mean… I mean *us*.'

Her eyes were on the glass in her hand, yet she was aware that Quinn's attention was fixed upon her. She lifted the glass to her lips again, but the heat spreading over her neck and face had nothing to do with the brandy. A little bubble of hysterical laughter escaped her.

'I am at a loss, my education d-did not include how one should d-discuss these things with one's husband, but you s-said that *when* we c-consummate our marriage must be up to me, that it m-must be my decision and I…what I am trying to say…'

The sofa creaked as he sat up suddenly.

'You are babbling, Serena.' Gently, he took the glass from her fingers, putting it down beside his on the sofa table behind them.

'I know, but I am very much afraid that if I do not speak now I will not have the courage again and then it will be too late—'

'Hush.' He put a finger to her lips. 'I understand. I have already told you, there is no hurry.'

He put his arm about her and pulled her close, until her head was resting on his shoulder. He stroked her hair, his large hand surprisingly gentle. Serena relaxed against him with a shuddering sigh.

'Oh, but there *is*,' she muttered, one hand clutching at his lapel. 'I *want* it to happen. I want it quite *desperately*.'

'Desperately?' He put his fingers beneath her chin and, obedient to the pressure, she looked up at him. He was smiling. 'Then let us see what we can do about that.'

He lowered his head, his lips gently brushing hers. She slipped one hand around his neck, pulling him closer. Her lips parted, she was relaxing, melting against him. He shifted his position and pulled her on to his lap while she curled her fingers in his hair. The silky strength of it excited her, as did the complex scent of the man, the smell of his skin mixed with spices and soap, and the taste of him, overlaid with just a hint of brandy. His arms tightened, she could feel the taut muscle of his body pressed against her, but despite the curl of pleasure deep in her core, panic began to gnaw at her.

No. She would not be defeated. She *wanted* this and would not be denied.

'Take me, Quinn,' she muttered against his mouth. 'Take me now. Quickly!'

The last word was an entreaty. Quinn raised his head. He was still holding her against him and she could feel the frantic thud of his heart. His breathing was rapid and she put a hand up to his cheek, feeling the rough stubble against her palm.

'I want you to do this, Quinn.' She was begging, afraid of the insidious terror creeping up on her. 'Please, before it is too late!'

He stared down at her. Then, as his breathing steadied he put his hand over hers and drew it away from his face. He settled her back on the seat beside him, but kept a firm hold of her hands.

'Tell me what you mean by that.'

'I w-want to please you,' she murmured, looking away from him.

He said gently, 'This is not how it should be, Serena. There must be pleasure for you, too.'

'No, no, I have to do this, Quinn. It is my duty, as your wife.'

'Your duty!' His grip on her fingers tightened. 'Duty be damned. If I wanted only *my* pleasure I could have taken you weeks ago, is that not so?'

She bowed her head. 'You have been too good, too kind to me, b-but it is no use. I c-cannot enjoy a man's embrace. I thought I could but...fear engulfs me and... and I w-want to run away.'

She blinked rapidly, but could not prevent a rogue tear dropping on to her lap. Her heart sank. Any moment now he would send her back to her room.

Quinn did indeed release her, but only so he could cradle her face in gentle hands.

'Let us do this another way,' he said, wiping her cheeks with his thumbs. 'You shall tell me what you want me to do.'

A fiery blush burned Serena's cheeks. 'I—I cannot. I have no idea. I do not know how...'

She twisted away and sat beside him, her arms crossed as if to shield herself.

Quinn cleared his throat. 'Very well, let me make a suggestion. I am no rake, Serena, but I know that most ladies like being kissed. You appeared to enjoy that.'

'Yes,' she said shyly. 'I d-did. I do.'

'Good. Then let us start again.'

He put one arm about her shoulders and kissed her, a long, slow, languorous kiss that melted her bones. When he lifted his head, she remained with her head thrown back against his shoulder.

He smiled down at her. 'Did that frighten you?'

She gave a little shake of her head.

'And do you think you might like me to kiss your neck?'

'I think I might,' she said cautiously.

'Good.' He brushed his lips across hers, then his mouth trailed light, butterfly kisses along her jaw until he reached the spot just below her ear. A little sigh escaped her as he gently nibbled the soft skin. She closed her eyes and tilted her head to one side to give him more room. The caress of his lips was soothing, relaxing. No dark fears stirred within her.

'How is that?' he murmured, his tongue flicking over her ear.

'It is very…pleasant.' He stopped and she added quickly. 'I l-like it. Very much.'

'Excellent.' She gripped his shoulder as his teeth grazed her earlobe. She snuggled closer, aware of a sudden urge to purr. He breathed softly, 'Shall we move on a little?'

'Oh, yes.' She sighed. 'If you please.'

He settled her more comfortably against the sofa before his lips moved slowly down the side of her neck in a series of featherlight kisses. She gave a little moan when he reached the hollow between the collarbones.

Quinn raised his head. 'Do you not like it?'

'Yes, yes, I do. But I have never felt like this before,' she said, greatly daring, 'Could we begin again, perhaps?'

'Of course.'

This time she returned his kiss, her lips parting, and

she eagerly tangled her tongue with his in a sensual dance that left them both breathless. By the time his mouth had worked its way back to the hollow at the base of her throat, she had thrown back her head and her eyes were closed.

'What would you like me to do next?' he murmured.

'Wh-what else do ladies like?' she gasped, her body arching as he trailed one finger down her breastbone.

'Let me see if I can remember.' His finger ran around the neckline of her gown and she shivered with delight. 'But a word will stop me, do you understand?'

She nodded and he dropped a kiss on her shoulder, then returned his attentions to her mouth. She responded eagerly, tingling beneath the warmth of his palm as his hand slid over her silk gown. When he caressed her breasts, they strained to break free of the confining bodice. His expert kisses made her senses reel as his tongue teased and explored, stirring up the pool of latent desire that was steadily growing deep in her core.

She was dimly aware of his hand moving down over her waist and her hips, then he was gently pulling up the silken skirts, but she was too intent on enjoying his kisses to care, until she felt his hand on her bare thigh. She tensed and immediately Quinn stopped.

'Would you like this to end now?'

He breathed the words against her cheek and she sighed, her fears melting.

'No.'

Her reward was another deep, penetrating kiss, made all the more thrilling by the way her body was reacting to his fingers on her thigh. Heat coursed through her, an aching need for more. His hand moved upwards and Quinn continued to caress her, gently brushing over and around the sensitive skin until at last his fingers slid gently into her and she welcomed him with a little moan of pure pleasure. She moved against him restlessly as excitement rippled through her, a trickle at first, but building, like waves pushing against a dam. It was too much. She broke away from his kiss and dragged in a long, gasping breath.

'Enough?' Quinn ran his lips over her neck.

'I d-don't know.'

His soft laugh sent a shudder of need running through her and she clung to him. His fingers began to work again, stroking, teasing, drawing responses from every nerve in her body until all the attention was fixed on the aching core that was pulsing with a rhythm all of its own. Serena was no longer in control. The dam broke and her body bucked and writhed while Quinn continued his relentless pleasuring, unpenetrating, until she tensed and arched and cried out. Then his large hand cupped her, holding her fast as the last shuddering spasms racked her exhausted body.

Serena clung to him, eyes closed and breathing ragged.

'There,' he murmured at last, gently straightening her skirts. 'Did that frighten you?'

'Yes.' She looked up at him in wonder. 'Yes, but in a good way. I never knew…'

He kissed her nose. 'I am aware of that. Now, would you like to finish your drink?'

Serena leaned against Quinn and sipped her brandy. He kept one arm about her, and the comfortable, companionable silence that enveloped them was as unexpected as her reactions to this evening. When she had followed Quinn to the drawing room she had expected a hasty coupling that would satisfy a need, rather than the raw, all-consuming delight she had experienced.

'I am confused,' she said slowly. 'It seems I have taken all the pleasure this evening and not given anything in return.'

'I wouldn't say that.' The smile he gave her sent the blood pounding around her body again.

She looked away, blushing. 'I w-would like to repay the favour, Quinn.'

'I shall insist upon it, one day, but not now. You need to rest.'

He stood up and drew her to her feet. She was not sure she could stand, but with his arm to support her they made their way without mishap up the stairs. At her bedroom door they stopped.

'Goodnight, Serena.'

She clung to him and forced herself to voice the question that was rattling around in her head.

'Do you n-not w-want me?'

Her eyes searched his face. With a sigh Quinn drew her into his arms and kissed her gently. 'More than you can ever know, Serena, but there are fears and memories to be expunged. We must take our time.' He reached behind her and opened the door. 'Now, off to bed with you.'

More than you can ever know.

Serena hugged the words to her as she allowed Polly to help her into her nightgown and when at last she snuggled beneath the covers, she sank into a deep, contented sleep.

Quinn was in no very good temper when he allowed Shere to help him into his dark blue evening coat. He had not seen Serena since last night, when she had come to him, wanted him to make love to her, but so very afraid. It had tested him to the limit, demonstrating to her the pleasure of man's touch while denying himself a similar release.

He wished now that business had not kept him out of the house all day, wished they were not engaged to go to the Beddingtons' this evening. Damnation, it would be the sort of evening he disliked most. Hot, crowded rooms where one could scarce make oneself heard, the women vying to outshine one another with the latest fashions, men looking for social or financial advancement and all of them eager to share the latest gossip and scandal.

Serena had told him Mrs Downing had called and offered her a place in their carriage, so he need not have gone to all this effort. It was another wet evening and the last thing he wanted was to drive a dozen miles to mix with people he barely knew. He stood pensively before the looking glass as his valet gave his shoulders a final brush. Why the devil had he allowed himself to be sucked into this?

The answer was in his head even before he had finished the question. Serena. She needed him, not only the protection of his name, but his support. It would not be for ever. Once she had regained her confidence he could leave her to attend such parties without him.

'Will that be all, my lord?'

'Yes. Thank you.' He turned away from his own scowling image and took the hat and gloves Shere was holding out to him. 'Don't wait up for me—it is likely to be late.'

He strode out of his bedchamber and ran down the

stairs, his mood as grim as the weather. Once Serena had recovered, what use would she have for the over-large, unsociable man she had married?

Serena was waiting for him in the drawing room and the iron fist about his heart tightened at the sight of her. She was wearing another of the new gowns, a glowing emerald shot silk. He was dazzled. Not by the diamonds that winked at her throat and ears, but by her smile, the luminosity of her eyes. He stopped in the doorway, staring at her.

She was more than beautiful—she was radiant. No man would be able to resist her. Would she still need him once she realised that?

'Will it do?' she asked, glancing nervously down at the shimmering skirts. 'The gown arrived less than an hour ago from Mrs Bell.'

He came forward and took her hand. 'I have never seen you looking better.'

'Thank you.' The anxious shadow left her eyes and she twinkled up at him. 'You must take some of the credit, Quinn. This colour was your choice.'

For the briefest instant he regretted his part in making her look so fine, until it hit him: even in sackcloth and ashes she would be irresistible. She was like a butterfly, emerging from its chrysalis. Once her wings were dry she would want to test them.

'So it was and a good choice, too.' He pressed a light kiss upon her fingers and felt them tremble. He might not be able to keep her, but she was his for a little longer yet. 'The carriage is at the door. Shall we go?'

Beddington Lodge blazed with light as the carriages drove one by one under the soaring, pedimented portico where the guests might alight, safe from the weather. Serena left Quinn in the marble hall while she went off to the retiring room. As she entered a group of ladies gathered there drew closer together, like a flock of colourful birds alarmed by the presence of an intruder.

Serena handed her cloak to the attendant and sat down to put on her dancing slippers, trying to ignore the murmurings of the other ladies.

'It's not that I blame her for marrying a fortune,' declared one, in a whisper that reached every corner of the room. 'But 'tis the manner of it. Quite shameless. Sir Timothy was heartbroken when she cast him aside. Not that I condone his behaviour in eloping, but still, he did it in good faith.'

'Just like her mother,' said another.

'At least her mama had the decency to wait until she was widowed,' tittered a third.

'Poor Lady Hambridge, no wonder she has retired to the coast. Too ashamed to show her face in town, I suppose. It must be such a blow, to have harboured a viper in one's bosom.'

'As I have always said, spare the rod and the child is spoiled.'

'And her poor husband! Besotted, I suppose…'

Serena straightened, an angry retort upon her lips, but the little group was already disappearing out of the door in a rustle of silk. She should have spoken out as soon as she heard Sir Timothy's name and denounced him for a scoundrel. Her shoulders sagged as she realised how unlikely the truth would sound. Tears started to her eyes and she hunted for her handkerchief.

'Serena, are you quite well?'

Elizabeth Downing was approaching with her mother and Lady Grindlesham. Serena made haste to wipe her eyes.

'We were just coming in as Mrs Pinhoe and her cronies left,' said Mrs Downing, sitting beside her. 'We heard something of what they were saying. Have they upset you?' She patted Serena's hands.

'Pay them no attention, my dear,' declared Lady Grindlesham, hovering around her. 'They are merely jealous because you have married well.'

'But Quinn,' Serena whispered, pulling her handkerchief between her fingers. 'I had not realised how this must look for him.'

'Now don't you worry your head over that,' returned Lady Grindlesham in hearty accents. 'Lord Quinn has never cared a jot what is said of him. Come along, my dear, you dry your eyes while Mrs Downing and I change our shoes, then we will all go out together and woe betide anyone I hear making disparaging remarks about you!'

Serena was grateful for their support and she endeavoured to put the incident out of her mind. Quinn was waiting to escort her into the ballroom and the warm admiration in his gaze did much to restore her confidence. They danced the first two dances together and when their host requested Serena's hand for the next set, she was pleased to see Quinn stand up with Lady Beddington.

As always, dancing helped Serena to relax. Frosty stares and sly comments were forgotten and by the time she met up with Mrs Downing and her daughter during a break in the music, she felt very much like her old self.

'I think your fears of the evening have been al-
layed now, Serena, is that not so?' said Mrs Downing, twinkling.

'Yes, thank you, ma'am. Your kindness and that of
Lady Grindlesham has done a great deal to help.'

'Nonsense, my dear, your own good manners and
quiet dignity have won over all but the most spiteful of
the tattlemongers, I assure you.'

They chatted for a few moments, before Serena excused herself and went off to find her husband. She
could not see him in the ballroom and thought he was
much more likely to be enjoying a quiet hand of piquet
in the card room. She had almost reached the big double
doors when someone stepped in front of her and flour-
ished an elaborate bow.

'Lady Quinn. Your most *obedient* servant, ma'am.'

Serena stopped, the blood turning to ice in her veins.

Chapter Twelve

Sir Timothy was less than arm's length away. He was smiling, but his eyes glittered with angry menace. Serena glanced quickly around, but there was no one in sight she could call friend. She must deal with this alone.

She fought down the dark terror churning inside and said with icy disdain, 'We have nothing to say to one another.'

'Ah, how that cuts me to the quick.' He clasped his hands over his heart. 'Oh, cruel, cruel Beauty.'

Anger and panic were rising in equal measure. The flow of guests in and out of the ballroom had all but ceased as people stopped to witness the interchange. Serena tried to step past Sir Timothy but he blocked her way again.

'Ah, fair tormentor,' he declared with a sigh. 'Can you deny you have shattered my life?'

'I do deny it,' she retorted. 'You tricked me—'

He spoke over her, his bright, malicious gaze flickering around the room. 'My heart is broken. Irrevocably. I sacrificed *everything* for you, madam.'

'You sacrificed nothing,' she hissed at him, aware

that the crowd around them was listening with obvious relish to every word.

'You call it nothing, when the lady of your dreams begs you to elope, to go against all the precepts of good breeding and risk the censure of society—'

He sighed and cast another anguished look around him. Serena heard someone mutter 'shameful'. She wanted to hurl herself at him and claw the spiteful gleam from his eyes, but she kept silent. She would not lower herself to bandy words with this villain.

'But I am not vindictive,' he continued, assuming an expression of deep melancholy. 'I will not blame you for passing me over in favour of another.'

Her lip curling, Serena pushed past him.

'I am pleased—aye, *delighted*—that you are now so comfortably established,' he called after her. 'You will always hold my heart, Lady Quinn. Now and for ever!'

Serena was shaking, but somehow she managed to leave the ballroom with her head up. As she crossed the marble hall, Quinn walked out of the card room. He frowned when he saw her.

'What is it?' he demanded. 'Who has distressed you?'

Serena used every ounce of willpower not to run to him.

'Sir T-Timothy.' She caught his arm, 'No, no, I pray you will not go in search of him. He...' She leaned against him. 'He is still pretending it was my idea to fly from town. Th-that he did it all for me...'

'The devil he is!'

'Everyone believes him,' she muttered, blinking away a rogue tear. 'I am lost. But what I regret, most bitterly, is that I have dragged you into ignominy, too.'

* * *

Quinn stifled his rage. He needed to think rationally. Much as he wanted to thrash Forsbrook to within an inch of his life, he knew that would only fuel the fires of speculation that were burning so brightly around his wife.

He said now, 'We have a choice, Serena. We can run away and leave the field clear for Forsbrook to spread whatever vicious slander he pleases. Or we can stand our ground. I am not ashamed of my wife. In fact, I am exceedingly proud of you and I want the world to know it. However, if you would prefer, I can order our carriage now and take you home.' He glanced down at her. 'Well, what do you say? Can you face returning to the ballroom?'

Quinn watched the colour ebb and flow from her cheeks. Her shoulders straightened and her head came up.

'I can do it, if you are beside me, my lord.'

Quinn led Serena back towards the ballroom and paused momentarily in the doorway, his eyes travelling around the room. There was no sign of Forsbrook, but it felt as if all the guests thronged beneath the blazing chandeliers had turned to look at them. He kept a faint, unconcerned smile on his face, ignoring the sly nudges and whispers. Serena's clutch on his sleeve revealed her anxiety, but she, too, was looking about her with apparent indifference. Damme, but he admired her courage!

The scrape of a fiddle was the signal for couples to take their places on the dance floor. A cheerful young gentleman with artfully disordered curls and shirt-points almost reaching his eyes came bounding up.

'Ah, Lady Quinn, I was afraid—that is, you may recall you did me the honour of agreeing to dance the next with me!'

'Then you will be disappointed,' replied Quinn. Belatedly he tried to soften his blunt words with a smile. 'I shall be dancing the quadrille with my wife.'

'Ah.' The young man fell back a little. 'Well, then. Perhaps the Scotch reel, Lady Quinn?'

'I'm afraid not,' replied Quinn, leading Serena on to the dance floor. 'My lady dances with no one but me.'

His announcement caused a ripple of surprise among those close enough to hear his words and a great many eyes watched them as they danced. Serena was a little pale, but her grace and composure never faltered. By the time the lengthy quadrille was over, she was glowing from the exercise and readily agreed to his suggestion that they should forgo the next dance and instead seek out a little refreshment.

The supper room was situated a little distance from the ballroom and as they approached the open doors it looked deserted.

'It shows the popularity of the Scotch reel that there is no one here,' remarked Serena as they went in. 'I—'

She broke off and Quinn felt her shrink closer. There was someone in the room, after all. Forsbrook. He cursed silently.

Sir Timothy was standing by one of the sideboards, pouring himself a generous glass of their host's brandy. He looked up, his florid countenance darkening when he saw them.

'Lord and Lady Quinn.' He raised his glass in a mock salute.

'I am sorry I was not present just now, when you spoke to my wife.' It took all Quinn's willpower to keep his voice level. 'Perhaps it was for the best. I might have been tempted to call you out.'

'For what?' Forsbrook sounded confident, but there was wariness in every line of his body. 'I was quite sincere.'

'We all know that is a lie.'

'Ah, but can you prove it?'

Forsbrook's purring response made Quinn want to cross the space between them and throttle the villain.

'I am afraid the evidence is on my side,' Sir Timothy continued smoothly. 'After all, it was not I who duped her friends, neither did I force the lady to go with me. Her reputation was ruined the moment she stepped into my chaise.'

'You know very well I thought we were going to Vauxhall!' Serena put in angrily.

'You see how she holds to her story?' Forsbrook shook his head, saying sadly, 'I fear she has you, too, under her spell, my lord.'

A chill ran through Serena. What if Quinn believed that plausible rogue? She felt rather than heard Quinn's angry growl.

'By God, Forsbrook, I shall take pleasure in exposing you for the villain you are.'

Sir Timothy retreated a step, but he said with a sneer, 'Really? And how will you do that, my lord, without making public just how you came upon Miss Russington that night at Hitchin? Will you admit that her reputation was so compromised you had no choice but to marry her? That she was soiled goods? Then everyone will know that you and I have shared her charms—'

With a roar Quinn launched himself at Sir Timothy. The brandy glass went flying as a single blow from Quinn's fist sent him crashing to the floor. The noise brought servants running into the room, but they stood, irresolute, while Quinn towered menacingly over the cowering figure on the floor.

'Quinn, no more, I pray you!' cried Serena, clinging to his arm.

She could feel the iron of his bunched muscles beneath the fine wool sleeve, hear the rasp of his heavy, angry breathing, but to her relief he stepped back. The servants helped Sir Timothy to his feet. His coat and breeches were stained with spilled wine and candlewax from the floor and he brushed at them angrily, throwing Quinn a look of pure hatred.

'That was very foolish of you, my lord. Attacking me can only increase the speculation.' He glanced down at himself. 'You have ruined my clothes, sir, but it is nothing to the dirt that will stick to your wife if you try to avenge her, Lord Quinn. Remember that.'

Serena held her breath, wondering if Quinn might yet shake her off and attack Sir Timothy. Instead he put his free hand over her fingers, where they still clutched his sleeve.

'Believe me, I will ruin more than your clothes if I find you anywhere near my wife again, or if I hear you have been maligning her. Come, my dear.'

Even as they walked away Serena heard Sir Timothy's mocking voice following them.

'Now why should I malign Lady Quinn, when everyone knows she will hold my heart for ever?'

* * *

Serena was shaking so much she was afraid her legs would not carry her. She did not object when Quinn suggested they should leave and was profoundly relieved when they were at last bowling north in their elegant carriage.

'I beg your pardon,' said Quinn. 'I should not have allowed the villain to accost you. I should have been with you.'

'You cannot be beside me every minute of the day,' she replied miserably. 'It is I who should be apologising to you, my lord. I have brought nothing but shame upon you.'

'Nonsense. This is but a little setback.'

He gathered her into his arms and she clung to him, burying her face in his coat. Gradually she began to relax, soothed by the gently swaying of the carriage and Quinn's large, calming presence.

'You must regret you ever met me,' she whispered.

'Not at all.' He drew off his gloves and tilted her chin up towards him. 'There are many…compensations.'

He kissed her, his mouth working over her lips gently but insistently until she forgot about the ball and Sir Timothy. Forgot everything but the pleasure of his touch. His tongue darted and teased, drawing up a fine thread of excitement from somewhere deep within and she returned his kisses, revelling in the taste of him.

Her body melted against him. His hands began to caress her and she felt the heavy longing tugging at her thighs. His hand found its way beneath her skirts and his fingers were assuaging the aching need. She was hot, excited, as pleasure welled up inside her. She explored him with her own hands, revelling in the contained, muscled strength of his body.

She ripped off her gloves, the better to feel him, yet running her fingers through his silky hair and over the rough stubble of his cheek was not enough, she wanted to feel his naked body pressed against hers. But it was too late, she was losing control and could do nothing but gasp as her body arched and strained, wave after wave of exquisite pleasure pulsing through her.

Afterwards Quinn pulled her on to his lap and cradled her in his arms. The carriage rattled on through the darkness and at length she gave a long, contented sigh.

'Serena?'

His voice was a rumble against her cheek and she smiled in the darkness, clinging to his coat.

'You held me thus when we first met. I feel so, so *safe* with you.'

'Good.' He dropped a kiss on her hair. 'I see moonlight glinting on water. We must be crossing the Thames. Time to make ourselves respectable, if we can.'

Serena giggled, but she tidied her clothes and tried to straighten Quinn's crumpled neckcloth.

'There,' she said, pulling on her gloves and sitting down beside him. 'That is the best I can do.'

'Thank heaven I told Shere to go to bed,' he muttered. He reached for her hand. 'Did I hurt you?'

'No.' She blushed in the darkness. 'I—I would have liked…more. I wanted you. All of you.' The blush deepened at the admission.

Quinn squeezed her fingers. 'That is not something for a cramped, rocking carriage. The first time I take you I want it to be in comfort, in a feather bed with silken sheets and glowing candlelight shining on your golden body.'

'You make it sound wonderful, Quinn.' She rested her head against his shoulder. 'But I have come to associate bad things—terrors—with the bedchamber.'

'I hope we can eradicate those memories, given time.'

'I hope so, too. But, Sir Timothy—' She broke off. 'Perhaps we should return to Melham. Just for a while.'

'I think not. To withdraw now would hand victory to Forsbrook. No, we shall stay, if you can bear it. I believe in time the world will know just who is telling the truth. Sir Timothy wishes to be seen as the jilted lover, but he is too much of a philanderer to maintain that pose for long.'

'Very well. If you think it best.'

'I do.' He raised her hand to his mouth and kissed it. 'Be brave, Serena. I will look after you. I give you my word.'

When they reached Berkeley Square Quinn escorted Serena directly up the stairs. Her body was still thrumming and she leaned heavily on his arm, unwilling to trust her legs to support her. She wondered if he would take her to his room. To his bed. Unbidden came the memory of a darkened room, heavy, carved bedposts and black, black shadows. It reared up so suddenly that she stumbled.

'You must be tired,' he said, holding her up. 'It has been a long day.'

She wanted to contradict him, but try as she might, the words would not come. At her door they stopped and Quinn looked down, his face shadowed, unreadable.

'Remember, I am only in the next room. You have only to walk through the door, if you want me.' He kissed her gently. 'Goodnight, Serena.'

He was gone. She wanted to run after him, but instead her legs carried her into the room. Polly was waiting for her and as the maid helped her out of her gown and into her nightshift, Serena recalled Quinn's parting words.

You have only to walk through the door, if you want me.

I do, she thought desperately. I do want you, Quinn!

Once Polly had left, Serena remained sitting before the mirror. Silence closed about her, thick and heavy. Finally, she pushed herself to her feet and walked across to the connecting door. She only had to open it, to go to Quinn. He would take care of her.

Her trembling fingers hovered over the handle, then with a sigh she rested her hand against the polished wood and bowed her head. She couldn't do it. Not yet.

Chapter Thirteen

A week of social engagements followed, with Quinn dutifully escorting his wife everywhere. Timothy was not in evidence, but his spiteful tongue had been busy and the altercation at Beddington Lodge was the subject of much gossip. No one gave Lord and Lady Quinn the cut direct, but several of their acquaintance were distinctly cool. Serena presented to the world a smiling face, but inwardly she raged and could not feel other than guilty at what Quinn was having to endure for her sake. When she tried to speak of it he brushed it aside, telling her not to worry, but the injustice gnawed away at her and cast over her days a cloud that rivalled the overcast skies.

A week after the Beddingtons' ball she was alone in the morning room, when Dunnock came in to announce a visitor.

He gave a slight cough. 'Mr Charles Russington, ma'am.'

'Russ!' Serena jumped up from her seat. 'My dear, dear brother, what brings you to town?'

'You,' he said promptly, holding out his arms.

Serena did not hesitate. With a sob she ran into them.

'And now I know I was right to come,' he continued, holding her close. 'I have never known you to be blue-devilled before.'

'Oh, Russ, I am so unhappy. I have made such a mull of everything.'

'So it would seem, if the reports that have reached Compton Parva are even half-correct. You had best tell me the whole.'

Quinn walked quickly along the streets, the rain dripping from his curly-brimmed beaver. Damn this weather, he thought sourly. He had spent the past hour with his lawyers, freeing up funds. The poor summer had resulted in a disastrous harvest and his tenants would not be able to pay their rents at Michaelmas.

He had discussed the matter with Serena and knew she agreed with him that payment should be waived for anyone in hardship. He had always kept his own counsel but over the past few months it had become his habit to share business matters with her. He had come to value her opinion and as he turned into Berkeley Square he found himself hoping that she was not entertaining visitors. That he might have her to himself.

The lack of carriages outside his house was encouraging. It was unlikely anyone would have walked here today to pay a morning call. A footman opened the door to him and he quickly divested himself of his outer garments as he demanded where he might find his wife.

'She is in the morning room, my lord.'

Quinn strode away through the hall. He expected to find his wife alone, and it was a surprise—nay, a damned shock!—to find Serena had company.

The gentleman sitting on the sofa beside Serena was everything Quinn was not. The fellow was lean and darkly handsome with black hair curling fashionably about his head. He was dressed impeccably in a morning coat of blue superfine and there was not a spot of mud on his gleaming Hessians or pantaloons. Quinn's mood darkened even further. That would suggest he had arrived some time ago, before the rain started. Which meant he had been alone with Serena for at least half an hour. Damn him.

Quinn stood in the doorway, taking in the scene. Serena was leaning against her visitor and looking forlorn, but when she heard the door open she jumped up, her face brightening.

'Quinn! Do let me present my brother Russ to you.'

He felt his hackles settling and moved further in to the room to greet Serena's half-brother.

'I came to offer my congratulations on your marriage,' Russ said to him. 'However, from what Serena has now told me, I think commiserations are more in order. The minx has dragged you into the devil of a fix.'

'Russ!'

'Well, you cannot deny it, Serena.'

Russington's plain speaking surprised a laugh from Quinn.

'It is not wholly Serena's fault,' he said. 'Forsbrook is a dashed scoundrel.'

'Yes, I am acquainted with the fellow,' replied Russ. 'A nasty piece of work and always has been—'

He broke off as the butler came in with a tray and there was a pause in the conversation while the butler withdrew and Quinn filled three glasses. He waved Russ back to his seat beside Serena.

'I take it my wife has apprised you of everything?' Quinn dropped into a chair opposite them. 'Including how we met?'

'It was necessary, if I was to make sense of it all,' said Russ. 'I pray you will not be angry with her.'

'On the contrary, I am glad of it. I have never liked prevarication.'

'Good.' Russ grinned. 'I always suspected the explanation Henry sent me at the time of your marriage was not the whole truth, but at that point I was not in any position to post south and find out for myself.'

'Ah, yes.' Quinn nodded. 'I trust your wife and the baby are now going on well?'

'They are, I thank you. I was telling Serena that Molly has invited you both to come and stay. Immediately if you wish.'

'While the gossip dies down, you mean?' Quinn finished his wine and got up to recharge the glasses. 'If it becomes unbearable we may well do that, but my instinct is to ride it out.'

'That is just what I said,' Serena put in, showing more fire than Quinn had seen before. 'I do not see why we should run away because of Sir Timothy, the little toad. But we will come north soon, Russ. I am longing to see baby Emma, and little Charles, of course. Why, he must be three years old by now.'

Quinn was happy to let the conversation move on, and when Serena asked Russ to stay for dinner he quickly added his voice to the invitation. He said very little during the meal, taking pleasure in the way Serena chattered happily to her half-brother. At one point she threw her head back and laughed, a full-throated, delightful sound that caught at his chest. This was Serena as she was meant to be. As he wanted her to be, not anxiously worrying over what the world might say.

At length Serena rose from her chair, saying she would leave the gentlemen to their brandy.

'But not too long,' she warned him. 'I expect to see you both in the drawing room well before the tea tray is brought in.'

'You have my word on it,' replied Quinn, his mouth twisting into a grin. 'Now, off you go, baggage!'

The twinkle in her eyes told him she was not at all offended by this style of address and his grin widened as he watched her glide out of the room.

'You appear to be very fond of my half-sister.'

'I am.' Quinn turned back to his guest. 'Your visit has made her the happiest she has been since our return to town.'

'The gossip is that bad, then?'

'Aye.' Quinn scowled as he poured brandy for himself and his guest. 'Some of the town tabbies have very long memories.'

'Ah,' said Russ. 'They have raked up stories about Eleanor, I suppose. Serena's mother.'

'Yes. I must have heard something of it at the time,' said Quinn, 'but around that time I had my own troubles. Was she as bad as they say?'

'Oh, yes.' Russington stared moodily into his glass. 'Eleanor married my father for his fortune. She was very charming to Henry and me until the knot was safely tied, then she ignored us, and once Serena was born she was left in the care of nurses and governesses. Eleanor craved company. When Father died, she lost no time in finding herself another rich husband.' His mouth twisted. 'Conte Ragussina, a handsome Italian with deep pockets and a nature as restless as her own. She ran off within months of my father's death, and was married before the year was out.'

'And Serena?' Quinn prompted him.

'Left to learn of her mother's defection from her governess. She was not quite nine years old.'

'Poor Serena.'

'Poor Serena indeed,' muttered Russ, taking a long pull at the brandy. 'She should have gone to live with Hambridge, but Dorothea wouldn't have her. Serena was sent to a succession of establishments, seminaries, academies for young ladies—not that she ever settled at any of them. My own dear Molly has proved as good a friend and guide as anyone. I regret now that we did not take her north with us when we married, but Henry insisted she must have her come-out. And what a mull he and Dorothea have made of it.' He looked up suddenly. 'Your marriage to my sister seems to be the best thing that has happened to her. And it was none of Henry's doing, I'll wager.'

'Not at all,' replied Quinn, unruffled.

Russ frowned. 'They should be here, supporting Serena, not hiding at Worthing.'

Quinn refilled his glass and pushed the decanter across the table. 'It doesn't help that Forsbrook is enacting the broken-hearted suitor. If I call him out the gossip will only intensify, yet while he is in town Serena cannot be at ease. I am tempted to have him abducted and pressed into service on one of his Majesty's frigates.'

Russ sat back in his chair. 'Oh, I don't think you need do that,' he drawled. 'I have a plan, which I hope will do the trick as far as Sir Timothy Forsbrook is concerned.'

* * *

Serena looked towards the door as she heard voices in the hall and moments later the gentlemen came in. The room seemed to shrink upon their entry, for they were both big men. Her half-brother was tall, but Quinn was a few inches taller, his broad shoulders and muscular body making even Russ's athletic frame look slender. Quinn was not conventionally handsome, with his craggy features, his crooked smile and not quite straight nose, but over the past few months she had come to regard him as the most attractive man of her acquaintance. She was shaken to realise how much he now meant to her.

Quinn was smiling at something Russ had said and Serena was pleased the two men were getting on so well.

'There is great sport to be had in Yorkshire,' remarked Russ. 'As you will see when you visit.'

'And we shall, as soon as our business in town is finished,' said Quinn. 'I cannot think it will take too much longer now.'

A glance passed between the two gentlemen, but Serena was distracted by the arrival of the tea tray and thought no more about it.

It was midnight before Russ rose to take his leave.

'Will we see you tomorrow?' asked Serena, walking with him to the door. 'Perhaps I might take you for a drive in the park. Quinn has bought me a new phaeton and the prettiest pair of match bays to pull it. I venture to think you would not be ashamed to be seen with me.'

'I should never be ashamed to be seen with you,' he told her, smiling. 'Unfortunately, I have another engagement tomorrow and must then return to the north. This was only ever going to be a fleeting visit.' He kissed her cheek. 'Bring this showy equipage with you when you come north and you can drive Molly in style around Compton Parva!'

With that he was gone.

'I was very pleased to see Russ,' said Serena, when Quinn escorted her upstairs to her bedchamber soon after. 'I was glad, too, that you liked him.'

'He is very different from his brother.'

'He is indeed. Russ has always been my favourite. That is why I thought—' She broke off, flushing.

'Why you thought a rake would make a good husband?' Quinn finished for her. Serena bowed her head, too mortified to respond and Quinn laughed softly. 'Goodnight, Serena.'

She watched him walk away, heard his firm tread going back down the stairs and misery cut through her like a knife. They had been getting on so well and she had ruined everything.

Serena entered the bedchamber, closing the door with a snap that made Polly jump out of her chair.

'Good evening, ma'am. I have your nightshift all ready for you.'

Serena looked at the garment laid out on the bed. It was made of the finest linen and decorated with mother-of-pearl buttons and exquisite Brussels lace. It had been vastly expensive, Dorothea insisting that a man of Lord Quinn's wealth would expect to his wife to wear only the best.

Serena thought of the painting of *Venus with a Mirror* that was now hanging in the library at Melham, the Titian she had seen that first morning. Quinn might find the naked form much more alluring than being covered neck to toe. Her mouth dried at the thought, but a sudden excitement fizzed through her blood like champagne. There was only one way to find out.

Somewhere in the house a clock chimed the hour. Serena paced her room and pulled the wrap closer, not so much from cold as nerves. The excitement and determination she had felt earlier had evaporated and if Quinn did not go to bed soon then she would not have the nerve to go through with this. Then she heard it. The firm tread along the passage, the rumble of voices from the next room that told her Quinn was in there with his valet.

She retreated to the bed and sat down on the edge, pleating the skirts of the raspberry silk between her fingers. When she heard the soft pad of Shere's feet in the passage she moved again towards the connecting door and pressed her ear against the panel. Silence. Perhaps Quinn had drunk too much brandy and was already asleep. She moved to the long mirror to rearrange the thin robe. The red silk, almost black in the candlelight, was wrapped snugly around her and tied with a single ribbon under the breast. Apart from her hair, which she had brushed out and left to fall loose down her back, she looked perfectly respectable. Until she moved, when the front edges of the robe fell away to reveal the nakedness beneath.

'If he is indifferent to me now,' she whispered, 'then I shall never try again.'

Straightening her shoulders, Serena crossed to the connecting door. It opened silently and she saw that Quinn was in bed, propped up against the bank of snowy pillows, reading. The shadows from the single candle enhanced the rippling contours of his bare chest and shoulders.

He did not notice her at first. She took another, tentative step into the room and he looked up. Serena was watching him closely, his face registered surprise, but not displeasure. He threw back the covers and slipped to the floor. In one fluid movement he pulled the banyan from the end of the bed and shrugged himself into it, but not before Serena glimpsed his athletic form, wide shoulders and deep chest, narrow hips and strongly muscled thighs. There was a shield of dark hair on his chest. It arrowed downwards over the tight, flat stomach. She recalled the sketches and paintings Henry had shown her of statues he had seen on his grand tour.

A Greek god, she thought wildly. He is built like a Greek god!

It was not the smooth, boyishness of Michelangelo's *David*, but a much more adult, muscled figure. A warrior. A champion.

'Did you want me?' There was a hint of amusement in his deep voice.

Serena forced her eyes back to his face. Nervously she ran her tongue over her lips.

Oh, yes, I want you!

Her cheeks burned.

'I—' She swallowed, trying to force the words from a throat that felt too tight.

Smiling, he leaned back against the edge of the bed and held out his hands. 'Come here.'

Slowly she moved towards him, trying not to think of the way her own robe parted as she walked, displaying a leg from toe to thigh. He was her husband. Who else should see her thus? She *wanted* him to see her. Besides, he had seen her naked before, when he had helped her from the bath. Her step faltered as the black terror of those memories resurfaced.

'I c-can't—'

Quinn reached out and took her hands. She clung to him, as if she was drowning, and he pulled her close.

'Come and sit with me.'

He guided her to a large chest with a padded top that was placed at the end of the bed. Very little light from the single candle reached this far, but even so her hands clutched at the edges of the robe, pulling them together as she sat down beside him. He made no attempt to stop her, merely keeping one arm about her. His forbearance was too much. She gave a little sob and buried her face in his shoulder.

'I thought I could do this,' she mumbled as her tears soaked his silk banyan. 'I beg your pardon, Quinn. I have failed you.'

'No, no.' He cradled her cheek and gently turned her face up towards his. He said softly, 'Now, what is it that frightens you?' She glanced past him. 'Ah, of course. The bed.'

She nodded and hid her face in his shoulder again. 'The shadows. He held me down. At the inn. He threw me down and t-tried to…' She shivered and his arm tightened around her, holding her firm, giving her courage. Her fingers clutched at his dressing gown. 'I want to please you, Quinn. I w-want to be your wife in more than name.'

'And so you shall be, Serena, in time. We need not rush this.'

She relaxed against him, sighing.

'Will you…?' She took a breath and looked up at him. 'Would you kiss me, please?'

Even in the shadows she saw his eyes gleam. 'It would be a pleasure.'

He pulled her to him, one hand about her neck as he lowered his head and captured her lips. He kissed her slowly at first, gently, until she began to respond. He teased her lips apart, his tongue exploring her mouth. She yielded, her body softening, melting against him as his hand caressed her neck, easing away her tension.

His mouth moved, light as a feather, along her jaw. She put back her head, closing her eyes as he continued those delicate, tantalising kisses along her neck. He tugged at the ribbon tie of her wrap and she felt the satin sliding away. Her body tensed when he stroked her breast but she did not flinch away, rather she pushed herself against him. His thumb began to circle the tip, oh, so slowly, then his mouth closed over its fellow and Serena gave a little cry. Heat shafted through her blood from her breasts to somewhere deep between her thighs, into an aching pool of desire.

He stilled and she clutched at him, begging him to go on. With a soft laugh he teased one hard nub with his thumb and forefinger while his teeth caught the other. Serena's body pulsed and shuddered beneath the onslaught. She had slipped to the edge of the seat, her body instinctively arching towards Quinn. When she opened her eyes, she was staring up at the shadowed canopy of the bed, but the darkness no longer frightened her. There was no hint of panic. Instead she felt more alive than ever, the blood singing through her body.

It was a revelation, so absorbing that she barely noticed Quinn had moved. He was holding her firm, one arm about her waist, and his free hand gathered both her breasts while his mouth roved lower, down across her ribs and on to the soft skin of her belly. He eased her legs apart and, glancing down, she saw that he had shed his banyan and was naked, on his knees before her.

'Quinn!'

At her whispered cry he looked up. 'Do you want me to stop?'

'Yes. No. I do not know.'

His eyes glinted wickedly in the candlelight. 'Then I shall go on.'

His hands slid down to her hips and he lowered his head, his mouth moving from one side to the other, then back to nestle in the curls at the hinge of her thighs. Her body froze with shock, but only for a moment. Then she was opening for him, shifting restlessly as his tongue flickered and teased. Another cry escaped her, but lest Quinn should think she did not like what he was doing to her she pushed her fingers through his hair, clutching at the thick, silky locks.

He gave a soft laugh. 'Do you like that, Serena?'

'Yes, yes,' she panted, offering herself up to him again. 'Oh, don't stop now.'

He obliged her with his mouth and tongue while the rippling excitement built inside her. She arched back against the bed, her hands thrown out on either side and gripping the covers as he continued the exquisite torture, holding her firm as she writhed against him. The ripples became a flood that carried her higher until she did not know if she was flying or drowning. She cried out, her body bucking and shuddering as wave after joyous wave swept through her.

At last the tide receded, leaving her sated and barely

conscious. All she could hear was her own gasping sobs. Quinn gently removed her silk wrap, then he gathered her up and carried her around to place her in his bed. He climbed in beside her, snuffed the guttering candle and pulled the covers over them both. With a sigh she reached for him and he took her in his arms.

'No more terrors?' he murmured, his mouth against her hair.

'No,' she whispered, one hand pressed against his chest, her fingers threading through the crisp, dark curls.

'Good,' he pulled her closer, 'because there is more.'

'More?' She managed a shaky laugh. 'Oh, Quinn, I do not think I could…'

He stopped her words with a kiss.

'Not yet then,' he murmured, pulling her into his arms. 'Sleep now.'

Serena stirred. Something was different. She opened her eyes and the grey light of dawn creeping in through the unshuttered window showed her that this was not her bedroom. This was Quinn's room. Quinn's bed. There was nothing to fear.

But, glancing up at the canopy, all she could see was an inky blackness. Icy fingers ran down her spine, fear gripped her. She could hear Quinn's deep, regular breathing beside her. She wanted to cling to him and let him comfort her, but black terror was enveloping her and she could not breathe. She could feel again cruel hands around her throat, choking off her life.

Trembling, she slipped silently from the bed. Without waiting to find her dressing wrap she fled back to her own room.

Chapter Fourteen

Serena sat up beside Quinn in the phaeton, doing her best to keep her distance, but it was difficult not to bump against him as he swung the carriage around the corners and negotiated the traffic.

'I am glad you accepted my invitation,' he remarked as he guided the bays into the park. 'We need to talk. About last night.'

'Yes.' She clutched her hands tightly in her lap.

'I thought it would be better done in private, and it gives me an excuse to drive your bays and be seen in this vastly fashionable equipage!'

Serena knew his attempt at levity was to set her at her ease, but it only made her feel more wretched. She had failed him. Again.

'It was very kind of you to buy it for me. Very generous.'

He said, 'You were gone when I awoke this morning. I want to know what I did to make you run away in the night. Did my passion frighten you?'

'No! It—it was not you, Quinn. You were all kindness.' He gave an exasperated hiss and she hurried on. 'I... I enjoyed your attentions. More than I can say. I

have never known anything quite as wonderful.' She
was thankful for the veil covering her cheeks, hiding
her blushes. 'I thought the bad memories had been exor-
cised, but when I woke, it was so very dark. All I could
see was shadows. And I panicked.'

She bowed her head, remembering how cold her own
bed had been. How empty. She had curled up beneath
the covers, shivering and feeling thoroughly wretched.

'I thought as much.' He tipped his hat towards the
occupants of a smart barouche coming the other way,
but did not stop. 'That is why I sent a note up with your
breakfast, rather than coming in person. Your room is
your sanctuary, Serena. I will not enter uninvited.' He
reached out and briefly put his huge, gloved hand over
hers. 'As long as it was not my...*attentions* that distressed you.'

Serena felt another swell of gratitude for his understanding. She tucked her hand in his arm and leaned
against him.

'No, Quinn, you have never done anything to distress me. I just wish I could be a...a proper wife to
you.'

'We have all our lives to work on that.' He flashed
a smile at her. 'But for now, we shall continue as we
are. I am yours to command, madam. But you must
trust me, Serena. I will never ask more of you than you
wish to give.'

She squeezed his arm and rubbed her cheek against
his sleeve. 'You are a good man, Rufus Quinn.'

'Nonsense.' His gruff response was followed by a
growl of annoyance. 'By heaven, let us get out of here.
Damned crowds and it is not even the fashionable hour.
The devil only knows how you stand it!'

* * *

The worsening weather brought more families back to town. Hostesses began to find their reception rooms filling up again and Quinn persuaded Serena that they should hold a party of their own.

'It need only be a small affair,' he told her. 'You may invite whomsoever you wish. Although we should include your brother Henry and sister-in-law.'

'Yes, I suppose we must.' A shadow of uncertainty flickered over her face. 'Dorothea has written to tell me they are returning to town at the end of the week.'

'You are not looking forward to that?'

'Dorothea disapproves of any sort of scandal.' Her hand fluttered. 'She disapproves of *me.*'

'If she had taken better care of you in the first place, there would be no scandal.' Quinn finished his coffee and rose from the table. Serena was still looking pensive and he stopped behind her and dropped a hand on her shoulder. 'You are Lady Quinn now, Serena. If your sister-in-law annoys you, tell her to go to the devil.'

That made her laugh. 'Yes, that is what you would do, Quinn, is it not? One would expect nothing less of the rudest man in London!'

She looked up at him, her dark eyes alight with merriment, and he caught his breath. He wanted to bend and capture those smiling lips, to kiss her senseless, then carry her off to bed and make love to her for the rest of the day. Even as his body reacted at the thought he saw the laughter die from Serena's face. And she shrank away from him, blushing violently.

'G-goodness, is that the time? I promised Cook I would discuss tonight's dinner with her, so I had best hurry and finish my breakfast...'

She began to cut the toast on her plate into tiny squares. Quinn stepped away. She had shown him more clearly than any words that his passion frightened her. Oh, she had denied it when he had asked her outright, but if that was the case why did she shy away from him? Every day he looked for some sign that she desired him. Every night he strained to hear the sound of the connecting door opening, but it remained firmly, obstinately shut. He had promised he would not rush her and he would hold to that, even though it was becoming more and more unbearable.

'I have correspondence that requires an answer,' he muttered, turning to the door. 'If you will excuse me.'

Serena kept her eyes on her plate, listening to Quinn's footsteps as he went out and closed the door behind him. How had she ever kept her seat, when she wanted so desperately to throw herself into his arms? The impulse had been strong and so sudden that it frightened her. Even now she was trembling so much she could hardly wield her knife.

And the worst part of it all was Quinn's disappointment. He wanted her, she read that quite clearly in his eyes. She was his wife and he had every right to expect to take his pleasure, but he was too much of a gentleman. It must be her wish to go to his bed and she *did* wish it, although for some reason she could never put it into words or actions. Every evening when she retired to her room she looked at the closed door between them, wanting desperately to walk through to him, but fear held her back.

Fear of the dark shadows that reminded her of Sir Timothy choking the life from her, fear of the terrifying panic that welled up, that made her want to scream and rip and tear at Quinn, to reject him and run away rather than allowing him to love her. And something else, too. The fear of irrevocably committing herself to this marriage. To committing to Quinn. Until it was truly consummated he might still walk away, find a wife who was worthy of him.

Serena pushed her plate away, her appetite quite gone. She had panicked again, blushed like a schoolgirl and shrunk away from Quinn. She closed her eyes. If only she had shown him by a word, a look, how much she wanted him then he might even now be covering her with kisses and making her body sing.

'I beg your pardon, Lady Quinn.' She looked up to find Dunnock hovering in the doorway. 'Cook was asking if you were ready to see her, because she was hoping to go to the market later.'

'Yes, yes of course.' Serena rose, pushing her own concerns away. 'I will go to her now.'

By the time Serena finished discussing menus with Cook, Quinn had gone out. He left word that he was dining out but would return in time to escort her to the theatre. She was disappointed, for the desire she had felt earlier was still there, a nagging whisper deep down. Heavens, she thought, a wry smile tugging at her mouth, how unfashionable, to yearn for a husband's company!

When she saw the clothes laid out on the bed, her new coral-coloured silk gown and the velvet opera cloak, Serena felt a *frisson* of excitement, as if this was her very first ball. Perhaps tonight would be different. She and Quinn both enjoyed the theatre and she was hopeful that afterwards…anticipation made her stomach swoop. Hope. She was *hopeful*. How long had it been since she had felt like this?

Serena stared into the looking glass as Polly dressed her hair and found herself smiling. It was as if she was waking from a bad dream, rediscovering the zest for life that had once been natural to her. And she had Quinn to thank for it. The curl of desire was still there, working its way around her body.

'There, my lady.' Polly stood back to admire her handiwork. 'You look as fine as fivepence, if you don't mind me saying.'

'Not at all.' Serena laughed.

She turned her head this way and that, regarding her reflection in the mirror. Her thick tresses were gathered up into a neat topknot with a few guinea-gold curls framing her face.

'Indeed,' said a deep voice behind her. 'As fine as fivepence!'

'Quinn!'

Her smile grew wider as she turned to see him standing in the doorway. He had changed into his evening attire of blue frock coat and white satin waistcoat, his muscular legs straining against the tight-fitting breeches and silk stockings. As he walked towards her a diamond sparkled from the folds of his snow-white cravat. That and the heavy gold signet ring, were his only ornaments, but Serena thought this only enhanced the magnificence of his physique.

'I had no idea it was so late.' Her hand went to the ties of her wrap. 'I have yet to put on my gown—'

'We have plenty of time yet.'

Serena glanced at her maid. 'Leave us, Polly, if you please. I will ring when I need you.'

When they were alone, Quinn came closer and held out a velvet box. 'I thought you might like this.'

Intrigued, she took the box and opened it.

'Oh.' She gazed down at a full set of coral and gold jewellery. 'It is a perfect match for my robe. How clever of you.'

'I saw this parure in Rundell's today and since I knew you intended to wear your new gown...'

She put the box down on the dressing table and lifted out the comb. Carefully she nestled it against the top-knot, the coral enhancing the deep gold of her hair. The ear drops followed, but when she reached for the necklace, three strings of fine coral beads, Quinn stopped her.

'Let me.' She kept very still as he placed the necklace about her neck. His fingers brushed her nape as he fastened the catch and her mouth dried. 'There. I hope you are not offended that I did not buy you more diamonds? I could have done so, I know that some women would settle for nothing less, but I thought that you—'

She lifted one hand to the necklace—the coral was warm against her fingers.

'No,' she said softly, meeting his eyes in the mirror. 'I have the diamonds you gave me as a wedding gift—I do not need more. This parure will set off the gown perfectly. Thank you.'

His hands moved to her shoulders and this time she did not shy away. Instead she turned her head and dropped a kiss on to the back of his fingers. His grip tightened and she felt his lips on her neck.

'Mayhap we should forgo the theatre this evening,' he murmured, his breath warm on her ear.

'Perhaps we should,' she whispered, amazed at her own daring.

He met her eyes in the mirror. 'Surely it would be a pity to waste all this effort. I know how much you wanted to see Macready playing Othello.'

'I think…' Serena swallowed. 'I think I would prefer to go to bed with you than see Mr Macready.'

Laughing, he pulled her up into his arms and kissed her, a long, unhurried kiss that turned her bones to water.

'Very well then. If you are sure.'

The blaze in his eyes set her heart racing even faster. She touched his cheek. 'I am sure, Quinn.'

He dragged her close for another searing kiss that left her dizzy. How could she have ever thought herself safe with this man?

'Well, madam, should it be your bed, or will you risk the shadows of mine?'

Held close against Quinn's chest she felt light-hearted and reckless.

'I think it must be yours, sir. Let us not waste time moving everything from mine.'

He threw back his head and gave a shout of laughter. 'You are quite wanton, Lady Quinn, and I love you for it.'

Her senses reeled. She felt quite faint. Love. Had he really said that?

He had his arm about her and was leading her through the connecting door. Pressed close against him, she could feel the barely contained power of the man. It was, she thought, like being too close to a powder keg.

Serena's cheeks burned when she saw the valet was in the room and she looked down, shrinking closer to Quinn.

He said coolly, 'You may go, Shere. I shall not need you again tonight. And you may tell Lady Quinn's maid she need not wait up.'

She heard the door close softly behind the valet, then Quinn was pulling her round into his arms. Slowly, with infinite care and myriad kisses, he unlaced her stays and removed every scrap of clothing until she was standing before him, naked save for the coral jewellery. Slowly he removed the comb and pins from her hair, watching as the heavy silken curtain fell about her shoulders.

'My Venus,' he murmured, gazing at her in a way that sent a delicious shiver running through her body.

He dropped his head to kiss her breasts, but Serena felt at a disadvantage. She scrabbled at the buttons of Quinn's coat and soon his clothes joined hers in an untidy pile on the floor. At last only the snowy shirt was between Serena and Quinn's glorious body. She plucked at it impatiently, feasting her eyes on him as he drew it off over his head. He pulled her close, skin to skin, then scooped her up into his arms.

'There is always the daybed,' he murmured, nodding towards the couch in one corner of the room. 'If you would feel safer there. It is your choice, Serena.'

A vague image of the inn flickered through her head, but she blinked and it was gone, it had lost its terror because this was not Hitchin. This was Quinn's room and when she looked towards his bed now all she remembered was the pleasure of his caresses. She slid an arm about his neck, smiling up at him.

'The bed, if you please.'

Holding her eyes with his own, he laid her gently down on the covers. She reached for him and he measured his length beside her, bringing his mouth to hers for a long, languorous kiss that drew out her very soul. Her hands roamed over him, marvelling at the silky skin over iron-hard muscle, and when he began a series of tantalising kisses down her neck she drove her fingers through his hair, clutching his head as his tongue worked its magic on her breasts.

They swelled, tightening beneath the teasing attention of his mouth, but this time she was not prepared to lie passive while he pleasured her. She began her own exploration, using her hands and her mouth, revelling in the salty spiciness of his skin as she worked her way across his chest and downwards, exploring, teasing, learning what excited him and how to make him groan with pleasure beneath her touch. He reached for her, drawing her close, sliding his fingers over her skin and down to the aching heat between her thighs. Urgent desire spiralled through her and she moved restlessly against his hand.

'Go on,' she pleaded. 'Go on, Quinn. Finish this!'

He rolled her on to her back and covered her. His fingers slid away and she felt him enter her. She bit her lip, anticipating pain, but there was none. Quinn was moving gently, slowly and Serena lifted her hips to push him deeper. She moved with him, matching his rhythm, her fingers digging into his shoulders as the now-familiar excitement took over. With each thrust he was carrying her higher. She was flying, soaring, and as she reached her pinnacle he tensed and held her there. They shared a brief, wondrous moment of ecstasy when his shout of triumph mingled with her own cries before she fell into joyous, heady oblivion and beyond. She subsided at last, trembling against him, and Quinn held her, a gentle giant, keeping her safe, cocooned against the world.

* * *

Serena stretched luxuriously and opened her eyes. It was not yet dawn. Quinn's naked body was wrapped around hers, his regular breathing soft against her neck. She felt a rush of emotion, a mix of happiness and affection so strong that tears filled her eyes. Wonderingly, she reached out and touched his cheek. It was rough with morning stubble.

'I love you,' she murmured.

He did not stir. She kissed his lips and his arms tightened around her. Smiling, she snuggled closer and sank back into a deep, dreamless sleep.

When Serena woke again, the sunlight shining into the room told her it was morning. A delicious thrill ran down her spine when she remembered how they had spent the night and she turned towards the large, warm body beside her. Quinn. Her husband. A smile tugged at her mouth as she watched him sleeping. His eyelids fluttered, the dark lashes lifted and his hazel eyes stared at her. He raised himself on to one elbow.

'Can you not sleep? Is anything wrong?'

'I was merely thinking how good you have been to me.'

One eyebrow went up. 'And that prevents you sleeping?'

'No,' she said, smiling. 'That is because I am not accustomed to sharing a bed with a man.'

'Ah, I see. And you find it an unpleasant experience?'

'On the contrary.' She felt a blush spreading through her, even to her toes as she added daringly, 'I should like to do it a great deal more.'

'Then you shall,' he muttered, pulling her against his hard, aroused body. 'As long as it is only with me!'

* * *

The following week passed in a happy daze for Serena. It was mid-October, but the sun seemed brighter, the days warmer than they had been all summer, and she found herself singing as she went about the house. Something had shifted inside her. There was no longer a black cloud of despair weighing heavily on her spirits and she began to take pleasure in living. She knew it was due in no small part to her husband.

Just the thought of Quinn made her smile, but it was not only the nights spent in his bed. She delighted in his company and could only regret that the more she was accepted into London society, the less she saw of Quinn. At first she had barely noticed the change in attitude towards her, but her own notoriety had been eclipsed by fresh gossip about Sir Timothy, as Miss Downing lost no time in explaining when Serena took her up in her phaeton for a drive in the park.

'He is pursuing the widow of a wealthy mill owner,' Elizabeth told her, with obvious relish. 'It is the talk of the town. They were at Covent Garden Theatre last week, for Mr Macready's *Othello*. Perhaps you saw them?'

'We did not go, after all,' said Serena, a rosy blush stealing through her as she thought of what she and Quinn had done instead.

'Well, I have seen her,' declared Elizabeth. 'She is a handsome creature with quantities of black curls and a passion for jewellery. One cannot help but notice her, for she is very loud and…and *flashy*. She is from the north, you see,' she went on, as if this explained everything. 'You will not find them at any respectable society parties. But he takes her to the Subscription Balls, where positively *anyone* can buy a ticket.'

'But who is the woman?' Serena was unable to resist asking. 'Is she so very unsuitable?'

'Oh, yes. Her name is Mrs Hopwood and she positively *reeks* of trade and bad breeding,' said Elizabeth cheerfully. 'Mama and I saw her shopping with Sir Timothy in New Bond Street and one could not help but overhear their conversation. Her voice is quite coarse, you know, her style of dress designed to attract attention and she was *dripping* with ornament! She looked like a jeweller's trade card! Sir Timothy was fawning all over her.' She shuddered. 'It was truly grotesque.'

Serena knew her friend was enjoying relating the story to her, but she could not share her amusement.

'Poor Mrs Hopwood. Someone should warn her about Sir Timothy.'

'What, when they are providing the *ton* with such amusement?' Elizabeth laughed. 'I am sure the widow can look out for herself and as Mama says, Sir Timothy's determined pursuit is turning opinion in your favour. No one believes he was ever in love with you now, Serena. No,' Elizabeth concluded, 'this little development can only be to your advantage.'

Serena knew it was true, but her new-found happiness brought with it a wish that others should be happy, too, and when she sat down to dinner with Quinn that evening, she could not help but mention her concerns.

'I do not like to think of any woman being duped, as I was, by Sir Timothy,' she told him, when the covers had been removed and the servants had withdrawn. They were in the habit of sitting together at one end of the table when dining alone and she cast an anxious glance up at Quinn, who turned his head to smile at her.

'Your kind heart does you credit, my dear, but I doubt there is anything to fear. If the widow is as wealthy as people say, then she will have an army of lawyers to advise her.' He grinned. 'Sir Timothy is certainly burning his boats in setting his cap at the woman. I saw him at Tattersall's today, buying a showy pair of greys on her behalf. It would appear this Mrs Hopwood means to drive herself about town in a phaeton and a high-perch one at that.' He glanced at her. 'Perhaps you are afraid she will cast you into the shade.'

She laughed. 'She may do so, with my blessing!'

He reached out and briefly covered her hand with his own.

'She won't do it,' he told her. 'You are a nonpareil. I have never seen a woman handle the reins better than you. And you may believe it. You know I will never lie to you.'

'Th-thank you.' She blushed, inordinately pleased by his praise. 'Nevertheless, I cannot be easy about this. Sir Timothy is a scoundrel and I do not like to think of him preying on anyone.'

Quinn growled. 'You know that nothing would give me greater pleasure than to call the fellow out and put a bullet through him,' he said, 'but that would reflect badly upon you, which is something I want to avoid at all costs.' His hand tightened over hers. 'Try not to be anxious about Mrs Hopwood, Serena. She will not come to any harm.'

With that she had to be satisfied, but it seemed that Serena could not avoid hearing about Sir Timothy and his new flirt. Her own escapades appeared forgotten, which pleased her, but it meant that Quinn no longer felt obliged to escort her everywhere. Serena missed his company at the balls and parties, but she tried not to complain, knowing that he did not enjoy such gatherings.

However, he would have to attend their own party.

Knowing Quinn would not enjoy a ball, Serena had decided upon a musical evening, where they could invite some of the young musicians with whom Quinn was acquainted to perform. But even here Serena could not avoid the latest gossip concerning Sir Timothy. During a performance by a promising young harpist, Lady Grindlesham dropped down on the sofa beside her, declaring, 'It must be a match. He is for ever in her company.'

'Yes, I have seen them driving out in the park,' murmured Serena.

'They are *everywhere*,' exclaimed Lady Grindlesham. 'Of course, she may not have entrée into the best houses, but they are together in every public place.' She leaned closer. 'They attend a great many private card parties and it seems the widow's luck is much greater than that of her escort! I understand he is so much in debt that only a rich wife can save him now. Yet he continues to live high. The word in town is that it can only be a matter of time before they are married.' She gave a little tut of displeasure. 'I hope she does not think that will make her any more acceptable in polite circles. Sir Timothy's standing is quite diminished, you know, which I am sure must be a great relief to you, my dear. Any man who could so shamelessly pay court to such a vulgar creature, however large her fortune, *cannot* be a true gentleman!'

Lady Grindlesham patted Serena's hand and moved

away as the company politely applauded the harpist's performance. Nothing more was said of the matter, but Serena relayed to Quinn all she had heard once the guests had departed.

They were alone together in the drawing room, where Quinn had persuaded her to sit down on the sofa and enjoy a glass of wine with him.

'Naturally, I am relieved that people now believe me rather than Sir Timothy,' she said unhappily, 'but it has nothing to do with truth and everything to do with the fact that the widow is not considered worthy of their notice.' She gave a little huff of disgust. 'Such hypocrisy!'

'Now you see why I dislike town so much.'

'I do, but…' she tucked her hand in his sleeve '…I thought it was also because Barbara died here.'

For a moment she feared she had offended him, that he would not reply, but at length he sighed. 'I have never been a great one for society, but I realise now I used her death as an excuse to withdraw completely.'

'Then it is very good of you to come back for my sake.'

'I confess I have enjoyed it more than I anticipated,' he said, relieving her of her empty glass.

'I am glad.' She sighed. 'But I cannot expect you to remain in town for ever, Quinn.'

'Of course not. We shall return to Melham Court in due course.'

Serena wanted to tell him that she was ready to leave town immediately, but at that moment he took her in his arms and kissed her, driving all coherent thought from her head.

Despite the exigencies of hosting her first social event in town, Serena was up and about early the following day. Now she was most truly Quinn's wife she felt much happier and much more alive. Perhaps it was the new closeness she felt with her husband. Having completed her household duties, she went to look for him and was a little disappointed to discover he had gone out and would not be back until dinnertime. Serena wondered what to do in the meantime and, looking out of the window at the fallen leaves dancing about the square, she decided a brisk walk would serve to use up a little of her restless energy. She ran upstairs to change into her walking dress and set off with Polly running to keep up with her.

'Where are we going, my lady?'

'Oh, I am not sure yet. I know,' she said, struck by inspiration, 'we shall go to the Pantheon Bazaar.'

'You've no need to go there, madam.' Polly sniffed. 'You don't need to watch the pennies.'

'Perhaps not, but I have not been there since I was a schoolgirl. It might be amusing.'

The exercise, and browsing the tempting counters in the Pantheon Bazaar, proved a perfect way to while away a few hours. Serena could not find anything she really needed, but she bought a pair of white evening gloves while Polly was looking about her, wide-eyed at the cornucopia of treasures. Serena took out her purse and gave her a handful of coins, ordering her to go off and treat herself.

'Ooh, madam, thank you, but I can't take this.'

'Of course you can,' Serena told her. 'Now off you go and find yourself something you would like. I shall be happy enough wandering around here. We shall meet back here, in half an hour.'

Polly went off, her money clutched tightly in her

hand, and Serena returned to browsing the selection of gloves laid out before her.

A flurry of activity caught her attention and she looked towards the doors in time to see a lady enter, a tall, striking figure in a modish promenade dress of scarlet wool decorated with quantities of gold frogging. It was Mrs Hopwood, Serena recognised her from her drives in the park. She took the opportunity to study her more closely. She had a pleasant face, although it was painted and powdered too heavily for Serena's taste. Her countenance was framed by an abundance of thick, dark curls that peeped out beneath her stylish bonnet with its scarlet ostrich feathers. She was accompanied by her maid, a dour-looking woman in a severe black gown and jacket, a complete contrast to her flamboyant mistress.

Serena bit her lip and after a brief hesitation, she approached the widow.

'Mrs Hopwood.' The woman turned, her brows rising, and there was a definite wariness about her. That was not surprising, thought Serena, for she was being accosted by a perfect stranger. 'Forgive me, we have not been introduced.' She coloured slightly. 'I am Lady Quinn.'

'Are ye now?' said the widow. 'Well, I've heard a deal about you, my lady.'

The voice was rough, uncultured and had an unmistakable northern burr, but a smile hovered about her carmine lips and her unmistakable friendliness caused Serena to relax a little.

She said, 'Can we talk, privately?'

Mrs Hopwood regarded her for a moment, then she nodded to her maid, who withdrew to a discreet distance. The widow turned towards the embroidered stockings displayed on the counter.

'Let's look at these and we'll be less conspicuous, perhaps. Well, Lady Quinn, what is it you wish to say to me?'

What indeed? Serena sought about for words that would not be insulting, or misconstrued.

'I have seen you driving in the park.'

'Have you now?'

'You are always escorted by...' Serena could not help her lip curling in distaste '...by Sir Timothy Forsbrook.'

'What of it?'

Serena's colour rose, but she had come too far to turn back now.

'I wanted to put you on your guard.' The widow gave her a searching look and Serena hurried on. 'I may be wrong. Perhaps he is indeed in earnest and means you no harm, but—' She stopped, her cheeks burning. 'You say you know of me. If you heard my story from Sir Timothy then it is lies, but I do not ask you to believe that. All I can say, all I would urge, most strongly, madam, is that you should be careful in your dealings with that man.'

There was a long silence and Serena wondered if she had offended the widow. After all, they were not acquainted, what business was it of hers? Serena was about to apologise and walk away when the widow spoke.

'Thank you for your concern, dear, but I know exactly what I am about.'

'I beg your pardon,' murmured Serena. 'It was presumptuous of me—'

'No, no, I understand and I am grateful. Truly. But

I pray you will not be anxious for me.' The voice had softened and lost its strong north-country accent, but the next moment it was back again. 'Now, you'd best move away from me, my lady, before anyone can remark upon our meeting.'

Serena nodded. She had half-turned away when Mrs Hopwood touched her sleeve.

'Bless you, my dear. It was good of you to warn me.'

With a swirl of scarlet skirts the widow went off to join her maid and Serena was left wondering if she had been wise to address a total stranger. But she could not regret it. Mrs Hopwood might be in thrall to Sir Timothy, but at least she had tried to warn her of the danger.

It was a Monday morning, overcast but dry, and Quinn was already in the breakfast room when Serena entered. His smile was intimate, reminding her of the night they had spent together. Of every night for the past few weeks, she thought, her stomach swooping delightfully, but his voice when he spoke was perfectly calm.

'Well, my dear, what are your plans for the day?'

'Why, nothing very much, my lord. I thought perhaps you might like to drive out with me later? November is upon us and I doubt we shall have many more fine days.'

'Alas, I have business in the city today.'

'Oh.' She tried to hide her disappointment.

'And I shall not be at home for dinner this evening.'

Serena looked up from pouring her coffee. 'You will be out all day?'

'I am afraid so.' He added, as an afterthought, 'It is Settling Day at Tattersall's.'

'Good heavens.' She laughed. 'Have you been playing deep, my lord? I had not thought that was your style.'

He bared his teeth at her. 'You know it is not. But I thought I would look in today.'

'But you will be back in time to come with me to Lady Yatesbury's rout tonight? We do not need to be there until later.'

'Alas, I fear I shall not.' He glanced across the table. 'Do you really wish to go? It will be a dreadful crush,' he told her. 'Yatesbury has no discernment and lets the world and his wife through the door. I would much rather you did not attend.'

'Then I shall not do so.' Serena bit her lip, more disappointed at not seeing Quinn than missing the rout.

'Good.'

He turned his attention back to his plate, indicating that the matter was closed, and Serena felt a little stir of alarm at his reticence. She had never known Quinn to gamble recklessly and she could not believe he had done so now, but there was something he did not wish to share with her. Dunnock came in with the post on a silver tray. Serena drank her coffee while Quinn sorted through the letters. He pushed his chair back.

'There is one for you,' he said, coming around the table to her. 'From Lady Hambridge. You may tell me later what she says. I must deal with my correspondence before I go out.'

He bent to drop a light kiss upon her hair and was gone, leaving Serena feeling restless and uneasy. Quinn was as kind and affectionate as ever, but he went out a great deal these days and rarely told her too much about where he was going. Perhaps he was developing a taste for town life, just when she had decided she would prefer to return to the country.

The day dragged. In the afternoon Serena sent for her phaeton and took a drive around the park at the fashionable hour. However, the house felt even more silent and empty when she returned. She went upstairs and while she waited for Polly to come and help her to change her dress, she stood at the window, looking out at the square. There was no doubt about it—she missed Quinn. Whenever he was away from her she was impatient for his return. It was foolish. It was definitely unfashionable, but there it was.

She went downstairs and instead of going to the morning room, where she usually spent her time alone, she made her way to the library in an effort to find some small crumb of comfort. There was no study in the town house and Quinn worked at the large mahogany desk in the library. She went in, smiling when she saw everything on the desk top was in order, inkwells full, a supply of pens trimmed and ready for use, the accounts journals piled neatly on one side.

At Melham she had been in the habit of helping Quinn with the estate business, but although they still discussed such matters, there was little to be done from London and she felt excluded. How foolish, she thought, going around to sit in his chair. She ran her hands over the carved arms, as if trying to feel some sense of Quinn from the polished wood.

He had never excluded her and, if he currently appeared preoccupied, it was because he was immersed in town life: dinner at the clubs, sparring with Gentleman Jackson at his famous boxing saloon in Old Bond

Street, perhaps even attending cockfights, although Quinn never mentioned such things. He must know she would not approve.

A sliver of paper protruded from the top right-hand drawer of the desk. Careless of Quinn and probably indicative of his hurry to be gone this morning. She pulled open the drawer. The offending sheet was the top one of a sheaf of opened letters that had been hastily pushed into the drawer. This morning's correspondence, she guessed.

As she reached forward to flatten the top sheet she noticed the flowery heading. Rundell, Bridge & Rundell. It must be the bill for her coral parure. She lifted it out, mildly intrigued to know how much the set had cost. The figure at the bottom of the page made her gasp, until she realised that beneath a detailed description of the parure were three further items: a diamond bracelet, ring and necklace.

Serena stared at the page, an icy hand squeezing her insides. Perhaps Quinn planned to give them to her later, but a far more persuasive answer presented itself. Quinn had bought the diamonds for his mistress.

Some women would settle for nothing less.

No. There must be some mistake. But she could not resist pulling the rest of the bundle from the drawer, bills from London tradespeople, mantua-makers, milliners, haberdashers and shoemakers. There were even two more bills from Rundell's. She scrutinised each sheet, but recognised none of the items listed. She reached over and took out the last document. Spreading it open on the desk Serena gazed at it in dismay. It was the lease of a house in Devonshire Place.

Carefully Serena put everything back in the drawer,

blinking away the tears that threatened to drop and smudge the elegantly written accounts. She had not even considered it, yet now she berated herself for a fool. Quinn was a man, was he not, and it was years since the love of his life had died. Why would he not have a mistress? And why would he give her up, merely because he had married? He had wed Serena to save her reputation and she was so damaged that it was only recently that she had welcomed his advances. It was quite understandable that he would want someone to give him the comfort that was lacking in his marriage.

It was too much. She collapsed on to the desk, sobs tearing at her body. The pain was intense, as if indeed her heart were breaking, but such powerful emotions could not continue and at length she dried her eyes. There might be another explanation for these purchases. She should ask Quinn. But even as she wiped all signs of her tears from the library desk she knew she would not do so. He had promised her he would always tell the truth and she was afraid that his answer would be too painful to bear.

Chapter Fifteen

As instructed, Quinn's driver turned the closed carriage into Devonshire Place and brought it to a halt a few yards along, from where Quinn had a good view of an elegant town house with its black-painted door, iron railings and ornate wrought-iron balcony on the first floor. He glanced at his watch. Ten thirty.

He looked up as another carriage rattled into the street, a hackney, which stopped outside the house. The cab drew away and Quinn watched a fashionably dressed gentleman run up the steps and into the house. Quinn picked up his hat and fixed it firmly on his head, then he waited a full five minutes before jumping down from the carriage and, after a brief word with his driver, he made his way towards the black door.

The manservant who admitted him answered Quinn's questioning glance with no more than a nod. Silently Quinn handed him his hat and cane then lightly ran up the stairs to the drawing room. There was only one person present, the fashionable buck who had preceded Quinn into the house. He was standing by the window, staring out, an open letter dangling from one hand.

'So, she is gone.'

Sir Timothy Forsbrook swung round.

'You!' He waved the paper. 'Are you behind this?'

'You have been duped, I presume.' Quinn ignored the question and stripped off his gloves, dropping them on to the small dining table in the centre of the room.

'You know damn well I have.'

Forsbrook's voice shook and Quinn noted that his usually florid face was very pale.

'Actually, I know very little. Why don't you tell me?'

'That high-flyer tricked me finely, the bitch!'

Quinn walked over to the side table and poured out a glass of brandy.

'Here, sit down and drink this.' For a moment he thought Forsbrook would knock it from his hand, but after an inward struggle he snatched the glass and tossed the contents into his mouth. Quinn took the glass. 'Sit down,' he barked again, waiting until Forsbrook had complied before turning to refill the glass and then pouring a brandy for himself.

As Quinn returned to the table Forsbrook looked up at him.

'Did she dupe you as well?'

'On the contrary.'

Forsbrook's face contorted and he swore viciously. 'I knew it. The moment I saw you here I knew you were behind this.'

'I am sure you did,' replied Quinn unmoved. 'The thing is, what are you going to do about it?'

'Devil take you, what *can* I do? If I don't show at Tattersall's and settle my account…' He trailed off, his hand grasping the brandy glass until the knuckles glowed white. Then with another curse he pushed himself to his feet. 'But you will meet me for this, Lord Quinn—'

'Oh, I don't think so, Forsbrook. I have a much better plan for you. One that will allow you to pay your debts of honour, at least.'

Quinn sipped his brandy, seemingly relaxed but alert, should Forsbrook attack, which the murderous look on his bewhiskered face indicated he would like to do. A minute went by. Quinn was aware of the noises from the street, the rattling of a carriage over the cobbles, dogs barking, the shout of a hawker crying his wares. At last Forsbrook lowered himself back into his chair.

'You have no idea how much I owe.'

'Tell me,' Quinn invited him cordially. 'I should imagine your debts are extensive.'

'They are.' Forsbrook emptied his glass, went over to pick up the decanter and brought it back to the table. 'That damned whore gave me to believe she was sweet on me. She was dressed like a swell and very free with her blunt. By Gad, I'd never seen so many jewels on a woman and all of 'em real, I swear.'

'Oh, they were,' murmured Quinn, but Forsbrook did not hear him.

'Naturally, I had to keep up with her. She was determined to be seen about town, too.' He threw another venomous look at Quinn. 'No doubt that was your plan, to provide fodder for the town tabbies. Well, it worked. They were scandalised. There was no hiding her inferior breeding, but I did not think that would matter overmuch to me. She might be as common as the hedge but once we were married I planned to set her up in a snug country manor and come to town without her.'

'Chivalrous.'

'Well, what do you expect? I knew I would be marrying beneath me, but we are not all of us born with a fortune!'

'So you did not tell her you were already living on the edge?'

'Of course not. She was very generous, so how could I be otherwise? Whenever she asked me to purchase some little trifle or go to Tattersall's subscription room and place a wager on a horse she favoured, how could I refuse? And she always paid up, next time we met. And at the card parties…' He shook his head. 'She would ask me to stake her, if she had not brought sufficient funds, but more often than not she won it all back that same evening.' He reached for the decanter and slopped more brandy into his glass. 'We'd talked about marriage. She didn't want a fuss, said her people might not understand about her marrying out of her own sphere. She asked if I could obtain a special licence, even gave me the blunt to cover it there and then!' He dropped his head in his hands. 'I arranged the whole for this morning…'

Quinn's lip curled. 'And no doubt you were going to take your blushing bride direct from the ceremony to Tattersall's.'

'No, damn you, it wasn't like that! I admit much of what I owe at Tattersall's is to cover bets placed—mine and hers!—but almost half of it is for those damned nags of hers. She wanted to set up her stable and asked me to buy the cattle for her. The first team didn't suit, so last week she asked me to purchase her another. Prime goers and damned expensive, too. What could I say? She told me she would have the money here for me today. And after that I was going to settle all my obligations. I would be home free.'

'Instead of which you face ruin. And worse,' said Quinn softly, 'disgrace.'

Forsbrook glared at him, hatred bright in his eyes, but behind that something else. Fear. He thought little of his fellow man—even less of women—but he set great store by his own standing. Gambling losses were debts of honour and if Forsbrook could not pay them, he was finished. Quinn was unmoved. It suited his purpose very well that the fellow considered himself at *point non plus*.

He said now, 'What sum would you need to clear your debts?'

Forsbrook slumped in his chair. 'It will take nothing less than eight, nine thousand pounds. How am I to come by such a sum without surety?'

'I will give you ten thousand pounds.' Forsbrook's head came up, hope and suspicion warring in his face. Quinn continued, 'I shall, of course require you to fulfil certain conditions.'

'Go on.'

Quinn fetched pens and ink from the writing desk, then he went back and pulled a thick sheaf of documents from the drawer and placed them on the table before Forsbrook.

'First, you will sign these letters for publication by the main London newspapers, to wit, the *Gazette*, the *Morning Chronicle*, *The Times* and the *Morning Post*. You need only read one—they are all identical.'

'You have gone to a great deal of effort for this,' sneered Sir Timothy. 'You must have been very sure of me.'

'Read it,' ordered Quinn. 'I will not have you say afterwards you did not know what you were signing.'

He watched as Forsbrook's eyes skimmed the neat lines.

'You would have your wife exonerated from all blame and at the expense of my good name.'

Quinn shrugged. 'We both know this is a man's world. Society will not think much worse of you for admitting you abducted an heiress.' He watched as Forsbrook scrawled his name on each copy of the letter. 'Your being duped by the woman calling herself Mrs Hopwood will do far more harm to your reputation.'

'I am aware of that.' Quinn heard the unmistakable sound of grinding teeth. 'I shall be obliged to remove myself from town for a while.'

'Which brings us neatly to the next condition.' Quinn moved the letters out of the way and replaced them with two more sheets. 'I will grant you the sum of ten thousand pounds, on the understanding that you quit England for the next five years, and never—mark my words, Forsbrook—*never* come near Lady Quinn or her family again. If you break either of these conditions, I shall serve a writ upon you for the repayment of this sum and pursue you mercilessly for it.'

'Leave England!' Sir Timothy sat back, his face suffused with anger. 'And what the devil am I to do for the next five years?'

'I neither know nor care. There is a chaise waiting at the Golden Cross to take you to Dover and thence to France. We are no longer at war, so you may travel the Continent, as many of our compatriots are doing.'

'Preposterous,' Sir Timothy blustered. 'I shall do no such thing.' He waved an accusing finger at Quinn as he folded each of the letters and placed them safely inside his coat. 'And do not think I shall allow those letters to be published without challenge. I shall refute them. I shall say you coerced me.'

'Then I shall be obliged to call you out,' retorted Quinn. 'Believe me, I should like nothing better than to put a bullet through you.' He paused another moment, then reached out for the agreement. 'Very well. If you are not minded to take up my offer…'

'No.'

Forsbrook stopped him and Quinn drew back, waiting. Forsbrook looked about the room, as if hoping the rich widow would appear suddenly and tell him it had all been a joke designed to tease him. At last he sighed and picked up the pen.

'Very well, since I have no choice.'

It took most of the day to settle Sir Timothy's affairs and the clock was striking ten when Quinn finally brought him to the Golden Cross.

'Damn it all, Quinn, there is no need for you to come with me like a blasted gaoler,' Forsbrook exclaimed wrathfully. 'We are agreed I will leave the country. Confound it, you heard me tell my landlady to have my things packed up and sent after me.'

'You are a slippery customer, Forsbrook, and I shall not be content until I have word you are safely in France.' He watched Sir Timothy throw his portmanteau into the chaise. 'You know the consequences of breaking our agreement.'

'Aye, I know it, damn you. By heaven, Quinn, this has cost you a pretty penny! I hope she is worth it.'

'Oh, I think so.'

Quinn pushed him into the coach and closed the door. Forsbrook leaned out of the open window.

'You are a fool, if you think you can keep her, Quinn,' he declared. 'Her family has always courted scandal and Serena Russington is no different. A beautiful pleasure-seeker.' His last, sneering words stayed with Quinn as the chaise drove out through the arch. 'A man such as you will never hold her!'

As his coach rattled towards Berkeley Square, Quinn leaned back in the corner, gazing out at the dark streets. He was dog-tired, but satisfied with his day's work, and he looked forward to telling Serena all about it. Serena. Just the thought of her revived him and when he reached the house he sprang out and hurried to the drawing room. It was empty and he went back to the hall, looking for Dunnock. Serena's maid was about to disappear into the nether regions of the house and he called to her.

'Is your mistress in her bedchamber?'

Polly turned and took a couple of steps towards him before bobbing a curtsy.

'She is gone to Lady Yatesbury's, my lord.' She observed Quinn's frown and twisted her hands together. 'A new gown was delivered and my lady said 'twould be a pity not to wear it out.'

Quinn dismissed the maid and went upstairs. When they had spoken at breakfast, Serena had not seemed eager to go out. In fact, she had told him she would not go. Yet she had changed her mind, just because her new gown had arrived. As he strode to his bedchamber, Forsbrook's words floated back to him.

A man such as you will never hold her.

Serena's head ached from the noise and chatter in Lady Yatesbury's overcrowded, overheated rooms. In truth, she wished she had not come, but when she had discovered that Mrs Bell had sent round her new evening gown, the angry rebellion simmering beneath her despair had erupted. Why should she remain in Berkeley Square, lonely and lachrymose, when Quinn was out who knew where, enjoying himself?

Some part of her, the dutiful wife she had tried to become, argued that she had no right to object if Quinn had a mistress. She should be grateful for all he had done for her. But the truth was that Serena did not *feel* grateful. She felt…jealous. Jealous of this unknown woman upon whom Quinn had spent a small fortune. She had donned Mrs Bell's white and silver gauze creation and set off for Lady Yatesbury's rout in a mood that could only be described as high dudgeon.

Serena took a surreptitious peek at the mantel clock and her heart sank. It was not yet eleven. To leave so soon would give rise to comment, but to remain, when it was an effort to raise a smile, was unthinkable. She would seek out her hostess, make her apologies and slip away with as little fuss as possible.

Lady Yatesbury was by the door, greeting two late arrivals. They made a striking couple, the gentleman tall and dark, with pomaded black curls and thick whiskers, his lilac coat heavily laced, and while Serena could only see the back of the lady, is was clear that her scarlet gown was heavily embroidered with gold thread. Fixed into her fair curls she had two bejewelled combs that matched the sapphires and diamonds around her neck. It could not be better, thought Serena. The appearance of such an ostentatious pair would mean her own absence would barely be noticed.

Serena drew closer and hovered, waiting for the newcomers to move away so that she could take her leave of her hostess, but Lady Yatesbury appeared to be in no hurry. She was waving her fan and blushing at something the gentleman was saying to her. Then she caught sight of Serena and called to her.

'Lady Quinn, well, how fortunate! Come closer, my dear, do.'

The lady in the scarlet gown turned and as Serena approached she found herself staring at a face that looked strangely familiar.

The lady held out her hands, beaming. 'My darling girl. Have you a kiss for your mama?'

Chapter Sixteen

Serena's world rocked. There could be no doubt. The petite frame, the chocolate-dark eyes and guinea-gold curls—it was like looking in a mirror. True, the face was a little more lined than Serena's, but the woman was still beautiful and when she spoke her voice was soft, musical and full of warmth.

'You must let me present my Eduardo to you, my love. Conte Ragussina.' She gave a tinkling laugh. 'I suppose he is your step-papa, now.'

The Conte made a flourishing bow and picked up Serena's nerveless hand.

'But I beg my Lady Quinn will call me Eduardo,' he crooned, kissing her fingers.

Serena gently withdrew her hand, murmuring something incoherent in reply.

'So, it is true,' marvelled Lady Yatesbury, looking from Serena to the Contessa. 'You had no idea you would meet here tonight?'

'None at all,' purred the Contessa, 'I had written to advise of my return to England, but one knows how easily letters go astray.'

'Indeed, indeed,' cried their hostess. 'And for this

happy reunion to happen in my house!' She clasped her hands in delight and Serena could imagine how the tale would have spread by the morning. 'But you will wish to talk privately with your daughter, Contessa. I shall take you to my boudoir on the next floor. You will not be disturbed there, I assure you.'

'Yes, yes, we must talk.' The Contessa slipped one hand through Serena's arm and waved the other imperiously at her husband. '*Caro mio*, you must go away and enjoy yourself while Serena and I become acquainted again.'

In a daze Serena allowed herself to be carried away from the overcrowded reception rooms and up the stairs to a comfortable little sitting room decorated in shades of powder blue. The Contessa Ragussina sank down gracefully on to a sofa and patted the seat beside her.

'Come, my dear, I will not bite, I promise you. How long is it, seven, eight years?

'Twelve,' replied Serena coolly, choosing a small chair opposite the sofa. 'I was but eight years old when you left me.'

A shadow of something that might have been guilt flickered across the Contessa's features.

'Ah, do not hate me for that, my darling. What was I to do? I knew your brother would never allow me to take you and I would be the first to acknowledge that the life Eduardo and I lived would hardly have been suitable for a little girl.'

'You have no other children, madam?'

'Good heavens, no. One was quite enough.' She gasped and put her hands to her mouth. 'Oh, my darling, pray do not think I did not want you. Nothing could be further from the truth, but I had such a *horrid* time of it, you see, and children are quite disastrous for one's figure, as you will discover soon enough, for you are married now. Lady Quinn. Well, I declare! And I am quite, quite furious with Hambridge for not informing me.'

'Oh?' Serena's brows went up. 'Does Henry correspond with you?'

'He does not, but he should. The Conte's *avvocati* have written to him upon occasion, so he cannot say he does not know how to contact me. Neither did he inform me of Russington's nuptials. I learned of that and of your own good fortune when I reached London. We have been here, what, four weeks now.' She made a little moue of distaste. 'I had forgotten how cold and miserable it is. We came at the invitation of the Hollands, you see, but it would not do to impose upon Lord and Lady Holland for too long so we have hired Kilborn House, near Hampstead. I know it is a little out of town, but it was the only house big enough for us to entertain in any style.'

'And do you intend to stay long in England, ma'am?' Serena marvelled that she could make such a calm, polite enquiry when she was still reeling from this unexpected meeting and her mind was seething with conjecture.

'Oh, no.' The Contessa chuckled. 'Although it would annoy your brothers immensely, which would be amusing! We remain another se'ennight only. But that is long enough for you and I to become acquainted.'

Serena arrived back at Berkeley Square just as the watch was calling two of the clock. She and her mother had remained closeted together in Lady Yatesbury's sitting room for over an hour and by the time they emerged

Serena had learned a great deal about the Contessa Ragussina, but felt very little affection for the woman who
was her mother. Papa she remembered as a bluff, jovial
man. Her mother was a much more elusive memory, a
golden creature whose painted cheek the young Serena
had been allowed to kiss, after first being warned that
she must be careful not to crush her gown. When Papa
died and Mama had quit the country, the eight-year-old
Serena had experienced no sense of loss. It had made
little difference to her life, except that her half-brothers
were anxious that no whiff of scandal should be attached
to Miss Serena Russington.

She had remained at the rout for another hour or so,
and by that time she had formed a pretty accurate as-
sessment of her mother. The Contessa Ragussina was
a charming, spoiled beauty who cared for nothing but
her own pleasure. Her delight in coming so unexpect-
edly upon her daughter appeared genuine, but Serena
thought it was more for the sensation it would cause
rather than any maternal affection. The Conte was an
inveterate flirt, but he seemed genuinely fond of his
wife and was rich enough to provide for her every wish.
They were louche, loud and most definitely scandalous, and she had no idea what Quinn would say when
he knew she had met them.

Quinn. Serena crossed the hall and made her way
slowly up the stairs. She very much wanted to go to
him. Twenty-four hours ago she would not have hesitated to go to his room, to wake him up if necessary
and tell him everything that had occurred at the rout.
But the fact that Quinn might have spent the day—and
most of the night—in the arms of his mistress gnawed
away at her. Knowing it was jealousy and might well be

unfounded did not help one jot. It just made the night spent in her own, lonely bed that much longer.

When Serena went into the breakfast room the following morning Quinn was already there, finishing off a plate of ham and eggs. She bade him a polite good morning and received nothing more than a considering stare in return. A servant served her with coffee and hot rolls, but once they were alone Quinn asked her if she had enjoyed herself last night.

'Thank you, it was interesting.'

He threw her a glance. 'You did not come to my room.'

'No.' She concentrated on buttering her bread roll. 'It was very late.'

'I missed you.'

The words were quiet, almost off hand, but they increased her inner turmoil. Did he really care about her, or did she merely feed some insatiable appetite? That thought produced a prickle of anger.

She said with ill-concealed bitterness, 'I thought you would be exhausted. After a day spent enjoying the pleasures of society.'

'What the deuce do you mean by that?'

'For one who professes to dislike town so much you are very reluctant to quit it.'

Quinn frowned. He put down his knife and fork and pushed away his empty plate.

'What is this about, Serena—have I offended you in some way?'

Tell him, Serena. Ask him to explain the bills, the lease of another house. There should be no secrets between you.

'*Something* has occurred, and I want to know what it is.' He bent a searching look upon her. 'Well, madam?'

The butler's cough interrupted them.

'I beg your pardon, my lord. Lord and Lady Hambridge have called. They wish to see you immediately.' Dunnock's sombre tones were overlaid with a hint of anxiety. 'Lord Hambridge says it is a matter of some urgency.'

For a moment she thought Quinn might tell the butler to go to the devil. Instead he nodded and pushed his chair back.

'Very well, we will come now.'

'I have shown them into the drawing room, my lord.'

'We will finish this later, Serena,' muttered Quinn as they followed Dunnock through the hall.

But she barely heard him. She was wondering about the revelations that awaited them in the drawing room.

When Dunnock opened the door for them to enter, Quinn saw immediately that something was seriously wrong. Henry was pacing up and down the room, while his wife was perched on the edge of a sofa, pulling a lace handkerchief between her hands with quick, jerking movements. His first thought was for Serena. He guided her to a chair and gently pressed her to sit down before greeting the guests.

'Good day to you, Hambridge, Lady Hambridge. When did you return from Worthing?'

The butler had withdrawn by this time and Henry wasted no time on pleasantries.

'Last night,' he replied shortly. 'And we were devastated by the news that awaited us. Poor Dorothea has been quite prostrate.'

Serena tensed and his hand tightened warningly on

her shoulder. 'I am sorry to hear that. I take it this concerns us?'

Hambridge stopped and fixed Quinn with a solemn gaze. 'Serena's mother is in London.'

'I see.'

'Such a dreadful shock,' exclaimed Dorothea, tugging at the unfortunate scrap of lace between her hands. 'She has been in England for a full month with that disreputable husband of hers! That foolish clerk of Hambridge's should have sent the letter on to us, but no, he must leave it for our return. I vow I was almost carried off by a seizure when Henry read it to me. They have hired a house out of town, thankfully, and there is little chance of them being invited to the sort of gatherings *you* will attend, Serena, so all is not lost.'

Henry nodded solemnly. 'And if by some mischance you should meet, on no account must you acknowledge them, Serena.'

'Indeed not,' declared Dorothea. 'I vow if I should happen to see that dreadful woman I shall not hesitate to give her the cut direct. That is, if I should recognise her.' She gave an angry titter. 'I have no doubt she is quite hideously raddled by now, with the debauched life she has been living.'

'Oh, I do not think you will have any difficulty knowing her,' remarked Serena. 'I do not believe she is much changed. And the likeness between us is quite unmistakable.' She added coolly, 'I met the Conte and Contessa, you see. At Lady Yatesbury's rout last night.'

So *that* accounted for her strange mood this morning, thought Quinn. His surprise at the announcement was nothing compared to that of Lady Hambridge. She shrieked and fell back on the sofa, while Henry scrabbled in her reticule for her smelling salts to wave under her nose. Quinn and Serena watched in silence.

'Thank God you don't subject me to such histrionics,' he muttered.

'You have met the Contessa?' Henry's outraged stare moved from Serena to Quinn. 'What the devil were you about, sir, to allow such a thing?'

'I was not at hand to prevent it,' Quinn retorted.

'Do you mean to say Serena was there *alone*?' cried Lady Hambridge, sitting up.

Quinn ground his teeth. 'I am not her keeper, madam.'

Dorothea sucked in a scandalised breath. 'You are her *husband*, my lord, and it is your duty to protect her reputation. What's left of it!'

Quinn saw Serena's hand come up, as if to ward off a blow, and he bit back a scathing reply. Dunnock came in, bearing a sealed letter on a tray. With admirable aplomb he fixed his eyes on his master and ignored everyone else.

'A note has arrived for you, my lord. The messenger insisted it should be delivered to you immediately and he awaits your answer.'

Quinn took the letter and dismissed the butler. He glanced about him as he broke the seal and opened the letter. Serena was sitting pale but composed in her chair, while Hambridge fussed about his wife, who had relapsed on the sofa.

'We must see how best we can resolve this situation,' declared Hambridge, plying his wife's fan as she lay back with her eyes closed. 'A single chance encounter at Lady Yatesbury's may not be so very bad, but we must ensure there are no further meetings. It would be best if you were to withdraw from society, Serena, until the Conte and Contessa have returned to the Continent. You must cancel all your engagements and Quinn shall take you back to Melham Court. Dorothea and I will make sure everyone knows the meeting was not of your making. I am confident that by next Season this will all be forgotten and you need think no more about that scandalous female.'

Serena sat up a little straighter in her chair. 'You forget, Henry, that *scandalous female*, as you call her, is my mother.'

'And a most unnatural parent,' declared Dorothea in scathing accents.

'But Serena's parent, nevertheless,' put in Quinn, coming forward. 'It is therefore up to my wife if she wishes to continue the acquaintance.'

'Out of the question.' Dorothea sat up. 'Serena's reputation is already damaged. To accept the connection with the Contessa, to be seen in her company, would put her beyond the pale.'

'Calm yourself, my dear,' Henry said as his wife snatched back her fan. 'The Contessa may not wish for the connection. After all, she has shown no interest in Serena until now.' He looked suddenly much happier. 'I doubt if she truly wants to acknowledge the daughter she abandoned more than ten years ago.'

'I hate to disappoint you,' drawled Quinn, glancing at the paper in his hand, 'but the Contessa wishes very much to see her daughter. She has invited us to dine with her at Kilborn House this evening.' There was a stunned silence. Quinn continued, 'Dinner, followed by a little dancing.'

'Out of the question!' The Hambridges both spoke at once.

'I will not allow it!'

'It is not a question of what *you* will allow, Hambridge,' barked Quinn. 'My wife is quite capable of deciding for herself.'

Henry's face flushed. 'Think, man. This is not only her reputation at stake, but yours, too, as her husband!'

'Reputation be damned,' Quinn snapped. 'I have never cared for society's good opinion and I am not about to start now.' He turned to Serena. 'Well, my dear, shall we accept the Contessa's invitation?'

Serena saw only understanding in Quinn's hazel eyes and it steadied her. She ignored Dorothea's gasp of outrage and her brother's angry mutterings and spoke directly to him.

'You would come with me?'

'Of course.'

'Then I confess I should like to go.' She wanted to tell him her first impressions of the Contessa, but she was loath to do so in front of Henry and Dorothea. It smacked of disloyalty to the woman who had borne her.

'Then I shall give the messenger our answer now.'

Dorothea barely waited for Quinn to leave the room before she gave a loud huff of disapproval.

'You have shocked and disappointed me, Serena. I thought we had taught you better than this. If you persist in your wayward behaviour, then I wash my hands of you!'

'Now, now, my dear, 'pon reflection I think 'tis natural Serena wishes to know a little about her mother and a private dinner is perhaps the best thing for it.'

'With dancing! How can it be private? The entire Holland House set might be present!' Dorothea's eyes went back to Serena. 'Never tell me Quinn mixes in that company!'

'I have no idea.' Serena looked towards Quinn, who had just come back into the room. '*Do* you visit Holland House?'

'I have dined there, in the past. The conversation is always stimulating. But I do not go there now.'

'Well, that is a small mercy, I suppose,' Dorothea conceded. 'The scandal surrounding Lizzie Webster has never been forgotten.'

'Surely it is to his credit that Lord Holland married her,' reasoned Serena.

'That merely shows he is as bad as she is,' flashed Dorothea.

'Poppycock,' said Quinn. 'If I do not go to Holland House it has nothing to do with the fact that Lady Holland is a divorcee, but because the Hollands are such avid supporters of Bonaparte.'

'But you are sure to meet them at Kilborn House and heaven knows what other scandalous company the Ragussinas may keep.'

'Then we shall soon find out,' replied Quinn, with what Serena thought was admirable calm.

Dorothea rose in a crackle of silks. 'I see there is no arguing with either of you. Come, Henry, we shall take our leave.'

'You must see our position, Serena,' said Henry, escorting his wife to the door. 'We cannot grant you more than a bow in passing, if we see you out and about in your mother's company. And what Russ will say when he hears of it…'

Dorothea gave a snort of derision. 'Knowing your brother, he will merely laugh!'

Serena caught the glimmer of amusement in Quinn's eyes and she said, 'Thank you, Dorothea, that gives me some comfort.'

'Well it was not what I intended! Come, Henry, take me home, if you please.'

'Oh, dear.' Serena sighed when the door closed behind them. 'I fear they are seriously displeased with me. I only hope they do not cut all acquaintance with us.'

'They will come about,' said Quinn. He grinned. 'You are a very rich woman now, Lady Quinn. That counts for a great deal with your brother and his wife.'

'But not if I continue to cause a scandal.'

'You won't.' He pulled her into his arms. 'We shall be the very model of marital harmony.'

Serena's heart skittered at the warm glow in his eyes, but she could not forget the bills stuffed into the drawer in the library. How could she lose herself in his kiss if she was sharing him with some unknown mistress? With a little laugh she twisted out of his arms.

'Heavens, Quinn, how droll that sounds,' she said lightly. 'But you must excuse me, if you please. This unexpected invitation to dine with the Contessa has thrown me into complete confusion. I must go and find Polly to help me decide what to wear.'

She made her escape and managed to avoid seeing Quinn again until they set off in the carriage for Kilborn House. When they arrived, she handed her cloak to the hovering footman and Quinn glanced at her coral gown.

'Beautiful,' he murmured. 'But why are you not wearing the parure?'

She put a hand to the diamonds at her neck. She had no heart to wear the coral set—it reminded her of the expensive gifts he had bestowed elsewhere.

'I thought these were more fitting,' she replied at last, adding with a touch of bitterness, 'after all, diamonds are what every woman loves most.'

She moved quickly away towards the lackey waiting to show them into the drawing room, leaving Quinn to follow her.

The Contessa greeted them regally before making them known to their guests. There were some half-a-dozen people in the room and Serena recognised only two of them: Lord Fyfield and Mrs Medway, a dashing widow with a reputation for stealing husbands. They were greeted with an enthusiasm that bordered on the obsequious, which Serena disliked as much as Quinn. Neither did she like the Conte's familiar attitude towards herself, but she hid her unease beneath a cheerful smile, accepted the glass of wine pressed into her hand and did her best to join in with the conversation, wondering how soon after dinner they might take their leave.

Quinn's countenance was impassive as he watched his fellow diners. This was just such an evening as he detested, inconsequential small talk and malicious gossip. The flight from England of Lord Byron and Brummell earlier in the year had been followed by a storm of speculation and even now the Contessa's guests were eager to pick over the bones of the scandals. Quinn took no part, neither did he respond to the advances of the widow on his right. Serena, he noted, was turning away the flirtatious remarks of the Conte and Lord Fyfield with a smile, but her cheeks were more flushed than usual. He wondered how much wine she had drunk.

A question from his hostess claimed his attention, but he answered it briefly and went back to watching Serena. She appeared to be avoiding his eye and unease flickered. Was he mistaken in thinking her liveliness was forced? Was she indeed enjoying the dissolute company? An icy hand clutched at his guts. Perhaps Forsbrook was right. How could he hope to hold the interest of such a vibrant, lively creature as Serena? She had wanted a rake for a husband, not a serious, unsociable fellow who preferred books to parties.

Throughout dinner, Serena felt Quinn's eyes upon her. He was seated between the Contessa and Mrs Medway but he made little effort to engage them in conversation. He was living up to his reputation, then, as the rudest man in London. She did not look directly at him, afraid to read disapproval in his face. The wine had made her a little light-headed and she had been flirting with the gentlemen sitting near her. Well, she thought angrily, if Quinn was jealous she was glad. It could be nothing to the pain she was suffering.

With each glass of wine, the idea that Quinn had a mistress became more fixed in her mind. It must be so. There could be no other explanation. He probably considered it a kindness to keep the fact from her. How strange, she thought, that she could laugh and talk as if she had not a care in the world, when inside her heart was breaking.

The Contessa rose to lead the ladies from the dining room and as Serena passed Quinn he reached back and caught her hand.

'Are you all right?'

No. I want to rip and tear and scream. I want to throw myself into your arms and cry my heart out, but I will not do that because I am sure those arms have been wrapped about someone else.

'Oh, Lord, yes. I am enjoying myself vastly.'

She gave him a glittering smile and walked on. This was to be their life from now on. A pretence of happiness.

The ladies disposed themselves around the elegant drawing room and the Contessa invited Serena to join her on the sofa.

'You do not seem to be at ease, my dear,' she said, taking Serena's hand. 'Are you wishing yourself elsewhere?'

'No, indeed, ma'am. I very much wanted to come this evening.'

'Then perhaps it is your marriage. Ah, I can see by the way you have coloured up that I am right.' She sighed. 'I cannot say I blame you.'

'I do not know what you mean,' Serena replied coldly, pulling her hand free.

The Contessa was in no way discomposed. She said, 'Lord Quinn is not easy in society. Why, he said barely a half-dozen words to me during dinner.'

Serena saw no reason to be polite. 'I doubt the insipid conversation was to his taste. He has never been one for tittle-tattle.'

'But, my dear, gossip is the most entertaining kind of conversation! Do not tell me your husband is a prig as well as a bore.'

'You must admit, Contessa, he does have a magnificent physique,' giggled Mrs Medway, overhearing.

'Does he have a mistress—oh, no need to look like that, Lady Quinn, we are all women of the world here. Of course he does. What rich man does not?'

Serena wanted to deny it, but jealousy swirled about her like a hot red mist and kept her silent. This could not go on. She could not bear it. She would talk to Quinn, discover the truth, however painful. But for now she could only pray that the subject would soon be dropped.

The Contessa touched her arm and gave a soft laugh, shaking her head at Mrs Medway. 'Now, now, Edith, you are putting my daughter to the blush. She and Quinn may still be very much in love.'

'Charming, but quite unfashionable,' smirked another of the matrons, disposing her skirts more becomingly. 'However, it will pass, it always does.'

'Not for the Conte and Contessa, apparently,' remarked Edith Medway. 'Do tell us your secret, madam.'

'That is easy. Constant amusement, including lovers! Wherever we are we surround ourselves with young people who entertain and divert us.' She reached up to caress Serena's face. 'With your looks I could make you the most sought-after woman in Rome or Paris. How amusing that would be!' The Contessa laughed. 'What do you say, Serena, why not quit this dull marriage and come to the Continent with me?'

Serena blinked, startled.

'I—I am flattered but, but it is quite out of the question.' Her eyes slid away from the Contessa's considering look. 'I c-cannot… I do not wish to leave my husband.'

'No, of course not. No need to colour up so, my love, it was merely an idea.' The Contessa sent a smiling look around the room. 'Enough of this. Let us talk of fashion before the gentlemen come in. I saw the most exquisite bonnet in New Bond Street today. A new milliner...'

Serena would have liked to leave as soon as the gentlemen joined them, but the room had already been cleared for dancing and good manners dictated they remain a little longer. Besides, she would do anything to put off the evil hour when she must talk to Quinn. She pinned on a smile and pretended an enjoyment in the evening that she was far from feeling.

She danced first with the Conte, then with the elderly roué whose wife was consigned to the pianoforte. After that Lord Fyfield approached, but Quinn cut him out.

'My turn, I think.'

Serena eyed him warily. She was feeling a little dizzy, which was possibly the wine, for her glass had constantly been refilled throughout the evening. Quinn was not smiling, but she could not make out if he was angry or merely bored.

She said, a little recklessly, 'I hope you are not going to scold me, Quinn.'

'No, why should I? You flirt very prettily.'

She felt a flash of anger, irrational, but too real to be ignored. Did he not *care* that she had been flirting? The dance separated them, but when she passed him she took her chance.

'Sauce for the goose, my lord!'

His brows snapped together. 'What the devil does that mean?'

They changed partners, skipped and pirouetted their way through the dance until they were facing one another again at the end of the line.

'Are you angry with me, Serena?'

'I suppose I should be grateful for your company

tonight. You have had so much *business* to attend to recently.'

'Yes. But this is not the place to discuss it.'

Serena knew that. Of course she did, but some demon was prodding at her and before the dance separated them again she sent one last, Parthian shot.

'Oh, no explanations, I pray you. How dull that would be!'

She saw Quinn's face darken as she turned away from him for the final movements of the dance and barely had they made their courtesies before he grabbed her hand.

'A word in private, if you please.'

There was confusion as everyone regrouped for another dance. With the iron grip on her hand Serena could do nothing but accompany Quinn out of the room. He spoke to their host in passing and the Conte's knowing smile made her blush vividly. In the hall, a footman directed them to a small sitting room, where candles burned and a cheerful fire blazed in the hearth.

'We cannot talk here,' she objected. 'What if we are interrupted?'

'We won't be.' His voice was scathing. 'A household like this will have plenty of private little rooms ready for use.'

'But you do not want to make love to me.'

'No, I don't,' he growled. 'I want to know what the devil is wrong with you tonight.'

Serena panicked. She was not quite sober and she needed all her wits about her when she confronted Quinn about his mistress.

'I am put out, that is all,' she said. 'Because you do not like my mother, or her friends.'

'And you do?'

Not for the world would she agree with him! She said airily, 'They are most entertaining.'

'Is that what you call entertaining? Gossiping, pulling reputations to shreds, flirting—'

'Hah, now we come down to it, my lord.'

'To what?'

Again, she retreated, hating her cowardice in not asking him the one question that was eating away at her soul.

'You object to other men taking notice of me.'

'Not at all.' His mouth twitched. 'Although I would object to you taking notice of other men.'

It was an attempt to lighten the mood but she ignored it.

He said at last, 'Are you sorry you married me?'

Yes, if you do not love me and only me.

When she did not speak his mouth twisted, he said heavily, 'I am not at ease in society, Serena, you know that. You appear to enjoy it.'

'It is the life I was brought up to expect.' The words sounded haughty, even though she meant it as an explanation.

His face darkened and he walked away from her.

'Idleness and indulgence,' he retorted. 'I thought you wanted more than that, Serena.' At the window he stopped and looked back, saying bitterly, 'Ah, but I was forgetting. You intended to marry a rake.'

'You are not a rake and nothing like one!'

'No, nor do I wish to be.' He sighed and turned to the window, staring out into the darkness. 'Perhaps you would be happier with your mother's set. Parties every night, touring the grand cities of Europe, with as many rakes as your heart desires.'

'Then you should leave me here!'

It was like watching herself from behind a glass wall. Serena wanted to scream at herself to stop, but instead she could only watch herself parcelling up the happy life she had been building with Quinn and pushing it towards a precipice.

'You should go,' she said, shaking with hurt and anger. 'Go away and leave me here with my mother. She has already suggested I go with her when she sails for France next week.'

'Then you must do that,' he barked, keeping his back to her. 'If it makes you happy.'

'It cannot make me any more miserable!' She threw the words at him, wanting only to wound.

'Very well,' he said, his voice brittle. 'I shall leave you to enjoy the company of your new friends.'

'You may tell Polly to pack up my things and send them to me.'

He had reached the door by this time, but her words stopped him and he turned to look at her.

'If that is what you want.'

She tried to glare at him defiantly, but the mixture of hurt and anger burning in his eyes made her look away.

'No, 'pon reflection, you need not bother,' she said icily. 'Pray do not send me anything from Berkeley Square. I shall require far more dashy gowns for living with Mama.'

For an instant she thought he would pick her up and carry her bodily from the house. Hope flared as she realised just how desperately she wanted him to do that. Instead he nodded silently and went out.

'I will not cry.' Serena muttered the words to the empty room. 'I *will not* cry.'

Blinking hard, she made her way back to the drawing room, where the Contessa gave her a searching look.

'Lord Quinn has left,' she said, keeping her head up and her tone cool.

'That is excellent news, *cara*.' The Conte took her hand and lifted it to his lips. 'We shall enjoy ourselves much more without him. *Che stupido*—he is a man most tedious!' She felt his hand on her back as he escorted her across the room to the Contessa. '*Tua madre* says you are coming to the Continent with us, no?'

She was surrounded by eager, inquisitive faces. Mrs Medway and Lord Fyfield would make sure the story would be all over town by the morning and what a titillating piece of gossip it would be. Henry and Dorothea would be scandalised, but that did not worry her. Only the effect on Quinn.

Suddenly she was no longer trapped behind the glass wall. She knew exactly what she wanted to do. What she wanted to say. Gently but firmly, she freed herself from the Conte's grasp and addressed her mother, her voice clear and steady.

'No, I am not going with you. You will think me unfashionable, but I love my husband, very much. And if it is not too late, I am going back to fight for my place in his life. If you have any feeling for me at all, Mother, I pray you will order a carriage to take me back to Berkeley Square with all possible speed.'

Chapter Seventeen

Quinn had told the driver to make all haste, but his rage was abating long before they had covered the four miles to Berkeley Square. He handed his hat and gloves to Dunnock, ignoring the old retainer's questioning glance. Time enough for them all to learn that Serena was not coming back.

It was only a few paces to the drawing room, but it was long enough for a lifetime of thoughts to race through his head. He had lost her and it was only now that he realised how much she meant to him. Over the past months he had watched the fragile, broken creature he had rescued from the inn at Hitchin recover her spirit. He had always known the docile, timid woman he had married was not the real Serena.

He had never wanted it to be. He wanted the fearless, passionate woman he had seen at their very first meeting, the woman who had ripped up at him, not caring for his wealth or rank. She had faced him as an equal, even though she barely reached his shoulder!

He had always known such a vibrant, pleasure-loving creature might not be satisfied with his quiet way of living. He had thought that once she had recovered her confidence he would go back to his books and his estates and they would live their separate lives. There was nothing unusual in that. He had thought himself prepared for it. Looking forward to it, in fact. Until tonight, when he had seen the old Serena, beautiful, alluring, irresistible, and he had discovered he could not bear to live without her.

The silence in the drawing room pressed in on him. He paced up and down, going over the events of the evening. He should not have lost his temper. Serena, too, had been in a rage, although at the time he had not seen that. He raked a hand through his hair. He had promised to look after her. He should not have left Serena at Kilborn House. Whatever she decided to do, he should not have abandoned her in such company.

Quinn glanced at the clock, then dashed out to the hall and past the astonished butler. He had been home barely ten minutes. If he ran to the mews he might be in time. They might not yet have unharnessed the team.

As he wrenched open the front door, the postillions of a travelling chariot were bringing the four sweating horses to a plunging halt outside the house. He stopped in the doorway, blinking to make sure he was not dreaming, but there was no mistaking the golden-haired beauty who stepped out of the carriage. She did not see him until she had hurried up the steps, then she stopped, uncertainty in her face.

'Quinn. I—'

'Not here.' He reached out for her hand. Gently, as if she would break. The initial soaring relief and elation he had felt had subsided a little, for the travelling chariot had not driven away. She was not yet his. She might never be. Silently he escorted her to the drawing room.

Once the door was closed, Quinn turned to look at her.

'You came back.'

'For the moment.' Her eyes were dark and troubled. 'There are things we must discuss. They will not wait.'

He said, clutching at the only straw he could find, 'If it is the thought of meeting Forsbrook in town that has made you want to leave, you may be easy—'

'Sir Timothy?' She looked faintly surprised. 'No, he no longer concerns me, but in any case, Lord Fyfield told me tonight that he has fled the country. No one knows the whole story, but it would appear the wealthy widow gave him his *congé*. I am relieved for Mrs Hopwood,' she added. 'I would not want to see her tied to such a man. I would not wish anyone to be condemned to an unhappy marriage.' Her eyes flickered towards him again. 'That is what we must discuss.'

Quinn said nothing. He squared his shoulders and waited for the blow to fall.

Serena moved restlessly about the room and drew off her gloves. She must choose her words with care.

'I am not leaving England with my mother. I have no wish to join her set.'

'Then why is her carriage still at the door?'

'In case I have to leave this house tonight.'

'Are you afraid of me?'

'You know I am not! I owe you such a great deal, Quinn. Even my life, I think. Perhaps we should never have married, but it is done and cannot easily be undone. We may not be able to live together, but I have no wish to disgrace you more than I have already. I thought, perhaps, you might put one of your properties at my disposal. Somewhere remote, where I might live quietly and cause no more scandal.'

'Wait.' He stopped her, frowning. '*Why* can we not live together?'

She took another turn about the room, fighting the urge to burst into tears.

'I thought I could do this, Quinn. I thought I could live with you, share your world, to help you with your estates, your people.' She stopped, knowing what must be said, and forced herself to look at him. 'I have fallen in love with you, Quinn. I know now that I cannot share you. If I cannot have you to myself, then I prefer to retire to the country and, and n-never see you again.'

He straightened, as if a great weight had been lifted from his shoulders.

'There is no one else, Serena.'

He reached for her but she held him off.

'Truly?' She looked up, her eyes searching his face. 'Do you not have a mistress?'

'No. I never have. Oh, I admit, after Barbara died there were others, but not recently. And certainly not since I found you.' He smiled. 'I did not know it until tonight, when you sent me away, but you have my heart, Serena. All of it. The thought of living without you is intolerable.'

She swallowed. 'But… Barbara?'

'I loved her, very much. She was my friend and my first love, and I will never forget her. But there is room for another in my heart, Serena. One last and enduring love.'

She shook her head at him. 'Quinn, I have tried to be a conformable wife—'

He put his fingers to her lips, silencing her.

'That is not what I want, my darling. I want the *real* Serena, the lady who will stand up to me, argue with me if she thinks I am wrong. I fear we will have battles royal, but is that not better than a life spent constantly in calm waters?' He smiled, his burning gaze turning her very bones to water. 'I love you, Serena. I love you for your warmth, your spirit, your courage, and if you will stay with me I shall do my utmost to prove it for the rest of our lives.'

'Oh, Quinn!'

He stifled the words with a kiss, swift, hard and impatient. Serena responded, but after a moment, and with a supreme effort, she pushed him away. She wanted to believe him. She wanted it so much that her heart ached, but she had to be sure.

'I have to know, Quinn. I f-found several bills and receipts in your desk...'

'Ah.' His brow cleared. 'Perhaps we should sit down.'

She allowed him to pull her down beside him on the sofa, but he had done nothing to ease her anxiety and she said impatiently, 'Explain to me, if you please!'

He grinned. 'Those, my dear, are the consequence of a highly improper deception I agreed with your half-brother Russington.'

'Then, you do *not* have a mistress in Devonshire Place?'

He lifted her on to his lap. 'Why would I want a mistress when I have you?' He kissed her. 'No. I set up the glorious Mrs Hopwood.'

'Sir Timothy's rich widow!' Relief flooded through her and a laugh bubbled up. 'So she was never in danger of being duped.' She sighed. 'And you planned it all for my sake?'

He shook his head. 'I cannot take the credit for it—that was Russ. His was the plotting and planning. I, er, merely insisted upon financing the whole. The lady is a friend of Molly's, one of the, er, unfortunate women from Prospect House. The cook, in fact.'

'Nancy! But I have met her. She is an earl's daughter.'

He chuckled. 'Not the drab that Forsbrook took her for at all. When Russ explained the situation, she was more than willing to play the role. She was confident no one would recognise her.'

'She was quite correct. I certainly did not! I spoke to her, you see, at the Pantheon Bazaar, but even then, I had no idea—what a good actress she is.'

'Aye, she drew Forsbrook in nicely. Dangled the bait before his eyes: a northern fortune that was not tied up in trust. She was very convincing, the more so because she was rigged out with no expense spared.'

'So that explains the bills,' she murmured. 'If only I had asked you about them.'

'I should have told you what was afoot. I beg your pardon.'

'It does not matter now. And Nancy has gone back to the north—she is safe?'

'Yes. She disappeared in the night, leaving Forsbrook open to…er…persuasion.'

'You paid him off?'

'I thought you would not be in favour of my murdering him.'

'No indeed, but all this must have cost you a great deal.'

'A trifling sum, when you think what Lady Hambridge would have had me spend on a grand wedding.' He kissed her. 'I forbid you to worry about it. The yellow phaeton and carriage horses are now stabled in the mews ready to be sold on, but I let Nancy take everything else with her. Most of it will be sold to provide funds for Prospect House. I hope you do not object? The gowns would be far too big for you and I did not think the trinkets were quite your style. Whenever you wish, I will take you to Rundell's and buy you all the jewels your heart desires.'

She sighed and snuggled closer. 'For now all I want is to stay here with you.'

'Truly?' His arms tightened around her.

'Truly,' she said, turning her face up to his, her eyes shining. 'I love you, Quinn. I want to live with you as your wife. As your lover. I want to have dinner with you in the stone tower, alone or with our close friends. I want to learn to play duets with you on the piano and sing with you. It would be wonderful to take the grand tour with you, but I do not need a life full of parties or a host of admirers. Only you, my darling. I want only you.' She drew his head down towards her for another kiss. 'Send the coach away, Quinn, and take me to bed.'

* * * * *

*If you enjoyed this story
you won't want to miss these other great reads
by Sarah Mallory*

The Duke's Secret Heir
Pursued for the Viscount's Vengeance
The Ton's Most Notorious Rake

*And why not check out her
The Infamous Arrandales miniseries,
starting with*

The Chaperon's Seduction